CHASE, THE BAD BABY

JOHN ELLSWORTH

Subjudica House Press

CHASE, THE BAD BABY

A Novel

by

JOHN ELLSWORTH

For all the Chase babies
For all their caregivers

FOREWORD

Bad baby.

That's the horrendous label that some birth defect lawyers and some doctors call babies that have been injured in childbirth. It is used in this book not because Chase Staples is a bad baby in the ordinary sense of the word, but because he is a "bad baby" as some of those in the baby industry might call him. As the author and creator, Chase Staples is my most beloved character I have ever created. He and those like him are precious.

If this book helps prevent what happened to Chase from happening out in the world even one time, then the pain we feel for him will have been worth it a thousandfold.

PROLOGUE

●

He wrestled the baby's head free of the womb.

Suction, suction again. Was it even breathing?

With great urgency he freed the torso and limbs, the sucking sound of the sac giving way as the doctor lifted the baby free. A silent pause as he watched the chest. Was it even breathing? He wondered again. The baby lay limp in his hands, heavily jaundiced, as orange as the sun his first grader had painted in his refrigerator artwork. Would this baby ever paint a picture?

Then the neonatal team was swooping in, wresting the infant away, suction and more suction, a rush to the NICU, thankfully out of sight.

The doctor swallowed hard and fought to avoid eyes as the mother swam toward him through the anesthesia.

She knew the caesarean had come late. He could see terror on her face, narcoleptic though she was.

"My baby?" she said. "How is my baby?"

Shocky, the doctor opened his mouth to answer, but no words came out. He had been in this situation one other time, and he had been sued. Soon—one day soon—it would happen again, because of this. A man would come to the door, ask his name, and hand him the court papers. Then he would have to explain all this. He swallowed again, fighting down the bile of the raw truth. Which was, there was no explanation.

Outside the Hudd Family Hospital, clouds were tumbling by, angry and low. Chicago snow was blasting sideways, and the rush-hour traffic snarled and buckled on the Dan Ryan, the Kennedy, and the Edens. It was the perfect backdrop for a newborn baby to be injured beyond repair. And for a negligent hospital and doctor to work magic. Magic that made them innocent. Magic made from doctor's reports, fetal heart strips, nurses' notes, and C-sections.

In the end, the medical providers would point the finger of blame elsewhere. After all, there would be a lawsuit, this they knew beyond all doubt. There would be fifty million dollars to pay if the baby's lawyers won. A conspiracy would rise up within hours of the catastrophic birth. Preparation for the inevitable lawyer feeding-frenzy couldn't begin soon enough. There was blood in the water. The game was definitely on.

The first records were shipped to the Special Claims Unit before mother and child were discharged.

The SCU receiving clerk opened the file on the Unit's network. Chase Staples, it said.

Chase, the Bad Baby.

1

Only minutes away from Lake Michigan, the Emergency Department at Hudd Family Hospital provided for 100 percent of the urgent health needs inside the Chicago Loop. The ER department cared for nearly 75,000 patients each year, including serious injuries, as a Level 1 Trauma Center. The walk-in entrance opened onto a busy Chicago sidewalk. Rich or poor, if it was urgent and you were downtown, you wound up at Hudd. Its entrance had once been used for the popular TV series *ER*.

Inside Delivery Room 404, Chase Staples was struggling. He was stuck in mama's pelvic girdle. At the worst possible moment, the umbilical cord had coiled itself around the unborn child's neck. With each contraction the cord tightened and completely shut off blood flow until releasing its grip. Only then would it allow oxygen into the baby's starving brain.

The staff attending the birth had seen this case many times before. The results were almost always tragic. Unless there was a doctor present who knew what to do. With appropriate case management by an OB doctor, the babies emerged without injury. But Chase's doctor hadn't arrived at the hospital during those minutes when the case was begging for proper management. Still, Chase was viable and without injury, though he found the womb hot and suffocating. His lungs maintained a stasis with the liquid inside Mama's womb, while his birth instinct fought to engage with the canal, to maintain oxygen to the brain, and to enter the world. It was all anyone could want. A fair chance at a new life.

Nurse Andrea Mounce shook her head. Latoya Staples, the birth mother, was poor and black. Not the best status for top-notch health care, Nurse Andrea knew. She watched as her patient's hips shot upward. Latoya Staples was in mid-contraction.

Her fists were balled, knuckles white, and her back arched against the battle rampant in her mid-section. She was twenty-six but right then would have passed for forty-five, by the pain lines on the face. A *"gravida 3, para 2,"*— three pregnancies, two births—she was expending everything she had for this baby.

In her chart it was noted that she had two other children, ages four and two, and that her husband, John, was ten years her senior and drove a Chicago tour bus for Blueline Tours.

Latoya was a graduate of Roosevelt University with a degree in early childhood education. She had taught preschool in Chicago when her own kids were in attendance. Teaching allowed her to do one thing that she loved more than anything: mothering. She was excited about this pregnancy and almost giddy to see her new baby, Chase, whom she knew was a boy. For husband John, who was thirty-six, this latest child was a welcome addition even though later in life by some standards. John suffered the Iraq strain of

PTSD, where he'd served with distinction as a Humvee operator. He was honorably discharged with partial disability. LaToya's hospitalization was paid by John's health Blueline Tours health plan, of which Hudd Family Hospitals was the Preferred Provider.

Latoya gritted her teeth against the contraction and clamped her eyes shut. "It takes everything I have, this time," she said to the nurses. "This one is special." With all strength summoned, she pushed down as instructed and continued to breathe on command.

The contraction passed. She fell back against the soaked sheets, now clumped beneath her low back. She lay panting, out of breath, like some animal run to the ground.

The delivery room looked like a military skirmish was underway. It smelled of sweat and urine, 4x4s littered the floor, and medical instruments mounted on the wall blinked like a chorus the mother's vitals and Chase's telemetry. The delivery team watched the silicon fireworks and exhorted Mama to PUSH.

Nurse Andrea Mounce leaned around the stirrups and found Latoya's dilated eyes. "C'mon, girl, push...push. Squeeze it out."

"Oh my God," Latoya answered. "Oh, my God."

"Let go my hand, girl," said Andrea, "I need to check the baby's heart rate. Nancy, give me digits, please."

Assisting at Nurse Andrea's elbow was Nurse Nancy, a student nurse all of twenty. She had assisted at these births dozens of times, but still her stomach was in free fall, cascading down in fear at the utter life-and-death of the scene. So much to lose, she knew all too well, so much to gain.

"Nancy, give me digits! Stat!"

"Fetal heart rate one twenty-two BPM pre- and post-contraction. Falling to ninety during contraction."

It was a teaching hospital, so Andrea's follow-up question to Nancy was predictable. "And we're checking this because—"

Nancy didn't flinch. "If the baby's heart rate falls below one hundred that means"—she caught Latoya's sudden fear—"that could mean danger."

Latoya gulped air. "Is...my...baby...okay?"

"Good heart rate, holding at one twenty-two," Andrea reassured her. But no sooner had she said the words than the fetal monitor beeped and flashed its angry eye for attention. Another contraction had compromised the baby's oxygen.

"Nancy—"

"We've got the baby dropped down—ninety-two beats per minute."

Nurse Andrea puzzled to herself, "We're mid-contraction, and I get that. But why's the heart rate degrading so low so fast?"

"Heart rate now dipping below eighty," reported Nancy. Then, as if anticipating her teacher's question, she lamely added, "Could mean the baby isn't getting enough oxygen. Could be variable decels. Variable decelerations are caused by compression of the umbilical cord." This time she avoided connecting with Latoya's fearful eyes.

Andrea pressed the hand-held Doppler ultrasound probe to auscultate the baby's heartbeat.

"Thank you, Nancy. Textbook. Mama, squeeze my hand when you first feel the next contraction letting up."

The nurses stood in silence for almost a full minute. Andrea was oblivious to everything but the baby's heart sounds. Her eyes followed the clock's sweep hand above the mother's head. Nancy passed a damp cloth over Latoya's forehead. Latoya managed a smile and a nod. Then Latoya nodded again. "It's worst right...now."

Andrea never broke stride. "Tell me when it ends."

"Oh...me. Oh, God!"

"Hang in there. Release my hand when it passes."

Nurse Nancy offered a tray of ice chips. Latoya batted it away. She grimaced and arched upward, pulling away from the mattress as if by some invisible connection to the ceiling. "You know where you can...put...the ice. Okay, it's passing now."

Her agonized expression relaxed, as did her grip on Andrea's hand.

Andrea waited thirty seconds. "Three minutes ten seconds," Andrea announced. She stepped to the small churning platen at Mama's bedside and examined the fetal heart rate strip. "What is this about now?" she immediately asked. She spread out the paper record for Nancy to see.

Nancy said, "Variable deceleration? What's going on?"

Wordlessly they repeated the entire process, the contraction, the timing, and the paper strip.

Nurse Andrea again studied the fetal heart rate strip. "Same thing again. Variable decels. Heart rate dropped to eighty-two. Mama, I'm going to get a doctor in here to check you out. You're fine but I want to be sure there's nothing I'm missing. I'm just a nurse. He'll be just a few minutes." Andrea pushed the PAGE button on the wall phone.

"Resident OB to Delivery 404. OB to Delivery 404. Stat!"

2

Sue Gartner, MBA, was the ER and Maternity Service staffing director at Hudd Family Hospital, where her office had just been repainted Institutional Green. She hated the color and imagined a light yellow glaze on the wall, with Gladiolus stencils. Her redecorating musings were interrupted when Gerry Springer, MD, entered her office without knocking. Sue scowled. Gerry was a mere intern and should have known better.

He got right to the point, a fact that Sue appreciated, since it would keep the interruption short. "We're getting variable decels in Delivery 404," he announced. "You must have heard the stat page."

"And you are telling me this because?"

"We need staff to get right on this. Someone's got a baby in trouble. Which brings us around to the topic of you. You're staffing and you better find someone with more experience in C-sections than me. Variable decels means you should be dialing that phone right now."

"Please humor me. Variable decels means what?"

"Means variable decelerations in the baby's heart. I was

just reading this stuff over the weekend. It means we've got a bad baby on our hands if we don't act immediately to staff that call. According to the literature, we'll need a C-section in the next half hour."

Sue turned her attention to her monitor, speaking as she scrolled. "Can you manage the case until we locate someone?"

"No can do. I'm only an intern. I've only delivered a dozen non-emergent cases."

"Then we better find someone who can." She clicked the mouse and scowled.

Gerry suddenly blurted, "Where the hell is everybody? Am I the only OB doc on the unit?"

"Hold your horses—OK. We've had two sick call-ins. Your boss and Doreen Abrams."

"I'm the only OB on tonight?"

"So it appears."

"Then I hope this lady's treating gets off his ass and drops by sometime soon. I've never done a C-section—I've never even assisted at a C-section."

Sue lifted her eyes from the screen. "Well, this might be your first."

"Uh-uh. GW hospital policy guarantees thirty-minute decision-to-incision for C-sections. I just learned this."

She shrugged. "You're staff. Handle it until the cavalry arrives. Just keep the lid on things."

"Interns are not considered part of that staffing, so that excludes me. As it should."

Gerry backed away from the administrator's desk.

"Who's the treating?"

"Let's see. Mama told me. Payne, Phillip. You can dial him. *You* get him pissed with *you* when his cocktail hour prematurely ejaculates. Better you than me."

"Hell with his cocktail hour. 404 is his patient and he can get himself down here now. I'll call him."

"Act tough."

"Screw off, buddy boy. I am tough."

She returned to her computer screen and clicked the mouse to dial the call.

Latoya Staples was exhausted.

Her hair was matted and any sign of makeup had long since disappeared from her pretty face. She was in good physical shape, having been a cheerleader in college who still played racquetball twice a week at the Y, but this delivery had dragged on so much longer than her first two.

Nurse Andrea pegged her patient's remaining strength at ten percent.

Nurse Andrea and Gerry Springer were poised at the foot of the bed, quietly conferring. Andrea was a certified obstetrical nurse. Andrea was a seasoned veteran of the nursing wars, somewhere in her mid-thirties, and held the rank of major in the Illinois Air National Guard. There had been talk of her medical unit being activated to Germany but so far it was all rumors. She had very blond hair worn pinned back on one side, and she chewed Juicy Fruit gum nonstop each and every day as she tried to distance herself from her two-pack-a-day Marlboro habit. So far the oral substitute was working; she hadn't smoked in over ninety days and had only gained three pounds. She wore green scrubs and a hairnet, having assisted at three C-sections over the shift. That night she was pulling a double for an old friend from nursing school who was getting married over the weekend. Andrea was tired but happy to help out a friend.

Dr. Springer studied the fetal heart rate printout. Student nurse Nancy Steinman was lifting Latoya's head from the pillow and placing a dry towel beneath.

Dr. Springer measured the dilation. "She's dilated six centimeters. Not near enough, Mama."

"And we've got variable decelerations," said Andrea.

Latoya looked from doctor to nurse. "Am I having this baby today? Have you called Dr. Payne? What about my husband: is John Staples here yet?"

Andrea said to Dr. Springer, "Let's talk in the hall. Be right back, Mama."

Andrea and Gerry exited, closing the door behind. Mother's cries could be heard coming through the door as another contraction set in.

Andrea cut right to it. "This is bullshit. Where is this fool Payne?"

"Sue Gartner dialed him. That's what I know."

"So did I. A good fifteen minutes ago. Has he even answered?"

"Unknown."

She already knew the answer, but asked anyway, "So what are we looking at here, Gerry?"

"Realistically the heart rate strip shows weird decelerations with short-term variability. Someone needs to cut her open stat or we're going to get a bad baby."

"How much time do we have?"

"That baby better be lifted out of her in the next thirty minutes or we've got brain damage. Maybe just twenty-five minutes." His shoulders slumped. "I hate hospitals."

"And you're just getting started. Anyway, I'll put it in the chart right now, that we discussed C-section."

"That's my call. Put it in the nurse's notes and I'll chart it too."

"I'm also paging over and over for an OB doctor. They'll have to get someone here."

"Let's do it. Make the page."

3

A t 6:38 p.m. Latoya Staples was still caught up in the violent throes of childbirth. Across town, her OB-GYN was relaxing with his wife in their hot tub. They lived in the Park Ridge neighborhood about twenty minutes from Hudd Family Hospital, even in rush hour traffic. Their home was a modest townhouse, pool and hot tub in the back.

OB-GYN Phillip Payne had seen Latoya Staples four times before that night. He knew her fairly well and knew her husband, John. Latoya had been sonogrammed and told her baby was a boy.

When the STAT page arrived from Hudd Family Hospital, Dr. Payne in the hot tub, accompanied by wife Monica, was savoring a Tequila Sunrise. All but blind without his glasses, the OB stood in the tub and groped around on the cool deck for his glasses while the beeper was going off. Across from him in the tub Monica looked tight-lipped and angry. She said, "Must you get that? We're talking here."

He responded with a very poor choice of words, given the moment and the discussion—interrogation—they were having. "It's my beeper. You know I'm married to the damn thing."

"I thought you were married to me. At least I thought you were until you hired Beverly Melendez as your nurse practitioner. Now I'm not so sure."

He tried ignoring her as he squinted at the page. She suddenly stood, reached across the water, and plunged the beeper under the hot churning foam. Through the tub's under-lit water the beeper could be followed as it settled on the Fiberglas bottom.

"Now what the hell did you do that for?"

"You know it's only some heaving cow who felt a twinge and wants to know if she should leave for the hospital."

"No, I *don't* know that. It could be someone in delivery right now. And I'll never know, not with my beeper shorted out."

"Well, I'll bet you had time for Beverly today. How about time for me right now? Let the hospital staff tend to the cow. Don't you get to miss a delivery every now and then just for the hell of it?"

"I always have time for you." He frowned playfully. "I suppose there should be two OBs on the unit tonight."

An opening! Monica suddenly turned amorous and teasing. "Then let's have another glass of Love Potion and grope each other. I'm hot."

Dr. Payne retrieved the beeper from the tub floor. He studied it for any evidence of the missed page. Nothing.

"You can call your service and get the page. But first you have to service me."

"That can definitely be arranged. You refresh our glasses and I'll hop out and call the service."

"Not so fast. You hold that pose and I'll go underwater and see what's what."

"Wicked girl."

Monica submerged and turned to face her husband. His face relaxed, his arms rose up out of the water in surrender, and the page was temporarily forgotten.

Later, as he was leaving the house for the hospital, she stepped between him and the door. The wife asked, "Aren't you forgetting something?"

"Not that I know of. Why?"

She pulled a damp curl of hair from her forehead and looked exasperated. "Tonight's Franklin's final Little League game. Under the lights. You haven't been to one of his games all season. You put in an appearance tonight or you'll hear from my lawyers."

"God, you can be so melodramatic."

"Don't test me. Be there even if it's only ten minutes. I'm not joking here."

"It's already on my calendar. See you there."

ANDREA AND DR. SPRINGER were poised at the foot of the bed, quietly conferring. Dr. Springer studied the fetal heart rate printout. Student nurse Nancy was lifting Latoya's head from the pillow and placing a dry towel beneath when Dr. Payne strode into the room, all business.

Dr. Payne almost shouted, "Latoya! How are we feeling?"

Despite her agony, a smile came to Latoya's mouth. "Exhausted. My first two were nothing like this."

"It happens. We don't know why but a third or fourth can be brutal. Maybe it's the mother's age." He laughed. She grimaced.

Dr. Springer reported, "She's dilated six centimeters."

Andrea added, "And we've got variable decelerations."

Dr. Payne slipped his hand under the sheet and probed. "I'm getting four centimeters, Doctor. She's probably four hours from delivery. At least four, I would predict. The strip looks within normal limits so I wouldn't worry too much about the decels. Just means the baby's getting tired like his mom."

Latoya moaned. "Four hours! Am I having this baby today? Can we just start the Pitocin and get it over with?"

Dr. Payne ignored her. He said to Dr. Springer, "Let's talk in the hall."

Outside in the hall, Dr. Payne tapped a cigarette from the pack in his jacket pocket but didn't light up.

"Look, Gerry. I've got a must-see. My kid's Little League. Last game of the season. The park's not twenty minutes. I'll run over, do the proud father bit, and be back before she hits eight centimeters."

Dr. Springer didn't look convinced. "Well...you're the expert. But don't third and fourths come faster sometimes?"

"No, you're right, it can happen. But I'm making my four-hour call based on how little she's dilated since admit four hours ago. She was one then, she's three or four now. I've got another four hours before she hits eight, at least. I'm leaving you in charge of the case. If those decels fall any lower just page me. I'm back here in twenty minutes if necessary."

"I can handle it. But I haven't done a Caesarean, so please eyeball the clock."

Dr. Payne exited and Gerry returned inside.

A half hour passed while the staff attended to Latoya's needs. Almost unnoticed, Andrea tugged at the doctor's sleeve. "C'mon in the hall, please." They left the room and closed the door behind. Mother's cries could be heard coming through the door.

"How long did Dr. Payne say he'd be?"

"Twenty there, twenty back, maybe twenty at the game."

"I hate these cases where the damn OB isn't on top of things."

Twenty minutes crept by while the staff tried again and again to make mom comfortable, squeezed her hands during contractions, and urged her on. Gerry Springer reviewed the fetal heart monitor almost nonstop.

Andrea watched him closely for a sign. "You saw the heart rate strip and I saw the frown. What are you seeing?"

"I'm not positive. But I think I'm reading it right."

"So what are we looking at here, Gerry?"

"As I read it, the heart rate strip shows late decelerations with short-term variability on every contraction. This is new. Someone needs to seriously consider taking the baby out now."

"How long do we have, best case?"

"Stat. I don't want to cry wolf and get Payne pissed at me. But if I had to give my opinion, I would say the kid should come out now or we're going to chance a bad baby."

"Best guess?"

"According to the textbook that baby better be lifted out of her in the next thirty minutes or we've got brain damage."

"I'll put it in the chart right now, that we called for a C-section within thirty minutes from right"—she checked her men's wristwatch—"now. Six thirty-five p.m. That baby has to be breathing on it's own by seven oh-five."

Five minutes flew by and they could stand it no longer.

At six forty p.m., Nurse Andrea, Gerry, two orderlies, and Nancy were rushing Latoya along the hospital corridor leading to the operating room.

Andrea shouted to the team, "It's six forty-five. This baby is due out in fifteen minutes."

By now they had given up all pretense of speaking truth

outside Latoya's presence. Whatever needed to be said got said right in front of her. Their joint consensus was that things had deteriorated to the most urgent situation possible.

Nancy smiled down at Latoya. "How you feeling, Mom?"

"Dear Jesus, just let my baby be OK."

Dr. Springer tried to reassure her. "Doctor Payne will be here any minute. He's probably parking right about now."

"He's paid in full. I don't know why he isn't here yet."

As they cornered the end of the hall and she found herself squeezed between the bed and the wall, Nancy barked, "Easy! Bring it around easy. All right, we're off!"

With that they rushed the bed into the OR. As a team they transferred mother to operating table.

The gloved anesthesiologist was already syringing his sleep chemical into Latoya's IV. Her eyes fluttered and closed in an instant. The team stood around, nervously whispering; everyone studied the clock on the OR wall.

At 7:00 straight up, Dr. Springer paged Sue Gartner. Would she again page the hospital for any other OBs that might be on-site? And where the hell's Dr. Payne? Moments later they heard Sue's page, but no one responded to the OR.

So, they waited.

4

The OR clock crawled to 7:16, at which time Dr. Payne floated through the door.

Immediately he was gowned and gloved. He straightway moved to the operating table and placed the scalpel against Latoya's belly.

It was noted but not recorded anywhere that he had a strong odor of alcoholic beverage, as the DWI cops would put it. Andrea carefully followed his work, ready to speak up if there was the slightest fault in what he was trying to do. She had had it with him and would risk a disciplinary complaint by him in order to make sure things went correctly from then on.

At 7:18 Dr. Payne lifted the newborn from the mother's abdomen. The baby was severely jaundiced and barely moving. It was clear to the attending staff there was something seriously wrong with this baby. They suctioned the infant and handed it off to the newborn unit. Dr. Payne closed the mother's abdomen and smiled at her as she came to.

Latoya was very groggy. "How is he? He was stuck in there so long!"

The doctor opened his mouth but was speechless. He shook his head and quickly closed and began bandaging the wound. "All right, then, I'm off."

"Latoya, are you ready to ride up to your room?" It was Andrea and her voice was strangely subdued. It didn't fool Latoya, who began crying, softly at first, then growing in volume as she reached greater consciousness.

"Where is he? How come I can't see him?"

"He's being cleaned up. It'll just be a few minutes."

Her face was wet with tears. "Where's my baby? Is he coming too? And where the hell is John? Why isn't my husband here?"

Dr. Springer said, "Doctor Payne said your baby is with the newborn doctors right now. They're assessing him and we should have him in to meet you very soon."

As they rolled out into the hallway, Nurse Andrea asked, "What's his name?"

Latoya, quietly crying, managed, "With all this running around and fuss, my baby's name is going to be Chase. My baby's name is Chase."

Two hours post-delivery, a neonatal team of physicians and nurses still worked on Chase Staples. They were chilling him in an effort to avoid further damage.

Dr. Amelia Henry, head of neonatology, said, "Whose baby is this? Who the hell let this happen?"

Frank Adamson, M.D., who accompanied the baby from the OR said, "Phillip Payne. It's one of his."

"Not the first one he's had."

"This is the second this year."

Dr. Henry softly grasped Chase's tiny hand and shook his head. "Gentlemen and ladies, we have a bad baby on our hands."

"A very bad baby."

Dr. Henry looked up. "Someone who prays, this is a great time for a prayer."

"You'll be charged with obstruction of justice."

"He kidnapped my little girl. Now she won't talk. He has to pay for what he's done."

"I knew this would happen." Special Agent Pauline Pepper was furious. She flicked a yellow lighter and fired up a Salem. She swore softly. Her dark green eyes flashed and she fixed Thaddeus Murfee with her thousand-yard stare. He met her gaze and they locked eyes. She dared him; he dared her.

They were seated at a twenty-person conference table, papers strewn before them out to the fifty yard line, and more documents on the way as office workers scurried about the Chicago FBI Regional Office, gathering all items demanded by Thaddeus in his *Freedom of Information Act* request.

"How about I don't respond to your written request? How about I make you take me to court?"

He shrugged. "I can do that. Happy to oblige, Miss Pepper."

"Asshole."

Their dispute was territorial. The *Freedom of Information Act* data dump had revealed the identity of his daughter's kidnapper. The girl had been located and brought home well and safe to Thaddeus and Katy. But Thaddeus was after the perps. The *FOIA* paperwork contained it all and now he had names and last-knowns.

The rest of the documents being brought into the room by the FBI's clerical staff were simply icing on the cake. More would be revealed once he had it all copied and back in his own office where he could silence the phones, kick off his shoes, and spend a couple of days going over each and every document and photograph with a microscope. When he was done, he would have a full and complete picture of Sarai's kidnapper. He would have the target's photograph—probably several. He would have his last known address, usual occupation, Social Security number (if there was one —who knew where the guy might be from?), and all the rest of the bits and pieces the world's greatest criminal agency had amassed about the guy.

The FBI sit-rep room in Chicago was quiet. An HVAC fan could be heard spinning in the ceiling.

"You're not hearing me, Thaddeus. You so much as follow this guy around the block and I will personally see to it that you're charged with obstruction of justice and arrested.

Thaddeus shook his head. "Funny thing is, the guy didn't kidnap *your* daughter. It was mine. Do you know she still won't speak? And she's five years old!"

"Nobody is sorrier to hear that than I am. Trust me."

"The doctors don't know what to do with her, the shrinks can't drag a word or a facial expression out of her."

"God." Her voice came down an octave. "What do they say it is?"

"PTSD is the working diagnosis. Katy thinks she's autistic. From the kidnapping."

"What do you think?"

Thaddeus grimaced. "I think I'd like five minutes with the guy. That's all I'm asking."

"Thaddeus we know your history. We know what you do to bad guys. But this guy is a matter of national security."

Thaddeus tilted his head. "What's that mean?"

"We believe he's part of a cell. That's all I can say right now. Except do not interfere. Do I have your word?"

"You have my word that I'll do whatever it takes to protect my family. Fair enough?"

"Brother, you've been warned."

"I will promise this. I won't do anything until after I've been through every shred of paper and had my own security people analyze what you've turned over."

Pepper slammed her fist against the table. "This *FOIA* does not entitle you to take the first shot. Ragman belongs to the FBI. We will hunt him down and bring him to justice."

Thaddeus could only smile. "You're starting to sound like your fearless leader, the President now. He's always about to 'hunt someone down' and 'bring them to justice.' That's cop talk for make an arrest, have a trial, Fed Fun Farm for 36 months, then back on the street. That won't work this time."

"Then interfere. You'll be the one headed to jail."

Thaddeus nodded. "That wouldn't be the worst thing that's happened to me since I sued the mob. Not by far."

Agent Pepper crushed the Salem and thoughtfully peeled the paper from the stub. She pushed around the overflowing ashtray, deep in thought.

"Tell you what, Thad. How about I promise to give you

weekly sit-reps on the guy if you keep out of it. That's something I never do, but I'll make an exception in your case."

"It's a start."

"Will that keep your dick in your pants?"

"I can't promise anything today."

She sighed and rubbed her eyes. "Let's get this stuff copied. We'll help load it in your car."

"My Tesla's downstairs. It won't hold much."

"How about we scan it and I send you a CD?"

"That'll work. By Friday?"

"Monday?"

"Done."

He extended his hand and they shook.

A temporary truce had been reached. Very temporary, he thought to himself.

Very temporary.

7

Four Middle Eastern men entered the famed Willis Building (ex Sears Tower) in Chicago. Four cell mates. One was an expert in nuclear engineering, one in computer networks, one in electrical engineering, and one in cartography. Sullen and angry they filed in, all wearing backpacks secured by locks requiring a thumbprint to open. They were dressed not as TV terrorists in black pajamas, sandals, and turbans. These four were dressed business casual: Dockers, Ralph Lauren Polo Shirts, tasseled loafers, and Gucci eyeglasses. They looked like the computer geeks laboring in the computer network room where servers whir and data gets deep-frozen for instant access by corporate masters.

In the football field–size lobby of the nation's tallest building they approached the bank of forty elevators and moved to the far end, away from the corporate types jammed together for a ride upstairs. There was no security to pass through, no X-rays of backpack contents, no electronic scans for weapons. At the concierge desk, four uniformed employees were lost in conversation, comparing happiness levels about the overtime game the Bulls won the night before against the Miami Heat. No notice of the four men was taken. The visitors were as plain vanilla as the thousands of other computer geeks and corporate servants who passed through the lobby 24/7.

Without a spoken word the visitors rode the elevator skyward eighty-five floors and exited into a lush hallway, deeply carpeted and lined with richly paneled walls. At one end was an unmarked door. At the other was an opaque glass door marked "Worldwide Expositions." They proceeded single-file to the glass door and entered without speaking to the male receptionist, who was wearing a holstered Colt .45 ACP. The foursome disappeared down a long hallway that terminated at an open conference room. At either side of the open door lurked hulking, swarthy men in expensive suits, unsmiling, but moving aside as the men approached. The four men entered the room, arranged themselves around the curved end of the forty-foot table, and removed their backpacks. Last man in turned and quietly closed the heavy steel-lined door.

"Exactly as ordered," said the man who chose the seat at the head of the table.

"Yes, Ragman," said the prematurely gray electrical engineer. He had a two-day growth and protruding eyes, giving him a haunted, owlish look. His name was Omar Kayem, affectionately called Kilowatt by his cellmates.

Ragman scowled. "Didn't even stop us and ask us our business. Who are these Americans? Don't they realize the sword of Islam is ready to fall on them?"

The computer scientist smiled. His real name was Maliki Al-Salim. "Ragman, NSA has intercepted every text we have sent over the last two weeks. Disinformation is in play." Named for Data of Star Wars fame, Al-Salim looked at their leader, hoping for his approval. Not everyone had a man placed inside the NSA with full access to all data. But Data did.

"Your man tells you NSA has our messages?" said Ragman.

"Yes," said Data. "And the reliability score is in the ninety-ninth percentile."

"The data score or your man's score?"

Data smiled and nodded, again seeking approbation. "Both."

"Excellent," said Kilowatt. "You have done well, Data."

"It's a team effort," said Data. "We must never forget."

"Precisely," said Ragman. He shot Data a quick smile, which relaxed all faces around the table.

The fourth man was Maps.

They used code names in all communications. All men were on no-fly lists; none was in the United States by visa. All were illegal; all were terrorists pursued day and night by Interpol and the FBI. To a man, all had proven his allegiance to Allah by the assassination of a family member. It meant nothing.

Now they had come together for the Final Solution.

They unloaded their backpacks.

There was a beryllium shell. Two hundred feet of wire. A dozen bars of C4 to implode the blast into the core.

And there was the Ragman's Ph.D. in nuclear engineering. He would assemble the parts into the whole. Kilowatt would create a network of wires with his electrical engineering. Data would disable the city of Chicago's emergency response network. And Maps. He would reverse all surface roads and freeways so traffic flow out of the city would be impossible.

A fifty-megaton bomb.

Capable of an airburst from atop the Willis Tower.

The plan was genius in its simplicity. No airplanes this time, no TSA comparing photos on no-fly lists, no hijackings. From the eighty-fifth floor they would have the perfect platform.

It would level the Loop plus two miles around. Seven hundred thousand would incinerate in the burst. Two million from radiation and burns. Allah would be pleased.

A core of fissile material would come across from Mexico in sixty days.

Then assembly could commence.

LATOYA AND JOHN STAPLES knew Chase had significant problems from the moment of his birth. But just how significant, they weren't told until finally, the third evening after his birth, a neonatology doctor met with them in Latoya's hospital room. She drew the curtain ring for privacy and launched into the case. She—Nancy Jarvis, M.D.—spared them none of what the doctors thought they knew about the baby up to that point. The findings on examination indicated severe mental deficits, but nobody was yet able—or willing, Latoya guessed—to fasten the blame for Chase's problems on any doctor or on any of the events of the birth. In short, the baby was damaged and so far they didn't see him progressing as normal.

On discharge they were referred to Armando Arroyo, M.D. He was a pediatric neurologist. His job was to follow Chase's case.

LATOYA AND JOHN liked Dr. Arroyo as soon as they met him. He was a middle-aged goateed Latino with a huge smile and piercing eyes. His hair was white and he wore trifocals. He also wore two turquoise rings, as he was a transplant from New Mexico some twenty years ago and loved that indigenous stone. His pleasant manner and exhaustive approach had impressed Latoya, and she had seen his preliminary reports. She thought the world of the man and totally trusted his opinions.

On that first visit he scheduled Chase for films. Images would be taken of the baby's brain and then they would all meet again.

8

S anford—Sandy—Green was the head of the Special
Claims Unit of Hudd Family Healthcare. He worked
out of the home office in Chicago. Special Claims
was special because it forged medical records. Never having
been one with scruples to interfere, Sandy loved the job. Its
work was secret, he operated without supervision, and he
hired outside counsel to defend the healthcare provider's
doctors, nurses, and hospitals. Payback for the $700/hour
legal work was extraordinary. The outside lawyers bought
gourmet meals, comped him to ski condos in Aspen, sun
condos in the Caymans, Super Bowl tickets, March Madness
seats, Bulls games—the list was endless.

Not to mention the cash they coughed up. It arrived in
actual brown paper bags.

Sandy Green was fast growing rich and nobody knew—
and nobody cared, either, as long as Sandy's Special Claims
Unit kept producing patient records and doctor reports that
were sandpapered and contained no evidence of doctor
screw-ups. Inside the four corners of the records there could
be no smoking guns. Keep the doctors and hospitals free of

negligence in their records, and anything went, as long as the IRS or FBI didn't snoop.

Sandy was an unvarnished college dropout whose own corners were rough. He preferred shiny, worn suits and scuffed wingtips to high fashion. Yet he answered to no one and how he dressed was nobody's business and so the hell with those at Hudd Family Healthcare who clucked their tongue at him. He performed work that was nobody's business and he would dress however he wanted, plus it was cheaper that way. And Sandy was always out to save a buck. Especially the big bucks at HFH. He treated the health care company's money like his own and the vice presidents doted on him for this.

Sandy's Special Claims Unit was responsible for the defense of all health care claims with a potential for costing the insurance company more than one million dollars. And he was excellent at his job. Not once in four years had a medical malpractice claim cost them over a million. The company's pockets were bulging with cash, and there was enough to go around to Sandy and his staff in bonuses, to make sure the cash piled up ever deeper in the vault.

Everyone at Hudd Family was happy.

SEVENTEEN CLAIMS HAD discovery deadlines running out. The plaintiff's lawyers wanted the medical records that Hudd Family had collected from its hospitals. The lawyers wanted the medical records for one reason: to find the smoking gun, the page or pages that would bury the health care company with a record verdict. But they would never find those smoking guns, not with Sandy's unit running interference. For him the entire litigation business was a game, a time-honored game that was played by the rules of Hide the Ball.

Here's how the rules worked. Sandy's group took in medical records from its doctors and hospitals and then washed those records—removing all taint of wrongdoing—before the records went public.

March 14 was like any other day at the office. It was rainy outside, which made some people glum, but not Sandy. In his peculiar shuffle gait, he stepped up to the desk of Amanda Barr, a cursive specialist working at one of the twenty-five cubicles under his command. It was quiet in the room; they labored behind locked doors and most of them wore headphones to enhance their concentration.

He waited until Amanda paused her writing. You couldn't pay these graphics folks enough money, he thought. They were worth every penny and he treated them with great respect. She finally noticed him and lifted an earphone. He said, "The Klinghoffer case. How are the doctor's notes looking?"

She smiled. She liked her boss. Everybody liked Sandy. "Just about rewritten. Dr. Johnson's handwriting is easy enough to copy." They always used the word "copy." It just sounded so much better than "forge."

Amanda and her co-workers in Special Claims had one thing in common. They were for the most part single parents in desperate need of money, thrilled to have jobs in a very down economy, and paid like kings. Hudd Family Healthcare took excellent care of these secret people. They were highly trained in the art of document forgery. They were sworn to secrecy. Before anyone's first day on the job they pledged a security oath that would have made even the NSA jealous. They passed rigorous background checks run on them by XFBI, Inc., weeding out those with any connection to law enforcement by birth or by marriage. They were paid as much or more than the company's junior vice presidents. They checked in and out each day with ID badges and were all but strip-searched randomly. No one knew when XFBI's door-keepers were going to run a strip. It could happen once in a week; it could happen twice in one day. The keen eyes of XFBI were on the lookout especially for floppies and flash drives.

XFBI enforced Hudd Family's policy of one hundred percent security. Even the staff computers were assembled without USB ports, so external drives or flashes could not connect up. Additionally, no employee had connectivity to the Internet so there was no chance of storing records on the cloud. The entire service was a closed loop.

Sandy handed Amanda a pale blue envelope. "This is for your excellent work this month on your three cases. SCU says thanks!"

She blushed. She knew there was at least $500 inside. Monthly spiffs were another aspect of the job where they were sworn to secrecy. The workers didn't know it, but the cash came from a secret company account in Costa Rica, impossible to trace, thanks to the forward-thinking foreign government and its labyrinthine system of national banking that rivaled the Swiss.

"What's the key to the case?" Sandy asked.

She rolled her eyes. "Dr. Johnson made the mistake of writing in Mrs. Klinghoffer's hospital notes that the clouds on the X-ray had never been visualized before."

"Clouds? Cancer?"

"Yep. The truth was, a radiologist had reviewed the same X-rays forty-five days earlier who warned of a neoplasm that was probably cancerous. That report was in her original file."

"So the doctor missed the cancer on the X-rays."

"He sure did."

"I see. How did you handle it?"

"Two things. First, I changed the radiologist's report to read the mass was benign. Second, I changed Dr. Johnson's notes to indicate he was relying on the radiologist's reading. He believed that mass was benign, according to my new record."

His brow furrowed. "What did India say?"

"I called India and spoke with Dr. Hasleym."

"Our radiologist."

"He reviewed the record and suggested that's how it be changed, that we pass it off as a radiology error."

"He wants to have the radiologist report the mass was benign?"

"Yes. So I followed his instructions and now we've got a new set of records ready for turnover to Mr. Klinghoffer's attorneys."

"And the radiologist?"

"Not connected with Hudd. He'll have his own cross to bear."

The case was now a wrongful death case. Mrs. Klinghoffer had in fact passed away after the mass had traveled through her body and attached to organs it then devoured. Mister Klinghoffer had lost his wife of thirty-eight years and he was about to lose her lawsuit as well.

Sandy patted Amanda's shoulder. "Nicely done. What's the next case up?"

"Chase Staples."

"Doctor?"

"Phillip Payne."

"Injury?"

"Uh—anoxia. Catastrophic brain injury. NICU says he'll never live independently."

"Look it over and then let's talk."

"Will do."

He was pleased with Special Claims, pleased with his workers, and pleased with himself for having the brains to do such important work.

Meanwhile, outside the locked doors of Special Claims, Hudd Family Healthcare aggressively pursued new patients through its shiny brochures and colorful advertising, churning out hospital stay after hospital stay, secure in the knowledge it would never suffer a knockout punch.

9

Hudd wanted Morgana Bridgman. Hudd was the second largest healthcare provider in the country, 107 hospitals and 36,000 physicians. Which meant they got sued habitually for medical malpractice. "Habitually" as in every day, several times a day.

Morgana was the ascendant medical malpractice defense attorney in all of Chicago. She was twenty-eight, a graduate of Cornell Law, women's NCAA basketball championship team, and a street fighter. They liked everything about her and wanted her to take over all their business in the Midwest. Hudd thought it a perfect match. She had responded positively to their feelers.

What Hudd didn't know, ironically, was her health.

Morgana was in trial the day she got the death sentence. Her own death sentence, it turned out. Which was unusual for a defense attorney in a trial that was not a criminal trial.

It was a three-banger trial—three days total, including jury selection, Bang-Bang-Bang, Jury Time. The plaintiff was a young woman whose nasal passages had buckled following surgery. Morgana's client was the plastic surgeon who had operated to remove a bump from the nose that the young woman had hated all her life. The surgeon followed routine protocols, packed the nose when he was finished, and left the surgicenter. The patient came in three days later complaining she could no longer breathe through her nose.

The doctor beamed a light up her nose. The passageways had indeed collapsed. Morgana's defense was that the patient had slept wrong, against doctor's orders, crushing her nose into her pillow. Result: no airflow.

Morgana paid an expert ENT $25,000 to testify. The expert was young, handsome, Harvard-trained, and admitted with special privileges to three Chicago hospitals. The jury loved him. What the jury would never know was that Hudd Family Healthcare had purchased three doctors for Morgana's case, two men and a young woman. They were all waiting in the wings, wondering which of them would actually be called to testify. In the end, the young doc was chosen because the jury consisted of eight women and four men. The women swooned over his good looks, and the men admired that he treated NFL Hall-of-Famers for injuries suffered in their Sunday brand of violence. Some of the players were Bears greats, and he named names. The men were hanging on every word. The women were hanging on every emotion he expressed, every turn of phrase, and his vulnerability. Perfect jury; the domino tiles fell as laid out.

Morgana wound up with a defense verdict and went 29-0. Better record than any NFL team would ever have.

What Morgana didn't know, however, was the defendant doctor's medical records were lies, compliments of Hudd Family Healthcare and Sandy Green.

In the defense of medical malpractice cases, lawyers like Morgana simply assumed that the records they had received from their clients, the hospitals, were genuine. It would never have occurred to her to suspect that the records were forged. So she had won the case using phony records. Did she know that? Absolutely not. Would she have used the records had she known they were phony? Morgana prided herself on the unconditionally ethical practice of law. She never bent the rules and she knew she would never run afoul of the Bar Association's ethics. So the answer was a loud "No!" she would never use forgeries.

When it was ended, she was tired. Way too tired for a twenty-eight-year-old who considered herself the picture of health. She jogged, ate right, didn't smoke, light drinks— maybe a couple of beers on Saturday while she washed the old Volvo, maybe an occasional wine with one of Caroline's fish dinners where her partner insisted a white was mandatory.

It had her perplexed, but not worried, the persistent voice telling her to lie down and nap. So she left for home after the trial, foregoing the office fly-by where you stick your head in, the partners shake your hand and fawn over your twenty-ninth defense verdict. And where the senior partner offers you a scotch and a one-on-one inside his office, door closed, reminding you how important you are to Jones Marentz, the medical malpractice firm known and feared throughout Chicago. She passed on all that.

It was a dull, overcast day, windy enough to blow you off the curb, with a blizzard-like snowstorm mixed with sleet mixed with ice. The kind of day that made you want to be inside with your family, shades drawn, coffee brewing, good book waiting.

She dropped off second-chair Manny Rodriguez on LaSalle and bolted north on US 41.

No sooner had she merged into the fast lane than her

cell chimed. Dr. Romulus' office. Right off she knew it was ominous, because the nurse said, "Please hold for Doctor Romulus."

"It's never good when your doctor calls you personally," she said to no one.

Turned out he was calling with the hospital workup. The information was conveyed in four short sentences. The jury was back and it was unanimous. It was leukemia and Morgana had six, maybe eight months. Unless chemo worked; which it did—sometimes. And didn't—sometimes. Come in Monday.

In shock, Morgana thanked him for the call, promised she would come in Monday, and ended the call. She balled her fist and slammed it into the dash. "Damn!" she cried. She fought back tears for several miles, trying to remain calm, avoiding the shakes by focusing on the road.

Finally she let a thought break through.

It was okay, in an odd way. It didn't exactly shock her. She had been raised Methodist and had some distant notion about a score on her life being kept somewhere. She was only just now beginning to question where that kind of thinking came from and whether it was valid for her anymore.

She was maybe a late bloomer about such things. But she gave herself a little breathing room in that category. She had been very preoccupied with other things than spiritual questions these past five years. Things like staying alive. Things like her relationship with Caroline. Sure, she had sent desperate people home without a dime, but that's what lawsuits were for. Winners and losers. Law school hadn't taught her to seek justice. Law school taught her to win.

She shivered though the seven-year-old Volvo was warm. The March roads were slick and getting worse by the minute, visibility down to maybe a half-mile. By 3:45 road-side lights were appearing in restaurants and farmhouses even as she drove further north toward Evanston.

Suddenly all she could think about was Caroline. They were coming up on their Paper (five years), and they were still going strong. She loved Caroline, who loved Morgana. She could still chase her around the bedroom; Caroline could make her warm on her coldest day; what wasn't to like? Morgana dreaded breaking it to her.

Absolutely dreaded it.

She took Ridge into Evanston.

Morgana didn't tell Caroline that night. She figured Sunday night she would ask Caroline to accompany her to see Dr. Romulus. She would tell her only that it "sounded serious."

No sense scaring her to death until they knew more.

10

After Morgana's collapsed nose trial, the courtroom had emptied, but two players remained behind. They talked in low tones. They were A.W. Marentz—Morgana's boss and senior partner at Jones Marentz—and Sandy Green. They had commandeered counsel table.

Sandy cast a quick look around the dark room and said, "Morgana *really* buried the broken nose lady."

"That girl's a thoroughbred," said A.W.

"You've done our bidding forty years, A.W. Is Morgana ready for the load?"

A.W. leaned back and removed his glasses. He rubbed the bridge of his nose. "She is. She'll do a super job. I want out of the rat race. I'm getting too old for this B.S., even second-chair is tough when you have to urinate every hour."

Sandy leaned close and almost whispered, "Does she know how we work yet?"

A.W. leaned forward. "She does not."

"Does she suspect?"

"She does not. She's no dummy. But does she know we're

doctoring hospital records? I think not. She would have raised hell with me otherwise—she's anything but shy."

"She's doing such a bang-up job we want her to take over from you. Do you think there's going to be a problem when she finds out about the records we've been feeding her all along?"

A.W. shrugged. "We'll find that out one week from tonight. She's been voted a partnership in the firm as of ten this morning. There's a party and announcement planned for one week from now. Before she gets in too deep I want to break the news to her. Carson's in agreement."

"Will you tell her how we do things?"

"All of it. Carson's been after me six months to break it to her. He wants to know if Morgana's going to bolt or stay around."

"Carson still managing partner?"

"Yep—he's Managing, I'm Senior. It's all good, as they say. We're both ready for Morgana to make our med mal defense practice her own domain."

"Well, Hudd Family Healthcare is behind that one hundred percent."

"But only if she performs. All we can do now is tell her and see how she responds. She can still walk on us, and just might."

Sandy nodded. "We can only hope. And pray."

"I better hop to it." A.W. lurched to his feet. He was old and obviously worn down, ready for a rest, though that wouldn't come for another week yet. "First things first. A grand announcement in one week, after she says yes and arrangements get made."

"Excellent. I saw Peter out front with your car when I hit the restroom."

"Being senior partner has its perks."

Sandy stood and stretched. "Well, Morgana is hungry enough to stick around. She devoured these witnesses today and looked like a Baptist preacher, kind and caring."

"Keep in mind, she owes Cornell Law over three hundred grand in student loans. And I've just made sure her payments triple."

Sandy whistled. "Triple. How did you pull that off?"

A.W. only winked. "I'm a big contributor to whichever party's in power. You never know when you'll have to call a favor."

ANOTHER TRIAL, another victory. Morgana Bridgman was now 30-0.

She smiled as she raced her assistant, Manny, back to Jones Marentz on LaSalle Street.

In the parking garage of the American United Tower, one parking space was marked Morgana Bridgman. Waiting patiently at the headstone was Carson Black, handsomely dressed in a three-piece Armani and Italian tasseled loafers. He smiled when he saw a red Porsche slowly nose in and park in Morgana's spot. The car was a brand new Turbo Cabriolet, a 500-horsepower monster with a top speed of 194 MPH. A young associate climbed out. The young lawyer lovingly looked over the car he had just gotten to drive from the dealership.

Carson clasped the young attorney's shoulder as he received the keys. "You won't soon forget that ride, Eddie Zarnoff."

"Maybe there's one waiting for me in a couple of years. You're the managing partner, what do you think?" This was said half-seriously but the young attorney paused in case there was an answer.

"It's taken Morgana five years to get hers. Plus she had a year clerking at the Court of Appeals. Give yourself time."

The associate nodded. The flashy Porsche key fob glinted in the fluorescent light.

MORGANA PULLED in two beats later. She stopped with the nose of her Volvo perpendicular to her parking space. Some idiot had left his show-off red Porsche in Morgana's spot. She imagined Carson was there to have it towed. She had to admit, her boxy Volvo looked dull next to the Porsche. She leaned over and rolled down the window.

"What gives? Who's in my space?"

Carson smiled. "You are."

"Come again?"

"Turn it off and come here."

Something was definitely up. She obeyed the managing partner and exited the Volvo. She leaned and inspected the Porsche's interior—who could resist?

"Great car. Have I been replaced by someone driving a turbo Porsche?"

"Nope. Guess again."

"I give—"

"It's yours, Morgana. A gift from your partners."

"My *partners*? Say that again?"

"Here." Carson tossed the keys, which Morgana snagged with one hand. Couldn't let *those* touch the ground. She stared at Carson like Curious George.

"This better be real 'cause you guys ain't never getting this car returned."

"Come on inside. Some people want to talk to you."

"No way, I want a test drive. Can I drive it first?"

"Come inside first. After that, you can drive it all you want. It's yours."

"Yes, sir."

Only too happy to oblige, Morgana followed the managing partner upstairs to the office. She clutched the keys tightly in her right hand. Caroline was going to faint over this. The woman loved Porsche anythings.

11

On the twelfth floor of the American United Tower the partners of Jones Marentz had begun celebrating in the large banquet room. A mahogany table shimmering under stained antique Venetian Lanterns centered the partners' room. The room reeked of rare and pricey.

When Morgana entered the room, a group of twenty-two partners, standing in rows at either side of the table, began soft applause that swelled in volume. Needless to say, she blushed head-to-toe.

"What gives?" Morgana said in her most apprehensive voice. "My going-away party? You're letting me go?"

A.W. seized her hand and led her forward. His courtroom voice commanded everyone's attention. "Welcome home, Morgana. Here she is, gentlemen! Back from the field, the deer slung across her shoulders. The hunter returns!"

She pulled up short. "Screw me. This is nothing but embarrassing."

A.W. Marentz swept her into the group of clapping, backslapping partners. "Get in here, genius."

Managing partner Carson Palmer followed close behind her. He placed an arm around Morgana's back. Everyone was just a little tipsy, Morgana was realizing, and they couldn't have been friendlier or happier for her. Someone thrust a Coors into her hand. Carson raised his hands for silence. The cheering and clapping faded away.

Carson, officiating now, began, "Morgana, meet your partners. These gentlemen and ladies and I are so impressed with your work that we have voted you a full partnership today. What do you have to say?"

All eyes were on Morgana as she instinctively made her way to the head of the table, where she raised her beer in a toast. "Gentlemen, to you and to Jones Marentz. May we all grow wealthy together!"

A partner at the far end of the table shouted, "We're already wealthy, kid. Try again."

Laughter erupted.

Morgana tried again. "Well then, may I grow wealthy too."

"Hear, hear," roared the bullish A.W. "Carson, would you tell the contestant what she's won?"

Extracting a sealed envelope from his inside jacket pocket, Carson carefully and with a flourish placed the envelope in Morgana's hand. This was the best part, the money part. The room was very quiet. "For openers, your base salary is two hundred fifty thousand per year. Plus bonus against billings."

Morgana smiled and wisecracked, "My Realtor's going to love hearing this."

Scattered laughter.

"Moving along. The Porsche is not a lease. It has been purchased and titled in the firm's name. Jones Marentz pays the insurance which, at your age, is unaffordable by mere mortals."

"Don't make her feel bad," someone offered.

"Full medical coverage, retirement fully funded after ten years, country club membership, health club membership, platinum American Express, and funding for two associates to do your bidding. "

She knew she looked confused. "Two associates? How the hell am I supposed to keep two associates busy?"

A.W. said, "Here's the best part. I just finished up with Sandy over at Hudd Family Healthcare. They want you to take over all their work, Chicago and downstate. You'll definitely need the two associates."

She stopped and turned. Morgana's heart flipped. This was what she had been working toward all these years. "You must be kidding. That's awesome."

Carson shook his head. "After your string of wins? They'd be fools not to grab your star and hang on."

Morgana's face reddened almost to purple with embarrassment. This went way over the edge; it was too good.

"Not kidding," A.W. said. "We spoke a week ago. Would I mind if they switched the account from me to you? Of course I don't mind. I'm almost seventy years old. I have nine grandkids I want to get to know. I'm richer than LeBron James. You're my heir-apparent—I've been grooming you for this. I told Hudd Family I approve a hundred percent."

"Here's one more thing," Carson said slyly. He handed Morgana a platinum VISA credit card. "This is a prepaid Visa card worth fifteen grand. Take this home to Caroline and tell her to go shopping."

"She accepts," Morgana said through a huge grin. Caroline needed something wonderful like that. Her happiness soared away to the sky. The timing was perfect; something for Caroline.

Plus she was pleased how the firm had accepted the fact of her and Caroline. There had never been even one raised eyebrow. She felt a special glow for these people.

"We want her to look like a charm on your arm."

"She tells me she does already."

"Then there's nothing like spoiling her just a little to keep the home life happy."

"She'll flip. Gentlemen, this may sound funny, but I've dreamed of this moment when I would win my spurs. And I'm flattered and shocked at your unbelievable gifts and the opportunity that's been laid before me. But more than any of these 'things,' I want you to know that I treasure your trust. I can promise you I won't let you down."

A glance passed between A.W. and Carson. A.W. leaned and whispered to Carson and Morgana. "Say, can we have a word in my office? I just need five minutes of your time then I have to run."

"Be right there. Just let me go pee first," Morgana said and she left the room, but not before yelping to the gathering, "Thanks again!"

Minutes later the three of them were assembled in A.W.'s office.

It was a huge corner office. In one corner stood a human skeleton supported by a steel rod, and in another corner was a treadmill. Morgana thought the space between the two—death and life—capable of a certain irony, but her mind passed the moment by. It was too engaged with just taking in these great moments.

Huge panes of glass overlooking the court buildings and city hall and lesser government buildings and landmarks separated the other two corners.

Plants sprawled everywhere, carefully cultivated and kept by A.W. himself, who still grew vegetables in the backyard of his home on LaRouge Street. The walls were lined with bookcases, packed with the usual trial lawyer tomes, including *Proof of Facts*, *American Jurisprudence*, and Federal Reporters from the Seventh Circuit as well as a good dozen or more volumes on insurance litigation, medicine and law, and trial reporters from across the country. The books were mainly to impress the visitors from the insurance industry who paid the firm's bills. All research anymore was computer-driven, and Jones Marentz had accounts with both Westlaw and Lexis-Nexis, your choice.

The office had a good warm feel despite the leather upholstery slathered around, thanks in part to the priceless art that adorned all but the Ego Wall, art hand-selected by A.W.'s better-half (his words), who carefully chose expensive New York and Paris artwork in oranges and yellows for emotional warmth and appeal. He wanted his wife and his visitors to feel the office was actually an extension of his living room where his own graciousness was always just a simple request away. Morgana would have killed for such an office.

They settled into comfortable client chairs arranged around A.W.'s desk. The room was very familiar and very comfortable to the young lawyer. She had spent hundreds of hours in there with A.W., who was really a mentor. They had plotted many of Morgana's trials around that desk, maybe not so much the last ten or so, but definitely at first.

A.W. started it off. "Everyone comfortable? Morgana, did you get a refill? Carse?"

Morgana held up her beer and shook her head. "I'm good. So what's up?"

A.W. nodded. "Well, we've had our fun, now we need to be serious for a few minutes."

What was this about? Morgana wondered. Probably more information about job duties. Fair enough, more money meant more hours to bill. She crossed her legs and pulled herself fully upright in the chair. Now she was all business. "Serious, like what about?"

Carson said, "Like what it really means to run with the wolves. You're about to find out what it really takes to be a partner at Jones Marentz. This is some truth telling time for with you."

The young lawyer didn't respond. She had zero idea where they were going with this. But she expected they wanted to see increased billables. Which she was willing to give, especially in light of the new partnership she'd been voted.

"Morgana, what you have seen tonight are the rewards that await someone who makes it around here. In this case, you."

"I'm astonished. I had no idea I could feel so good about sending widows home without a dime. Young women with failed nose jobs. It's not a bad trade."

"Is that sarcasm?" A.W. asked.

"Yes. I was only joking. Right now I'm ready to take the Porsche out onto the 90 and run with the wolves."

A.W. selected a cigar from the desktop humidor and automatically passed one to Carson. He lifted the wood box to Morgana, who waved him off. The men lit up and blew swirling plumes over the expanse of teak. It was all very back-roomy, very dramatic. They were definitely out to impress the young lawyer with something or other.

She shivered reflexively. She had never been so close to the inside of important matters in her life. For a kid who had come from a modest background, it could all really grow on her in a big way.

A.W. continued in a somber tone that sounded like Eisenhower planning the Normandy Invasion.

"The defense of insurance companies and their negligent doctors and hospitals sometimes transcends the law. Insurance companies are special institutions, with fine, long histories and honorable goals for their insured's. Sure, they get bad press now and then but so do all American companies. In the end they demand—and deserve—the very best legal services available. So, in a very real sense their needs sometimes transcend the law."

"'Transcend the law?' What's that?" Morgana cautiously asked. "That sounds like something out of Emerson."

"I mean that if we're going to keep winning for our clients we occasionally have to skirt around the law."

Morgana's back stiffened. *Come again? What did he just toss out at me?* "Like how? What on earth does this mean, 'skirt around the law'?"

"Like sometimes not telling the whole truth about the case."

"Well, I'm down with that—we keep our clients' secrets."

A.W. shook his head. "I'm not talking about keeping secrets, Morgana. At least that's not all of what I'm talking about.""

"So, what else do we have to guard?"

"Bottom line? Our partners at Hudd Family Healthcare will clean the doctor's and hospital's files before we begin the defense of a case. Sometimes we revise things just a bit. It's only good business. We're professionals and we're often called upon to clean up someone else's mess. So we do whatever it takes to save our clients money."

Something was looking wrong here. Morgana smelled rotting fish. "Meaning what?"

Carson held up a hand. "Let me take a shot at this. Morgana, remember in *Pulp Fiction* where Harvey Keitel comes to pick up the dead body that John Travolta's character inadvertently splattered all over the back seat of the car. Remember that scene?"

"Sure."

"Well, that's us, we're Harvey Keitel. Except we have law degrees and we're licensed to do what we do. We clean up others' mistakes. We make our own meaning out of the meaning that's presented to us. Do you follow me?"

"Carson, I hate to say this, but that sounds—"

A.W. interrupted. "—That sounds difficult to follow. Maybe. Let's be blunt."

"Meaning what?"

"Meaning we omit smoking guns."

Carson jumped back in. "We hide documents. We revise things like nurses' notes."

"We cover up. We protect our clients. It is a religion around here that we do not lose cases. We do whatever it takes to win."

"Imagine Harvey Keitel letting the mob get caught with its pants down? Well, neither do we."

A look of incredulity had settled on Morgana's face. Her eyes were wide and her pupils dilated in disbelief. She knew she was easy to read at that moment yet didn't care. Her stomach flip-flopped in her abdomen and she realized she was slightly nauseous at what she was hearing.

"This is getting very thick in here. Let's back up and take a deep breath. Okay? Are you telling me you have been destroying documents in litigated cases? *Revising nurses' notes*? Are you serious?"

A.W. was finally blunt. "Dead serious. And that's not all. When the dollar exposure calls for it we will manufacture evidence."

Morgana's astonishment etched into her face. She looked about her like someone expecting a clown to jump out and scream Surprise! "I hope to God this is a joke. You are bullshitting me, right?"

"Hardly. We'll revise nurses' notes, change times and measurements; we'll reprogram electronic monitors so we get the values we need to win. We'll dummy up X-rays and MRIs so they show no cancer. We do whatever it takes."

"Whatever it takes, Morgana, we're up for it."

Morgana was ready to jump and run. This *had* to be some huge put-on. "Jesus Christ." It was said like a prayer.

"You see—"

Then Morgana got angry. Slowly, but then it really poured out. "Hold on! I haven't had to dump documents or manufacture records and I've won thirty trials in a row. I've turned over everything."

Carson's face couldn't help smirking. All this Wonder Woman fluff heaped on the kid that night had not impressed him. "Have you? You really think you're special enough that we've let you use actual records? Dear girl, really."

A.W. said, "Who do you think doctored up your files before you were ever assigned to the case? That's what my job called for, Morgana. As of tonight, that's your job."

The roof caved in on her. It was not a joke. These assholes were serious. Now her look was one of complete disbelief. All she wanted was to run from the room, run somewhere safe, somewhere these things weren't being said. Her hand shook as she reached and placed the beer on A.W.'s desk. She stood and began pacing.

She abruptly halted. "Let me get this straight, A.W. You're telling me I wasn't going to trial with real records?"

Carson, still smirking, said, "Oh, they're always real records—"

Morgana had suddenly had it with the little weasel. She wheeled on Carson as one who had nothing to lose. "Shut the hell up, Carson. This is between A.W and me. This man is supposedly my mentor. Is that OK with you?"

"What Carson's saying is that our records are always real. They're just not original. Things get moved around. You might say we like to rearrange the furniture before the elves start the defense of the case."

"I can't believe what I'm hearing."

"It's time to face reality, Morgana. This is the way of trial practice in the United States. It wasn't always this way but it sure as hell is now, now that an insurance company can lose fifty million dollars to the wrong patient. The stakes are too damn high not to stack the deck."

Morgana flopped into her chair but then came bolt upright. A sudden inspiration had hit and she thought maybe this could be salvaged at the last second.

"Hold it. What if I tell you that I can win my cases without all the criminal activity? Do I get a chance to prove that?" She looked from man to man. Surely they could at least give her the chance to prove what she could do. That she didn't need their dirty dealings.

A.W. shook his head.

"Oh, you would win your share, but you would lose your share too. There are lots of negligent doctors and shoddy hospitals out there. Hudd Family can't take that chance. Like I said, fifty million—"

She finished it for him. "—Fifty million dollars is too much to risk. I get that."

Morgana looked to Carson. Maybe he understood what Morgana was willing to do, to give it a try the honest way. She doubted it, but she was desperate for a sympathetic ear.

But Carson said, "How else do you think you can earn two hundred fifty grand a year with a Porsche, country club card, tennis club membership, and a month off, all on us? Did you think we're all just an extraordinarily gifted group of lawyers who never lose?"

"Yes, I did. Up until five minutes ago, I actually did think that. I was proud to be here."

A.W. rolled the tip of the cigar in the ashtray. "I'm a bottom line kind of guy. Bottom line is, are you with us?"

"Actually, I'm with me. You of all people should know that." She pulled herself fully upright and straightened her shirt and jacket. "I won't practice this way. What comes next?" Again she looked at each of them in turn. Waiting for resolution, something decent to happen, a light to go off, an acceptable compromise to be served up.

Instead, A.W. said simply, "We won't accept No. Hudd Family would leave us. You're either all in or all out with them. Nothing halfway, Morgana."

Carson added, "Hudd Family is ten percent of the firm's annual billing. If we lost them we'd all suffer beyond imagination."

With a long sigh, the young lawyer surrendered to her conscience. She knew that if she went along, Caroline would get it out of her and then she'd be toast. Worse, her own conscience would devour her. It just wasn't doable. Even without Caroline looking over her shoulder, she just couldn't pull it off. "I won't do it. Life's too short to practice that way."

"Like A.W. just said, if you're not with us, you're against us. We cannot have that."

Morgana stood and straightened her suit jacket as if she were about to address a judge. "Gentlemen, I'll be around to clean out my desk in the morning. For now I'm going to go downstairs, find my Volvo, and go get drunk."

A.W. shushed her with his hand. "Please. We want you to think this over. Discuss it with Caroline. Look at your financial obligations and imagine trying to meet those obligations without your firm."

"You have no idea how sorry I am to have to tell you, A.W. But you've got the wrong kid. Damn it all, I'd rather sell insurance than send my life down the money river. Kiss my ass, both of you."

Morgana turned and left the two men hunched together in a cloud of cigar smoke, the oranges and yellows adorning the walls all at once looking not so warm after all.

She stormed out and fled downstairs to the parking garage.

Tears flooded her eyes and she had trouble finding the ignition.

Too much too late with too little to give. They had made their run at her and she had walked.

It just wouldn't fly any other way. Now to face Caroline.

Guess what, honey? I quit my job, lost my health insurance, and I have very narrow niche skills in medical malpractice defense. Plus I have leukemia. Maybe it's treatable; maybe it's not. What do you want to do this weekend?

She fought back the tears for a good two blocks. Then she collected herself and drove it on home.

12

C hristine Susmann was on top of her game. Since leaving the Army she had worked for Thaddeus as his key paralegal. But she was more than that. She had taught him how to arm himself, how to shoot, and how to protect what he believed in and what he loved. She was tough with an icy calm interior, clear-eyed, ready to do whatever it took to win a case, and she had the highest respect for her boss, whom she had watched mature from a boy lawyer into a giant of a litigator and client-smart attorney. Christine had received the CD from Pauline Pepper on Monday; it was now Wednesday and she had devoured its contents.

Together with Thaddeus, in their Chicago office in the American United Building, they were going over what they had learned. Outside the window the clouds were low and boiling past as the Windy City lived up to its name and winter departed with a flourish of howling wind and ice-specked rain. Inside it was warm, coffee was flowing, and the conference table all but hidden under the mass of documents printed off the CD and now in the process of falling into the system of categorization invented by Christine.

The CD had proved to be a gold mine.

HIS TRUE NATIONALITY WAS UNKNOWN.

Ragman had entered the United States in 2009. Tijuana ICE agents admitted him on the passport of one Luis M. Sanchez. The real Mr. Sanchez existed, if at all, in a parallel universe because he no longer existed in this one.

The real Mr. Sanchez had been a street soldier for a local drug wannabe who got crosswise with the Tijuana Cartel. They had separated his head from his torso, doused it with gasoline, and rolled it through the front door of La Oficina Federales in Tijuana. By the time a fire extinguisher shot forth and the flames abated, the identity of the head was indeterminate. The Mexican police had far fewer forensic tools than American crime labs and far less interest in keeping score of who killed whom in the narcotics collective. In short, the Mexican records had it that Sanchez was just another low-life, a bad guy, a *puta*.

With one redeeming characteristic. An important one.

He had been born in San Diego.

Which made him every bit as American as Senator Dodge from California (D). Which meant in his afterlife he was able to apply for and obtain an American passport. Which he did—*in absentia*, of course, because he was dead. The passport photo belonged to the new and improved Luis M. Sanchez, lately of maybe Pakistan, though the FBI had no firm idea about this part. It would be easier to trace your own ancestry back 400 years to the *Mayflower* than to trace the new Mr. Sanchez a month earlier to Pakistan or Iran or Saudi Arabia or Afghanistan or—that's the idea.

They coughed up twenty-three photographs of him, including two headshots from inside a tail car, and one of him leaving La Spondia, a mid-list eatery in Los Angeles. That had been in late 2009. Then he had fallen off the face of the earth for two years.

Sometime in 2011 he turned up again, this time in Chicago.

There were two police reports with his name, one fingering him as the assailant of a sophomore coed from the University of Illinois-Chicago, wherein it was reported by the young woman Sanchez had raped her at knifepoint. Unfortunately she had waited two weeks to report the incident. She had been ashamed and, frankly, scared to death of the guy returning to kill her. He had promised no less if she reported the attack.

The other police report had him living on Milwaukee Avenue, in a duplex. A thirty-year-old prostitute had run nude from the duplex, screaming and crying for help. The downstairs tenants had come to her aid and called the police. Details were fragmented, but there had been a knife and a long cut across her right breast that would leave a scar but wasn't life threatening. The police questioned Luis M. Sanchez, but he with his roommate swore to the officers the prostitute had cut herself in an attempt to extort money. A report had been taken and lost in the morass of unconfirmed police reports that swamped the Chicago police computers every night of the week.

Upstairs in the duplex, away from the madding crowd, Sanchez appeared to be sharing space with a French Canadian. The Frenchie was another man. He too was thought to be Middle Eastern. The second man had a Canadian passport which the agents had traced to another deceased gentleman, a Lavalle X. Fleuve of Montreal. Mr. Fleuve had perished at the age of thirty in a traffic accident while visiting Toronto. A wife and three children survived him. The widow had moved on and quickly remarried. Mr. Fleuve's resurrected self surfaced in Chicago, sharing the walkup with Mr. Sanchez.

Welcome to the afterlife, Messrs.' Sanchez and Fleuve.

Christine Photoshopped everything. Resolution shot up fifty percent. She saved her work in Sanchez's file on the cloud. Same process with Mr. Fleuve. This made the men's likenesses immediately accessible, tablet or smartphone. Thaddeus would be able to positively ID or disregard in an instant. Then she began building the Sanchez profile. Age, Physical Characteristics, Nationality, Names, Addresses, and, most of all, Associations.

Right out of the gate Christine knew that "Sanchez" was associated with at least five other men, interchangeable in looks and backstory. All were using false identities, all lived in Chicago, two had Ph.D.'s (one in nuclear engineering, Sanchez himself), one programmer, one mapmaker (she couldn't understand how that fit into any pigeon hole), and one operated as a gopher. The latter would be a man who had no visible means of support, who whiled away his days at some mosque or other, meeting with Imams. The FBI had infiltrated the mosques and turned over more names, phone numbers, addresses, and employment than Christine and Thaddeus could have hoped for. *FOIA*, they laughed, you have to love it. The Fibbies said these were Sunni Muslims, the same breed that was about to take over Iraq and throw gasoline on the Mideast bonfire.

Going in, Thaddeus only wanted the one guy, Sanchez. But one had morphed into six. Being an American who was suspicious of everything Middle Eastern since 9/11, the young lawyer's curiosity kicked in.

What were they doing here? He lay awake wondering. Christine said the big action for guys like them would be going on in Iraq, Iran, Syria, and Pakistan. Chicago? Really? *Why Chicago?*

And why did Luis M. Sanchez kidnap Sarai and abandon her in the Nevada desert alone, no food or water, on a day when the temperature blew by 105F?

Of course Thaddeus had paid to get her back. He paid $350 million. Which went overseas to an account in Zurich, not to Luis M. Sanchez, at least not that he knew.

He had to conclude that Sanchez had been a pawn. Someone had used him. And, Thaddeus was certain, he had been extremely well paid for his service.

In the week following the *FOIA* record dump Thaddeus and Christine put their heads together. They reviewed, scanned, and compiled. Then they went outside the record for third-party information.

He filed a lawsuit in District Court. The named defendant was Luis M. Sanchez. Thaddeus made no effort to serve the lawsuit—had no reason to serve it. If anything, they wanted Mr. Sanchez never to be aware he'd been sued.

The lawsuit was pure baloney, of course. Not a word of it true, none of the allegations, none of the complaints, nada. But the lawsuit gave Thaddeus and Christine access to many doors.

So she opened the first door. She sent a notice of deposition with subpoena *duces tecum* to Fifth Third Bank's home office. "You can," said the subpoena, "avoid appearing at the office of Murfee and Hightower in Chicago by simply forwarding the requested records." She was referring to his bank records, of course.

Fifth Third complied. A week later Christine received a five-inch stack of Sanchez's bank statements and check photocopies. Then she set about scanning each and every document into the Luis M. Sanchez profile, and began the laborious task of dragging and dropping where matches could be made. Was the check made out to his landlord, Gilbert and Betty Hildebrand? If so, it was inserted into his profile > addresses file folder. And so on, *ad nauseam*.

One week later the young lawyer and his paralegal came up for air and by now they had the goods on Mr. Luis M. Sanchez.

Turned out his name wasn't Sanchez at all. His true name was Ragur Amman Hussein.

Ragman, to his associates.

His daughter's kidnapper, to Thaddeus.

It was time to pay him a call.

"How do you want to run this?" Christine asked. She gave him a hard look, her "I'm up for anything" look.

Thaddeus returned her look. "I'm open to ideas."

"Well, the FBI is watching you. They're not watching me."

"And you know this how?"

She shook her head. "Please, Thaddeus."

"Sorry. So what would you do?"

"Let me locate them. Follow them. Try to figure out their game."

"I hate to think what they might really be up to," he said.

"Wouldn't surprise me they're getting set to blow something up. Or poison the city water supply. Or hijack a busload of school children. Some asshole ploy."

"No kidding," he said. "I'm beginning to think we should go after all of them."

She drank a slug of coffee. "Eliminate all of them?"

"Why not?"

She slowly answered. "Well, it *is* a joint venture of some kind. Something horrible where innocent people will suffer."

"That's what I mean. They already hurt Sarai. That got my attention."

"I have to agree."

"So we take them all out?"

"Whatever you think."

He nodded slowly and smiled. "I think."

"I'm on it, boss."

13

T he night after Morgana left Jones Marentz, there was a phone conversation between Sandy Green and A.W. Marentz. Sandy had just come off a twelve-hour marathon at SCU, forging records and creating X-rays from healthy actors. He was tired but it was important he talk to A.W.

They discussed Morgana, now that she had jumped ship and told them where they could put it. She wasn't going to cheat. The car and the huge salary hadn't been enough to lure her in, so they were sweating bullets.

Sandy was restless. He was getting a great deal of heat from the Hudd powers-that-be about Morgana walking out on the Jones Marentz law firm. He immediately launched into A.W. "So she walked. Truth be told, I'm not that surprised."

A.W. sighed and there was exhaustion in his voice. "I guess I shouldn't be either."

Sandy rubbed his eyes. He'd been up all night dealing with the VP of security. "You know, A.W., the Hudds won't allow this. Morgana's too dangerous to us now. Look what happened to Garrett Donovan, for god's sakes."

"Meaning?"

"I shouldn't have to spell it out. You already know what it means."

"Look, tell the Hudds I just need a few days. Let me work on the girl."

"I've got my orders. She's got until Monday to come around."

"Give me a week. Just make it a week. She'll get hungry and come crawling back."

"Then they're after me."

"A few days then. Give me four days."

"Wednesday she's back behind her desk or I step in. That's it."

"What does that mean?"

"I can't say. Not over the phone."

"You're not talking about hurting her?"

"I'm talking about keeping her quiet. We don't know what that means yet, do we? But so far you've struck out. Now it's up to me and I will not—I promise you—I will not let this young woman destroy an industry leader."

"So you would hurt her."

"Not over the phone. I told you that."

A.W. shook his head and hung up. Now he had to get to work on Morgana or things were going to get very ugly very quickly.

He was feeling too old for this crap.

He would have given anything if he had just stopped it right then.

But he didn't.

14

S cared to death.

Leukemia does that to cowards. Leukemia does it to the brave, as well.

Morgana came clean with Caroline on the drive to the doctor. "He said leukemia, now I get to find out what that means."

Caroline had been hanging on to the Volvo's passenger grip, showing white knuckles, since then.

They parked out front, trudged through the morning snowfall, and elevated up to the third floor.

Dr. Romulus was African-American, maybe ten years older than Morgana, wire eyeglasses, and a large turquoise bolo tie on his denim shirt. Spotless white lab coat, stethoscope coiled in his side pocket, showing blue jeans and sandals with socks below. He knocked once, came bouncing into the examination room, and shook hands. Caroline was introduced, and then they got down to it.

"Morgana the news is not great, but there's hope."

Morgana's heart jumped. "The tests are back, I take it."

Caroline slumped. "God. Start with the hope, please."

He raised a hand. "Let me ask Morgana a few questions first, please. I'm going to suggest symptoms, and you tell me if I hit one that applies, okay?"

Morgana was perched on the exam table, stripped down to suit pants and tee. Goose bumps rippled along her arms. "Okay."

"Swollen lymph nodes? Notice any?"

"No."

"And I don't palpate any."

"Next, fevers or night sweats?"

The young lawyer smiled. "Night sweats the night before a trial starts? That count?"

"Nope. We're talking about more than one, unrelated to any known stressors."

"Then no."

"Fair enough. Feeling weak, tired?"

"No more tired than usual. Well, maybe. Definite yes."

"Bleeding and bruising easily?"

"Nope. Sometimes when I floss, there's a little blood. But I floss every night for a few days and that goes away."

"Swelling or discomfort in the abdomen?"

"No."

He sighed. "Pain in bones or joints?"

"My knees. After I jog, my knees swell up. Especially the right one."

"That's the knee that was scoped after the accident?"

Morgana had been rear-ended and it drove her knee into the dashboard. "Yes, that was injured in the wreck. And scoped."

"Fair enough. Really none of the classical symptoms."

"Of what?" Morgana asked, thinking it might be an infection, mono, something like that.

"Leukemia. You have leukemia, that's my working diagnosis. Confirmed by an oncologist I spoke to. And the biopsy, of course."

Morgana shivered violently on the exam table. There it was again, the unspeakable word. Her head was suddenly spinning and she saw spots. Her mind raced backwards, day by day, looking for symptoms, unusual complaints, anything that confirmed what he was saying. But her mind came back empty-handed. She had noticed nothing. Except for the tired. There was that.

"Leukemia," she said to her mate. "I've wondered all my life what would finally get me."

Caroline rubbed her hands over her eyes and fought down a sob.

The doctor said, "We all wonder that. You're not alone in that."

Morgana shook her head. "But for me, I figured I would cash it in by drunk driving or maybe blowing my brains out if Caroline left me. Never thought it would be something like leukemia."

"Let me tell you what we know."

"Please."

Caroline retrieved a note pad and a pen from her bag. Note-taking time.

Dr. Romulus crossed a leg in the steel-frame chair he occupied. The mandatory computer screen was behind him, and it looked like a long form that was partially filled in.

Morgana studied the screen, what she could make out. Her history, exam findings, workup, she guessed. It was all right there, in electronic measure, tapping out the beats left in her life. Did she have a will? Did she even need one? They owned very little. Just the condo, the 401(k), a few thousand left from the accident, and the paid-for Volvo. Nothing else. Maybe she would do a will online.

"Okay, here's what we have. You came in two weeks ago for your annual physical. You'd had blood work done, my orders. The lab did a CBC—complete blood count, to check the number of white blood cells, red blood cells, and platelets. Came back terribly skewed, off the charts elevated white blood cells. Plus very low levels of platelets. 'Danger,' it said. 'Danger.'"

He was studying Morgana as he spoke. Probably deciding if Morgana was hearing what was being said.

She was.

"So we immediately performed a biopsy. A sample of your bone marrow was aspirated from your hipbone. The path doc studied the sample under a very powerful microscope. Leukemia cells present. Report sent to me, diagnosis followed. That's what we know so far."

"What else is there to know?"

He smiled. "Glad you asked. It means you're hearing me."

"Oh, believe me, Doc; I haven't missed a word of this."

"Good. Let's talk treatment. People with leukemia have many treatment options."

"Thank God."

"Yes. The options are watchful waiting, chemotherapy, targeted therapy, biological therapy, radiation therapy, and stem cell transplant. At least that's most of what we have in our arsenal."

"So which do I do? Or do I do them all?"

"That's between you and Donald Rabinowitz. He's the oncologist I refer my leukemia patients to. Best man in Chicago. Out of Northwestern Med. Like yours truly."

"That's good to know. That's who I'd want."

"Of course. Sometimes a combination of the treatments

I've mentioned will be offered. But really, the choice of treatment depends on the type of leukemia."

"Type?"

"Whether yours is chronic, myelocytic, or lymphocytic. And your age is a factor. What are you twenty-six? Twenty-eight?"

"Twenty-eight, almost twenty-nine."

"That's a good number. That plays in your favor."

"Okay. What else?"

"It also depends on whether leukemia cells are found in your cerebrospinal fluid."

"So I see Doctor Rabinowitz. Then what?"

He spread his hands and peered at Morgana over his spectacles. "Well, people with acute leukemia need to be treated right away. The goal is to destroy signs of leukemia in the body and make symptoms go away. We call this remission—you've heard the term, I'm certain. After the symptoms go away, there's maintenance therapy. Your case might be different, because you don't have symptoms. So you may not need treatment right away."

"Without treatment, how long do I have?"

"If it's acute leukemia? Maybe six months. Maybe eight."

"Shit."

"But it's not acute, right Doctor Romulus?" Caroline asked, almost pleading. "Plus," she added and pointed at Morgana, "you're getting treatment, of course."

They both stared at the young lawyer, who nodded and said, "No problem there."

Dr. Romulus continued. "But you will of course opt for treatment. We've called Doctor Rabinowitz for you. Monday, nine a.m. This is his card with address. Do not reschedule. You need to get in stat."

"I won't reschedule. I'll be there Monday."

"That's about it, for my part so far."

"My God. Now I go for treatment?"

"A bit more study and then treatment, possibly, yes. Doctor Rabinowitz will make his treatment plan with your input. This guy won't leave you. He's the best we have."

"And what do I tell Caroline?"

It was asked as if she wasn't there. She wanted Caroline to hear it directly from Dr. Romulus.

"Tell her you have the best internal medicine doc and the best oncology doc money can buy. Tell her you're in great hands. Tell her you're scared to death. Trust me, Caroline will know what to do."

Morgana wondered why she herself couldn't ever remember that.

Caroline grabbed Morgana's arm and steered her for the door. "Let's go to Starbucks. We need caffeine and words."

15

Caroline didn't take the diagnosis as well as Dr. Romulus had predicted.

Morgana couldn't blame her. They had been girlfriend-girlfriend since they were sophomores in high school. They were like twins in love.

A week later they kept the appointment with Dr. Rabinowitz. He was quick and direct. "Chemotherapy, beginning one week from today and not a day later. This is a difficult type of illness to control."

They rode home in silence. Caroline drove, Morgana stared out the window and tried not to think.

At first Caroline tried to comfort Morgana. "Nobody really dies of leukemia anymore," she told her.

She prowled the Internet for the next six hours, reading everything she could find on her disease and treatment modalities.

It was seven at night. They had ordered ribs and fries, delivery, thrown it down and washed barbecue sauce off hands and table. Bones were dumped in the trash, the rest of it down the garbage disposal.

They were sitting in their kitchen at the large round maple table. Morgana hated the captain's chairs with their bony backs, but Caroline loved them. Morgana had long ago made a case for chair pads, but so far Caroline was sticking to her guns. She wanted only wood. It looked better, cleaned better, and so on. So, they had wood and they hurt Morgana's back, especially that night. Then it occurred to her that maybe she was overly sensitive to pain because of the cancer. Or maybe it was in her back too. Was that possible?

It was pitch-black outside, there was a TV playing in the family room, and supper had been brief.

Morgana was trying to hold all her feelings inside, and then the dam burst.

"Who the hell told you nobody dies of leukemia anymore?" she cried. She was frustrated and just about ready to take it out on Caroline, which would have been the wrong thing to do. It wasn't Caroline's fault she had leukemia. During the course of just a few hours Morgana had invented her own explanation for why she had received the devastating diagnosis. The way she saw it, the disease was punishment she had coming for the trials she had been winning where the little guy got screwed over. In her panic, she felt her whole life slipping away in the knowledge that there was such a thing as karma and that she had played the game one time too many. Now she had to pay and she was in a rage inside. She was angry and she thought it was up to Caroline to help her keep it together.

Caroline stood and positioned herself behind her. She began slowly massaging her shoulders. "It's okay," she whispered. "If you have to be angry, I get it. Go ahead and vent."

She began humming softly. Her college degree was music performance, voice, and she was the lead singer for a group called Rosemary. Who was Rosemary? Nobody, just a name. Her voice was somewhere between Bonnie Raitt and Janet Joplin, and her range would make Mariah Carey jealous. All Morgana ever wanted to do was listen to Caroline's guitar and voice weave their magic. It was a dazzling fabric, the combinatory art that issued. Rosemary had four CDs out and toured in a bus all year. They were sixty days on the road, then fourteen days at home. That day was day seven.

But this leukemia thing was throwing both of them right out of the gate. Caroline was talking of canceling the rest of Rosemary's tour and Morgana wasn't trying to discourage her.

Communicating was fast becoming difficult. Morgana could tell that Caroline didn't really know how to talk about it and didn't know all Morgana might need to hear from her. That first night neither gave a damn about any of the relationship stuff anyway. Instead they were focused on whether Morgana was actually going to survive to see her next birthday. That was going to be big for them.

"What did Doctor Rabinowitz say?" Morgana asked as if she hadn't been there. In her fright she had missed things. She was trying to go back over, to rehash, and to make sure.

"He said there is a lot of help for you."

Morgana stared blankly. "I think we're doing chemo and something else."

"He said chemo and maybe a biological transplant. Bone marrow."

Caroline was right. She had been there with Morgana, of course, and had heard what the doc had to say. Morgana was so scared she had missed some, but Caroline hadn't. Caroline said Morgana was in her amygdala loop, that that was why she couldn't remember some of it.

"Now I remember."

"And there was something else I talked to him about. While you were in the bathroom giving your ones and twos samples."

"What was that?" Morgana asked. This was curious, she could tell by Caroline's voice.

"I want to have our baby. In case something happens to you."

Morgana tried clamping her hand over Caroline's mouth but she jerked away.

"What?"

Tears flooded Caroline's eyes. She pressed up against Morgana and nuzzled her face in her hair. "I want to get pregnant before you start treatments. Just in case."

"In case what?"

"You know. In case of something horrible."

"Oh, Jesus. You want to get pregnant? Now? Can't I even have my damn treatment first?"

Caroline was crying into Morgana's hair. "In case something happens to you, Morgana. I want our baby to stay with me. There. I said it and it's cruel and selfish but I had to tell you. It's been eating me alive."

"Oh, crap. I cannot believe this bullshit! I don't even have a job and I'm probably dying!"

Morgana stormed out of the kitchen and went upstairs to her office, where she slammed the door, slumped in front of her computer, and began Googling "leukemia and life expectancy."

She read for hours.

Finally she turned in. Caroline was already asleep.

Morgana stayed as far away from her as possible in the bed that night.

It was just too much to comprehend, having a baby in case Morgana didn't make it. Hell, they didn't even have a sperm donor picked out.

Didn't even compute.

16

T he weekend passed slowly—too slowly, for Morgana.

Monday she would start chemotherapy and she was dreading it. In her world, when she would have a trial coming up, she could prepare. She would depose all the witnesses, review all documentary evidence, handle and make her notes about all physical evidence. She would hire and depose expert witnesses, learn from them, learn how to cross-examine the other side's experts from her own experts, and visit premises, hospitals, doctor's offices, and surgical suites. She would speak with doctors and RNs, radiologists and lab rats. All of it in preparation for the moment she would get to stand up in front of a jury and say Ladies and Gentlemen, what I am about to tell you is....

But there was no such preparation for chemo.

All she knew was that she was going to be sicker than anyone could be and still survive. She knew there would be chemicals that would ruin her digestive tract, cause hair to fall out, keep her wired and awake all night (steroids), and all the rest of the calamities she had read about and discussed with others in support groups who had survived the same ordeal. But there was nothing she could actually *do*. She had to put her life in the hands of other people and for a trial lawyer that's the hardest thing on earth.

And her foul mood and silence affected Caroline. For one, Caroline was terrified, though Morgana wouldn't find out just how terrified until much, much later.

Also, Morgana was anxious to get on with her next move, her new life, now that Jones Marentz was in the rearview.

Caroline encouraged her to slow down. "Take it out of overdrive, baby, and enjoy the beginnings of a new life with me and with a baby"—an idea Morgana was slowly warming to. "We're going to beat this thing and we're going to create a family."

"Is this really the time to have a child?" Morgana asked for the hundredth time. The reality of possible parenthood settled over her, and she found herself struggling to see how she was going to pay for a child and make their monthly nut without a steady income. Maybe it was time to update the résumé? Talk to some other med-mal defense firms?

Saturday noon she finished studying the *Post* and her page twenty trial article. Then she changed into sweats and bounced a basketball over to the HOA court, where she spent an hour working on her jump shot. Still had it cold. She tried ten shots from beyond the three-point line and made four of them. Forty percent, not all that great, though most driveway players would kill for that.

She returned home, showered, and set off with Caroline for a slow afternoon of a game they called Tourista. What it was, was they would prowl Michigan Avenue and watch the tourists as they drove by and gawked. When the car was directly beside them the next up had to yell out which state the plates were from. As the car passed and the license plate rolled into view, they kept score. First to twenty-one won. That particular Saturday there were the usual majority of Wisconsin's, Indiana's, and Missouri's, of course. Occasionally a Maryland or New Mexico stumped them. No one ever got an oddball like North Dakota or Idaho.

"It's hard to tell, anymore," Caroline said. "Americans are all starting to look the same wherever they're from."

"I like the bucking bronco plate from Wyoming," Morgana said. "That should be worth ten points right there. Wildcard thing."

At 3:30 they headed over by the Art Institute, found a small restaurant, and got a table on the sidewalk. It was still cold out, but Chicagoans prided themselves on seeming not to feel cold weather. Sub-zero Bears games were the norm. Morgana ordered a longneck Coors and Caroline scowled at the menu and raised her eyes at Morgana. There passed between them a quick understanding: what if there was a baby on the way? No more alcohol, not that Caroline ever drank more than one wine anyway. Caroline settled for Diet Coke. "And an order of wings, bleu cheese," she added.

To which Morgana also added cheese fingers.

Not much else was said that afternoon. Caroline was into baby world, but Morgana knew she was actually trying to ignore the upcoming chemo. As for Morgana, she was into chemo and work world. First one, then the other, then back to the work issues. Chemotherapy was less than forty-eight hours away, but Morgana refused to let her mind dwell there. It's fourth quarter, seven seconds left, LeBron guarding you, down by three, and the throw-in comes right at you.

So they talked about everything but. They would work it out.

They always did.

Morgana went to bed feeling a little more peace. Time spent with Caroline always gave her that.

And that night Morgana was very grateful and slept very peacefully, untroubled by the dreams that lately had her coming awake in the wee hours gasping and struggling for air.

17

The thing about her leukemia was, she was feeling fine. But when she woke up Monday morning she was apprehensive. Fear was understandable because her brain didn't want to accept that while she was feeling okay she was soon going to voluntarily trade that for being sicker than a dog. That's what chemo did. The coming change didn't make sense and that part of her mind was really struggling.

"How you doing?" Caroline casually asked as Morgana shrugged into the sweats the oncologist's office recommended she wear to the chemo.

"Fine."

"Fine? Isn't that an acronym for Fucked-up, Insecure, Neurotic, and Extreme?"

"So I've heard."

"Are you any of those?"

"Probably the first one."

"Fucked up?"

"Probably."

"I would be too."

"Probably."

Caroline drove her to the low, dark building on the edge of Evanston, north on Dewey Street. It was a commercial-looking area, more like a commercial park than a shopping area. They parked at A-III (how clear things are when you're super-stressed) and went inside.

Her hands were shaking as she signed in. Caroline put her arm around her back as she jittered her first and last onto the clipboard. Caroline kept it there and guided Morgana to a waiting room chair. Morgana knew she was in no shape to have to decide even something as simple as which side of the waiting room to choose.

There were two other people waiting. One was a forty-something woman wearing a turban and reading a *Cosmo*. The other was a young boy, maybe twelve years old, with a totally bald head.

Morgana looked at him and smiled.

He didn't return her smile, didn't acknowledge the women, nothing, just kept staring at a spot on the floor between them. Morgana realized the kid had an iPod plug in his ear and he was lost in the music. She was glad the kid had something to help calm him. She was also wondering where in the hell a parent was. He shouldn't have had to be there in that situation alone. Even Morgana had somebody and she was almost thirty years old. At which moment Caroline, reading her thoughts, took her hand and gave a squeeze.

For several harsh moments Morgana fought back the tears that welled up in her eyes. This wasn't going to be easy. She was already feeling sorry for herself and she hadn't even received a drop of the chemicals yet.

Soon a nurse came for her and led her through a door

and back into a room with ten recliners. She told her to remove her shoes and sit back. Which she did.

A phlebotomist materialized and pricked her for a blood sample. The oncology nurse said they were going to determine whether she was well enough to have chemotherapy that day.

"Well enough?" Morgana said. "Are you serious? Hell no, I'm not well enough. I have leukemia, for the love of God! Is anyone following all this?" The oncology nurse—whose name was Karen—smiled and tweaked Morgana's shoeless toes.

"We're on it," she said softly and followed the phlebotomist through the far door.

Karen returned and unsheathed a set of headphones from plastic. "These are brand new. They'll be waiting for you every time you come in. You can watch the little TV screen on the arm of the chair while we dose you. The headphones give everyone privacy to watch whatever they want."

Which Morgana could probably have figured out for herself. It was then she realized that she was fuming inside. Her fear and dread had boiled up into rage. This wasn't fair! *How did this happen to me?*

Karen gave her a paper cup brimming with anti-nausea medication and a plastic cup of water. "Take, please," she said. "These will keep you from throwing up all over yourself and our chair."

Great. Protect their property, that's what she was all about. Later she would learn that it was the little things in life, like keeping her vomit out of crevices and crannies, which were the important things in life. That was a lesson yet to come.

Then she settled back and settled in. She sat in the sleek white chair at the Weinstein Clinic and watched as if in a dream. The oncology nurse returned with another nurse, who inserted a needle and cannula into her hand. They took turns explaining what they were doing and what she was going to feel.

For the next two hours, Morgana watched ESPN on her private TV screen as a cocktail of drugs infused into her veins through a long tube. It was an uncomfortable but not painful process and the strong anti-sickness drugs ensured she didn't feel any nausea.

Her first chemotherapy session coincided with the day the NBA all-star selections were announced. So she watched the announcements and followed the film of the stars' performances during the first half of the season. Being an ex-point guard herself, she was engrossed in the announcements—which were a welcome distraction from the various tingling and cold sensations she experienced during the chemo.

The last needle came out just as the national anthem started for one of LeBron's games as LeBron, D-Wade, and Bosh were shown on the lights-out basketball court just moments before being introduced to the adoring crowd.

All she could think about was how vigorous and healthy they all looked. Compared to how she must have looked right then, three hours after the needle bit into her arm.

She silently gave herself an All-Star pat on the back for getting past the first quarter in her game. Actually there would be six sessions, each a week apart, so it was one down and five to go. She had survived.

∼

ON THE DRIVE HOME, feeling sicker and sicker as they rode along, Morgana seized the last vestige of remaining normal health, and called A.W. and told him the truth about her health. She talked about the chemotherapy. She talked about the six weeks it would take.

A.W. was tremendously empathetic and told her they still considered her a member of the firm, no matter what had been said. A.W. expressed how he thought a cooling-off period might be helpful. In all honesty, Morgana was too sick to argue and didn't respond, just thanked A.W for his support and let it go at that.

So, she thought as Caroline drove them homeward, that door was still open. She could still go back to Jones Marentz if she had to. She thought it must have been how Butch and Sundance felt when they found they could return to the gang of murderers, robbers, and thieves they ran with. Not a healthy place, but familiar.

She'd had a girlfriend like that her freshman year in college. They lasted the whole school year, having great times one week and then having the blowup and being estranged and hating each other the next week. They would make up and get back together. This went on for nine months. Finally she realized that the girl's name was Chaos and, if they kept at it, her whole life would be like that, topping the waves from crest to crest, high time to high time. But there was always the trough below, where you always came crashing down. That was Jones Marentz. You could never be at peace there. Not anymore.

For all her ambivalence brought on by her physical ills, the knowledge that she could still return to the law firm somehow made her feel better anyway.

"It'll be six weeks before I can even talk about all that," she told A.W.

"Take all the time you need, Morg. They just want you feeling better and cancer-free. We'll all be praying for you."

Who could argue with that? She thought as she rode along, feeling more nauseated by the block. In her fear and upset she noticed they didn't sound like criminals. Not as much, anyway.

Which made her think of the scorpion that hitched a ride across the pond on the frog's back. At the other side, the scorpion stung the frog to death. Just as he was departing this world, the frog managed to ask, "Why did you sting me? I helped you!"

"You know what?" said the scorpion. "It's just my nature."

So it was.

And they pulled over at the next corner so she could stick her head out and throw up.

The fight was definitely on.

THAT EVENING IN BED, it took every ounce of strength in her body not to vomit. She hummed and sang to herself as she tried to get through the constant waves of nausea and the pounding in her head. The feeling of not knowing what was next was the worst, and she kept a bucket by her bed just in case.

After a steroid-induced night of insomnia interrupted by fifteen-minute islands of sleep, she woke up with what could only be described as a combination of the worst hangover in human history—a horrific migraine, and food poisoning in India. (She had never been to India, but she had had more than her share of hangovers back in her youth at one time.) She spent the morning in the bathroom, on her knees praying to the porcelain, imploring forgiveness for all wrongs and sins. Seriously, she would have called on

Houdini if she'd thought he could stop the process and restore her normal life.

She had completely gone off tea and coffee and sweet foods but her appetite remained strong for anything savory she could get her hands on. She remained in bed the entire day with a pounding headache, light aversion, and terrible nausea. She also had terrible constipation—a common side effect—and she almost fainted after spending yet another hour in the bathroom.

At dinnertime, a home health nurse came to the house to inject her in the stomach with a powerful drug to boost her immune system. Her skin had gone a funny gray color and the acne she had fought at thirteen had flared up like a teen's.

Later she opened her Kindle and pretended to read. This made Caroline feel better, as she was trying not to hover and baby her. Caroline was giving her the room she needed to be sick and face the reality of chemo for herself. Morgana did read a couple paragraphs of Martin Cruz Smith, one of her favorites, but the description of the bodies found under the snow had her quickly running for the toilet as the nausea overwhelmed her. She set that aside when she stumbled back to bed.

By 10:30 she realized that she was bored to death and nowhere near sleepy. It occurred to her, this was her life now.

She had a terrible urge, almost a panic, to call A.W. and tell him she'd made a huge mistake. It took every bit of logic Caroline could impart to keep her from making that call.

Just please keep paying the premiums on her insurance.

She really needed that health insurance. Especially now.

18

She made it to week six of chemotherapy.

The treatment had depleted every last ounce of reserve strength—and then some. She was exhausted mentally and physically. And it was taking its toll on Caroline as well. Too often they snapped at each other over what once what had been mere nothings. Now, under the pressure of Morgana undergoing the literal hell of cancer therapy, the mere nothings were often larger than one of them could grin and bear. So they snapped back and forth and then, at times, held each other and cried, forgiving each other for what they had become. But now it was week six—the magical week six—and the race was nearly run.

It was just after noon when the mail arrived. They tore right into it. Which was a good sign. Morgana usually couldn't have cared less what arrive by USPS. But she was actually coming back to life. Hey, she thought, she might actually survive this thing!

But her exuberance was short-lived

"Uh-oh," Caroline said, glancing over a letter. "You're going to love this."

"Let's see."

"Take a deep breath."

"C'mon." She scanned the document. "Student loan —*what*?"

She slumped at the dining room table. "So, should we just declare bankruptcy right now and get it over with?"

"What the crap! They've raised my student loan to over five grand a month. I've got to call them!"

Suddenly she was back. Full-bore, head-on, toe-to-toe— she was back.

"And when they tell you there's no mistake, then what?"

She crossed to the refrigerator and popped a longneck. That was another good sign. She hadn't had a beer in almost two months. "I'll figure something out."

Caroline swiped the beer from Morgana's hand and replaced it in the refrigerator. "Drinking beer isn't going to help anything. We've got to be clear-headed right now. Give it a rest."

"Give what a rest? It's only one beer."

"And one leads to two and ta-da-ta-da. I know you."

"But you don't know me like this," she indicated, holding out both arms to emphasize her new scarecrow physique. "Down thirty-five pounds in just six weeks. It's amazing what not eating can do for your weight."

"I know you, that's all I'm saying."

Morgana's face flushed. "Yeah? So just what is it you think you know?"

"I know how you sometimes dodge issues. You don't always face things head on."

"I did six weeks ago. I walked away from the greatest job I'll ever have. By the way, I can't believe they'd just let me walk. I'm surprised A.W. hasn't called to check up. But he did say I could return."

"I could hear what he was saying that day. You managed to leave that door wide open. No sympathy from me, Miss."

"But I'm not going back. At least I wasn't until this student loan disaster crashed through the roof and took me out."

"Don't even go there. The student loan changes nothing. Those are dangerous people at Jones Marentz and I don't trust them. Not one damn bit."

"Well, don't forget. I'm complicit. I used forged records in dozens of cases."

"What on earth are you talking about? You haven't done anything wrong."

"It's not about me. I haven't told you this; I didn't want to scare you. One of our partners was murdered just before I left. Garrett Donovan. Shot to death in a steam room."

"Didn't want to scare me? My God!"

"I doubt it means anything except he was in the wrong place at the wrong time. Probably a robbery."

"In a steam room? Are you delirious?"

Morgana nodded. But the memory made her so sad she could feel tears in her eyes. Great sorrow about the whole thing and she didn't even know why. She had barely known Donovan. "I know. I don't like it either."

"Jesus, Morgana, if they'll forge records they won't stop at anything to keep that quiet. You could be next!"

"Whoa, you're jumping the gun here."

"Am I? There's huge money at stake here. People like that will stop at nothing to protect their secrets and their money. These aren't people you should be doing business with. That's not who you are!"

"According to them, that's who I am. I've been winning with forged documents. God help me."

Two days passed. The huge new student loan payment

worked on them both. On Thursday morning Caroline opened her eyes and said, "When are you going to figure something out? You've been lazing around here for almost a week now since your final treatment. The vomiting and nausea are past. You said so yourself, you feel better than you have in ten years. Has your next move revealed itself?"

Morgana was groggy but she was instantly on.

"Bite me."

"Bite me. Stupid."

"I guess it doesn't get much worse than this. It is stupid. I'm sorry."

"My God, just figure out what comes next. We'll both be happier. At least you will and then I can lighten up too. So far this imaginary pregnancy is no fun. I just worry about money. I should go back on the road."

Right about then Morgana realized Caroline was being serious. Caroline was worried about Morgana's next move. She had probably been fearful about this the whole time Morgana was so sick. Now Caroline just couldn't hold it in any longer.

Morgana propped up on one elbow, facing her. "Linus, maybe I made a huge blunder resigning my job. What was I thinking? I didn't even give it a chance to see what kind of compromise we could make over lawsuits. Duh."

"No, they asked you to hide records and forge records. It was no mistake."

"I don't know. Maybe it's grow-up time for me."

"Meaning your next move hasn't come to you out on the basketball court."

"Hasn't revealed itself yet, no."

"From where I stand, you're too good and decent to throw in with those wolves. We'll find some other way to pay five grand a month. Maybe my dad will help."

Morgana moaned. The thought actually made her nauseous. Again. There was no love lost between Mr. Merriweather and her. Morgana actually still called him "Mister" and her father-in-law still hadn't suggested Morgana use his Christian name. Even after all these years of Morgana sleeping with his daughter. On the other hand, maybe that was why he preferred "Mister": he hated Morgana.

"I can't be in debt to your dad. He already thinks my rising star will flame out at any second."

"He loves you."

"Wrong. He's stalking me. He's waiting for an opening and then he'll jump."

"My dad doesn't stalk."

"Caroline, you really mean he loves you. I think I'm going to go back to A.W. and see if they'll maybe let me do it my way."

"Meaning?"

"Play by the rules and win by the rules."

"And lose by the rules. Not a chance. They're not throwing away a million-dollar judgment just because you're a decent girl."

"Hey, it never hurts to ask. Besides, we need the money. Look, we're both ready for a baby and I've got student loans out the rear. What if I swallow my pride and get back in there and prove that I can win by the rules. They don't have to know I'm turning over original records AS-IS."

"Not scrub the files? What if you get hit for twenty million? Then what?"

"I think I'm good enough to prevent that from happening."

"Hey, it's your career. If you think this might work for you, so be it. I just want you to know that I'm here for you.

We're here for you. She patted an imaginary fetus in her abdomen. "In my dreams, eh?"

"Let me sleep on it." She buried her face in her pillow.

Caroline slapped her across the rear. "No, I need you to go maternity shopping with me. My wardrobe calls."

"We're really doing this baby thing, aren't we." It wasn't a question.

"We are. It makes no sense but at the same time it makes great sense. Whether we do or do not get pregnant, you're going to take care of us. I trust that because I trust you."

Which was when it all became clear to her.

She would definitely call A.W. She would definitely return to Jones Marentz and pick up where she left off. She was a star and right now that sounded like everything to her.

She wouldn't get hit, either. Not even a judgment for one dollar.

19

I t was early spring when Christine confirmed their location.

The duplex on Milwaukee Avenue was two-story, white-face, wrought iron bars on the downstairs and upstairs windows, entrance in the middle of the building, double driveway on the north side that ran back along the duplex to what Christine guessed was the garage. But who could tell? They were Pakistanis; they could be assembling a nuclear weapon back there for all anyone knew. Hadn't the FBI said national security was in play?

Next-door south was a one-man pizza joint, Bud sign in the window, and next-door north was a Mobil station and Quik Stop. Christine pulled into the Mobil and cleaned her windshield.

Now she had to ask herself, if I were going to shoot someone, how could my legal training help? Obviously, she knew she didn't want eyewitnesses. No-brainer. Second, no demonstrative evidence such as guns or photos, no papers such as receipts from gas stations in the vicinity, and no circumstantial evidence. Circumstantial evidence equaled opportunity, in the prosecutor's arsenal. Did the defendant have the opportunity to commit the crime? Which meant Thaddeus and Christine couldn't allow anyone to place them within ten miles of the killing zone when the shots were fired. This requirement guaranteed that any alibi story would hold up.

But most of all, Thaddeus had to get the FBI off his tail, if he was to be the shooter. Which he was demanding.

She returned the windshield scrubber to its tank. She looked back up the block. All clear.

She pulled her VW bug boldly into some stranger's driveway as if it belonged there. She called Thaddeus and told him what she had found. He didn't know if the agents were tailing him, but since the run-in with Agent Pepper he would have bet money they were with him 24/7. What are a couple more sharks to a government that owns a whole ocean? It was time to make a judgment about the troops committed to the pursuit.

So he hopped on the Kennedy and drove from Chicago west. Ten miles flew by. He took the ramp for Arlington Heights. This was a small city west of Chicago. Still following him? He had no way of knowing, but the assumption was always positive.

He found the Arlington Heights Metra train station and parked right beside the tracks. Inside the station he sat down across from the Avis window. For an hour he sat there and counted noses and memorized faces. After an hour the waiting room crowd had turned over a hundred percent. None of the original twenty-five faces remained. Satisfied he hadn't been followed inside the building, he ambled up to the Avis counter, where he rented a Lincoln. They gave him the key and he headed back outside. But instead of claiming the Lincoln, he found his Volvo down at the other end of the parking lot and climbed inside. He took his time, in case they were following, because now he wanted them to vacate the lot with him.

He turned the key, drove back through Arlington Heights to the freeway, and jumped the Kennedy heading eastbound right back into Chicago. The day was warm so he cranked the sunroof and dialed in NPR. Maybe he made them behind, maybe he didn't. From all his criminal work he knew it was very hard to spot a vehicle tail. Reason was, more than one vehicle would be used to pursue you. Sometimes three or even four. And when that was the case, eyeballs could not be trusted.

Besides, at that point, he didn't care.

Downtown Chicago. He beelined to the Northwest Train Station. Twenty minutes later he was through gate eleven jumping the stairway into a westbound Metra Train.

The Metra to Arlington Heights was much slower than the drive. It made umpteen stops and passengers crawled on and off. Still, he had been unable to guess which of the passengers were special agents and which were accountants, commodities brokers, or computer geeks. His next move would sort all that out.

Finally they made the Arlington Heights stop. He rushed forward through the cars and reached the exit closest to the Lincoln. He jumped down the stairs and ran, jumped inside the Lincoln and floored it. In a great rush he tore out of the lot and flew to the freeway. Making a right on red, he hit the onramp at 65 MPH. Then he was in the fast lane and the huge engine quickly shot him up to 85. He took the next off-ramp, went north across the overpass, and pulled into an Exxon. He parked alongside the Men's and waited. Nothing came and nothing went, nothing was waiting back across the overpass. After ten minutes he was sure he had lost the tail. It looked like his scheme had paid off.

He raced the Lincoln back up toward the duplex on Milwaukee, where he swerved into the Mobil. He parked in the service lane, four back, where he could see the duplex.

Twenty minutes passed. But he was patient. He prepared his camera.

At last an occupant appeared and jumped into a red SUV. For one instant he caught a look of the man's face and shot a picture with his 300 mm lens. He swung out of the service lane and fell in behind the red SUV. As they began making their way south on Milwaukee Avenue, Thaddeus compared the camera shot to the *FOIA* pictures. Instantly he made the guy. His name was Maliki Al-Salim, code name Data.

According to the FBI file, this guy had helped arrange the transfer of money from mobster Mascari in Chicago to Ragman. Which meant that Maliki Al-Salim was a key player in Sarai's kidnapping.

Which also meant that he would be the first to leave this earth.

Thaddeus was all over it.

20

Thaddeus followed Maliki Al-Salim from Niles west and south to Wood Dale. His prey parked in a racquetball club parking lot. Thaddeus watched as he went around to the rear door, removed a gym bag, and loped up to the clubhouse. The handle of a racquet could be seen protruding from the gym bag as the guy disappeared inside.

Thaddeus waited. He studied his cell phone for texts while he passed the time. Nothing new. So he texted Christine and told her he was over east, in Indiana, checking out antique stores. Anything to throw them off. She texted back. Had he found the duck decoys he wanted for duck season? He replied that he had and that he was studying the prices. She texted back that he should not overspend and he replied that he certainly would not, that he knew the value of the decoys. She replied, "Good hunting!"

It was ninety minutes before Al-Salim reappeared. Same clothes, same gym bag, sunglasses, hurried walk. He darted several looks around at parked cars as he made his way back to his red SUV. Thaddeus, at the far end of the lot, went unnoticed.

Or so he thought.

The Paki pulled up to the exit, but before crossing the sidewalk he suddenly put it in park and opened the driver's door. Thaddeus, who had been following close behind, saw the parking lights suddenly flare and saw the door open and saw the guy walking directly back to him. What the hell, he thought. This guy's made me!

He jammed on the big Lincoln's brakes, threw it in reverse, and then roared forward and around Al-Salim. He purposely cut it very close and he could see the guy jump back behind his SUV.

Thaddeus pulled his cap low across his face as he went around, so his face was partially covered. Then he floored it and headed for the freeway. At the on-ramp there was no one following and he jammed the pedal to the floor; the Lincoln shot up to 110. What the hell, he thought, it's a rental. The guy will never see the car again. But the downside was if the guy made the license number. It didn't take rocket science to trace the plates back to Avis and then pay someone for the driver's name and address.

Thaddeus felt a cold chill race up his spine as he realized that he might very well have again put Katy and Sarai at risk. He cursed himself and slammed his fist against the dash. He would have to get rid of the guy and fast. He could only hope the guy missed the license plate. But here he was again, operating on hope, something he loathed to do where his family's well-being was involved. They were his blood and he owed them his life in the fight for their safety and well-being. Never mind, he would make it happen for Al-Salim.

And soon.

But it was too damn close, nevertheless. He would have to get a lot smarter and fast.

That racquetball club gave him an idea that slowly formed in his mind as he made his way west to Arlington Heights.

Racquetball would be perfect.

21

M aliki Al-Salim, code name Data, loved racquetball.

If he had any weakness, drilling an adversary squarely between the eyes with a 90 MPH racquetball coming off the far wall did it for him. Data played in Wood Dale, a small town south of Niles. It was a private club but, Thaddeus found, allowed day-guests to play there as long as they were willing to pony up the hundred-dollar court fee. Thaddeus entered through the front doors, inhaled the overpowering smell of steam mixed with chlorine coming from the steam rooms and spa, and told the drowsy young girl working the register that he'd like to just stick his head in and check out the courts. Without a word, she nodded and waved him through.

A plastic map on the hallway wall led him to the courts. There were twelve courts, it turned out, six down, six up one floor. All were vacant except one, where a father and son batted the ball around, the father constantly interrupting the workout to instruct his son on the finer points of where to hit the ball in order to make it unreturnable. He stood in the hallway and watched for five minutes, studying the hallway traffic, studying who came and went, studying which employees were nosing about: the kind of information that would prove invaluable later.

Then he returned to the front desk. "I need lessons," he advised a young man who had replaced the original clerk.

"Sure, one?"

"I need a week's worth, starting today, if that's possible."

"Let me check." The young man lifted a microphone, clicked the button, and paged "Chuck" to the front register. Within minutes a very hairy young man with a sweatband, wearing a white tee and white shorts, came bouncing up.

"Yes, Skipper," he said, ignoring Thaddeus. "What's up?"

"This gentleman wants lessons starting today."

"Can do!" said Chuck. He extended a hand to Thaddeus. They pumped hands like old friends and Chuck sized him up. "Ever played before?"

"Never. But I'm anxious to learn."

"Grab your gym bag and get changed. We'll meet on the practice court. That's last court upstairs, far end of hall. See you in ten."

Thaddeus registered under the name of George Aulistta and paid cash. No ID was requested and none was given.

Thaddeus changed, took the forty-five-minute lesson, and cleaned up in the dressing room. The entire time, he was committing to memory all hallways, stairwells, steam room, locker locations, shower rooms, entrances, and exits. By the time he pulled out of the lot an hour later, he knew the place by heart.

He returned the next five evenings and carefully improved his game under the watchful eye of Chuck.

Chuck thought Thaddeus was a natural; Thaddeus was certain Chuck looked at him and saw dollar signs. When the week was over, Chuck wanted to continue, promising to take Thaddeus' game to "the next level." Thaddeus politely declined, saying he was happy with the level he had reached.

Regretfully, Chuck watched his big fish saunter off to the locker room. He slapped the wall and returned to the weight machines where he could watch a certain young trainer working the stations with an obese older woman. It was a great place to work and within ten minutes Chuck forgot he had ever met the attentive young man who wanted to learn the game as quickly as possible. Chuck had bigger fish to fry. Romance was always just a station away.

Maliki Al-Salim was a champion racquetball player in his age bracket, and a Ph.D. candidate in computer engineering at Northwestern. His club racquetball tournament record was 40-0. He had become a millionaire at twenty-seven, thanks to a software startup that located parking places and electric car charging stations. At twenty-seven he became a father, and married at twenty-eight.

Scrambling forward and back, left and right on one of the 1,200 racquetball courts in Wood Dale, Maliki Al-Salim was a muscular man whose face, even at play, showed worry lines beyond his years. His opponent inside the four walls of the racquetball court was a nondescript, brown-haired thirty-something who had barely broken a sweat. Suddenly there was a loud banging on the glass and Maliki Al-Salim raised his hand to pause the game. He poked his head out the door. Two Middle Eastern men waited to speak with him. Unknown to Maliki Al-Salim, the two men were undercover FBI agents who had infiltrated Maliki Al-Salim's terrorist cell.

The shorter, bearded agent pressed close to his face. "Congrats, Maliki. I hear it went quite well in front of the Ph.D. committee today."

Al-Salim checked up and down the hallway before responding. "Well as could be expected. The dissertation defense is presented. How did you men find me here?"

"Relax. We've got your back. We are your guardian angels. We will make sure nothing comes up. Not until the event. Then, who cares?"

"We will receive our reward from Allah. Paradise awaits."

Al-Salim scowled and backhanded sweat from his brow. "The package is in place. The core is on its way from Mexico. Please stop following me. I am good."

"Ragman asked us to protect you until the package is assembled. You're safe and tonight we'll even drop around and tuck you in bed."

"Yeah? How do I know they're not outside planning to arrest me while you're in here talking to me?"

The smaller man smiled. He'd heard all this before. "We have more brothers, Sayed. Or maybe you didn't know that. When I say we've got you covered, we've got you covered. Is that your classmate you're playing against?"

Al-Salim turned and looked at the sweaty man, who was nonchalantly evening up the strings on his racquet.

Al-Salim said, "No, that's just some guy I met in the locker room. The desk hooked us up, both singles looking for a match."

"He looks fit enough. Look, get back to your game, don't worry about a thing."

"If you say so. I'm just having doubts about you two. Maybe I shouldn't have joined."

"Relax, you did the right thing. The package just needs your attention when the core arrives."

"If you say so. OK, back to the game."

The ball-swatting resumed with all its former fury and a half hour later both players were in the steam room chatting about the game when Al-Salim's opponent slowly unrolled his towel and pointed a silenced pistol at the engineer.

He fired once and Al-Salim's head exploded against the tile wall. Two more to the heart and the opponent was satisfied his work was completed. The young man casually exited the steam room, glancing back at the body as he left.

He skipped the showers, dressed in shorts and a tee, and exited straight out the front doors, where he climbed into a black Tesla and roared out of the club parking lot.

Thaddeus looked back once in the rearview mirror. No one following, none expected. He swiped the headband from his head and stuffed it in the console.

One down, five to go.

A promise kept.

23

Murfee and Hightower got the call from Chase's mother when the baby was two months old.

They met in Thaddeus' office and he got to know Latoya. She was about his age, give or take, had her degree in education K-12, no military service, but a year in the Peace Corps, right out of college. She had done a year in Micronesia, learned to speak Chuukese, and taught the islander's early childhood education theory and methodology. She had helped in several schools and won a fellowship upon returning, the Paul D. Coverdell Fellowship, though she hadn't followed through on graduate education. That was still down the road, because at the moment she and husband John were struggling with Chase.

She was a Halle Berry look-alike and told Thaddeus she was occasionally mistaken for the actress. Like Halle Berry she had won a beauty pageant. That was in Chicago. Unlike the actress, however, she had never tried to have a career based on how she looked. Thaddeus found her to be very down to earth and they chatted for probably fifteen minutes, while Chase squirmed in her lap.

Chase was unlike any baby Thaddeus had ever seen. Latoya had told Thaddeus in their initial phone call that she was exhausted and Chase hadn't been home quite two months. But Thaddeus wasn't quite appreciative of how Chase consumed every bit of his mother's attention, until seeing them together. While she and Thaddeus spoke, it was a constant struggle for her to remain engaged, as Chase cried, then threw up, then wildly flailed arms and legs and cried some more. "It's always like this," she said, sounding desperate. "When he sleeps it's for fifteen minutes, max, then I'm back at it again."

"Do you ever get time for yourself?" Thaddeus asked. Soon he would learn what a lame question it was.

"Never. At night he sleeps on my lap, almost upright. If I move or take a deep breath it jolts him awake and he's off and crying again."

"How does he do with food?"

Tears came to her eyes. "It took him a week to learn how to suck. I tried breastfeeding him once he learned about the nipple, but that was a huge struggle. We finally gave up. Now it's the bottle only."

"Has Chase been evaluated yet by a pediatric neurologist?" Thaddeus asked.

She shook her head. "He's only seen his pediatrician. That's partly why I called you. I didn't want to go out and create a bunch of medical records like a paper trail. Not without talking to a lawyer first."

The young lawyer nodded. "What made you think you needed to see a lawyer?"

"That fool doctor was late at the hospital. Chase was delivered late. It took everything the nurses had to get him to show up at all. You could hear their 'stat!' pages all over the hospital. They were frantic to get an OB on my case."

"What do you mean late?"

"They told me they had thirty minutes to deliver by C-section once something happened about his heart rate. I think it was his heart rate. So they wrote it down and gave it thirty minutes. But Doctor Payne came in after thirty minutes. I think that's how Chase got hurt."

"Has anyone told you what's wrong with Chase?"

She shook her head. "His pediatrician just says Chase needs to be evaluated. He gave me the name of a pediatric neurologist. We went there once, Doctor Arroyo. Now it's time to go back for the results of the tests they did. But I wanted to talk to you first."

"All right. Let's go ahead and set up that meeting. Then we'll meet again and discuss what comes next. Fair enough?"

"Okay."

Thaddeus called the office of Dr. Arroyo.

Thaddeus dreaded hearing what he knew he was going to hear.

But Thaddeus was anxious to get a lawsuit on file, as things were rapidly coming undone in the Staples household. Latoya and John were exhausted. They were bickering and fighting almost constantly. John had suggested they might be happier if he got a room elsewhere.

They needed serious legal help.

Now.

24

M organa returned to Jones Marentz without further discussion of how it would be played. She had decided that whether she turned over actual records or forged records would be her call, that she simply wouldn't address the issue with A.W. and Carson. She thought she was attorney enough to avoid any huge casualties anyway, and if she did, well, they'd have to discuss it at that time. Likewise, A.W. didn't broach the subject with her, which, in one way, was surprising to Morgana, but she also understood that all he really wanted at that point was retirement. *Make no waves* seemed to be his mantra. Turn over the keys and don't look back. Six months later there were still no catastrophes, so all was well.

It was a Friday morning when they discovered the Chase Staples records.

They were in Morgana's office, door closed against prying ears. Morgana was at her computer reviewing a screen full of hospital records. Manny was sprawled on a deep leather couch, texting on his phone.

Reading aloud, Morgana said, "So here's a new file. Kid

by the name of Chase, plaintiff claims brain damage caused
by late C-section."

"What do the records look like?"

"Let me see. Okay, they sent us two sets of nurses' notes.
Reading...reading."

"Take your time. I'm ordering lunch over here. Two tacos
again?"

"Two tacos. Still reading."

"Two tacos and a green chili burro," Manny texted. "Plus
two medium Dr. Peppers."

"This is funny," Morgana said. She was studying the
records and shaking her head. "I'm guessing the original
notes are the ones that place the C-section late after the
Decision to Incision page. And the...let's see—"

—Flipping pages onscreen—

"—The notes on yellow paper are the scrubbed notes.
Right on, this set shows the doctor arriving on time. They've
changed the records, Mano. But they screwed the pooch.
They gave us copies of the originals and the forgeries. This
is cute. Shit, what whores. So which records do we give the
plaintiff?"

"How the hell did we get unmatched records? Let me
see."

Morgana turned the screen to Manny.

Morgana shook her head. She was scowling and tight-
lipped. "This case has the potential for a fifty-million-dollar
verdict. Caroline is due in three months and we've got to
have health insurance, plus my student loan is running five
thousand two hundred fifty a month. Which records do you
think we turn over?"

"I'm afraid you're going to tell me the phony ones."

"This time. Just this time. We can't lose this puppy.
Mommy has bills to pay. Which reminds me, we're off to the

doctor for Caroline's sonogram. I'll be back in around four, we'll stay until nine, then we'll grab a beer and adios. And don't forget I see my oncologist in the morning, so don't schedule anything before noon tomorrow."

"You have tacos coming."

"Stick them in the fridge. I'll nuke them when I get back."

"Done."

25

Claney's voice purred into the earpiece, "He's westbound on the Kennedy. Maybe running the Arlington Heights stunt again."

Agent Pepper's voice came back to Claney. "Just stay with him. If he hops the train again, Xavier, you stick with him on the train and Claney you stay with his car at Arlington Heights Metra parking. Andrees, do you copy this?"

A third voice came up. "Andrees. We do copy. We're three car lengths behind Claney and ready to move up. Claney, request you take the Addison turnoff and let us roll with him next four interchanges."

"Roger that," said Claney. "Departing Addison."

"Copy that," said Pepper. Her own black Crown Vic was parked a block away from the Ragman duplex. She had a clear line of sight to the double driveway and a second government car was two blocks south, same side of the street as Pepper.

It was a Saturday which, the FBI agents had noticed, seemed to be Murfee's favorite day of the week to call on the

Muslims. While they couldn't prove it, they calculated that he was responsible for the hit in the racquetball club in Wood Dale. Maliki Al-Salim, aka Data, had been shot dead in broad daylight in the steam room and nobody had seen anything. The Fibbies had run ads in the *Wood Dale Press* asking any witnesses to come forward and tell what they might know. But there had been zero responses. Which meant the guy who had pulled the trigger was very good. And right now the full focus was on Thaddeus Murfee, for it was he who had the motive to shoot up this particular group of bad guys. No one else had been anywhere near them, so the FBI had tagged Thaddeus.

Which was why they were following closely that Saturday morning.

They followed him all the way to Schaumburg, where he went inside the mall, bought a hot cinnamon bun from Mrs. Field's, and devoured it with a cup of coffee at a metal table. He then slouched on the escalator, checking for text messages, and rode upstairs to the Barnes and Noble. He purchased one book, a volume guaranteeing instant success in day trading, and left the store. Skimming his new book, he rode the escalator back down, went outside to his car, climbed in, and then shut the ignition off. He left the book in the car and hurried back inside the mall. At the Jungle Zone he spoke to the hostess then hurried back to the restroom. Emerging five minutes later, he returned to his car and drove straight back home. All the way back to Evanston.

Come clear over to Schaumburg from Evanston for a book he could have purchased in Evanston? Pepper was amazed.

Really?

The only explanation was that he had made them.

How, they couldn't say.

But he was good. He was quite good and they were going to have to get smarter if they were going to catch him blowing someone away.

It was proving to be more difficult than Agent Pepper had anticipated.

But it always did with this guy.

26

F riday nights at the Woodton Mall in Schaumburg were bedlam. Every school-age kid within a ten-mile radius showed up, pocket full of daddy's cash and ready to do some serious retail damage. Some even carried credit cards that bore their own names, courtesy of the old folks at home.

But it was no different than the Friday night mall scene in any other American city. The biggest hit with the middle school crowd at the Woodton Mall was the Jungle Zone. It was a restaurant that, when you entered, had the look and feel of a jungle—aptly named—complete with thunder-storms that came and went, macaws that swooped down over the heads of the diners, and upland gorillas that prowled and roared when you least expected it. All mechanical, of course.

Tonight was Sayed Abu-Nidal's turn with his daughter, nine-year-old Erika. This was a gentleman with a degree from Purdue in electrical engineering, a dues-paying member of the IEEE, and an applicant for the Ph.D. program at Carnegie Mellon. Divorced three years, father had tacitly agreed with daughter that Friday nights would be spent first in the Jungle Zone for an early dinner, followed by the latest middle-school-appropriate movie at the Woodton Thirty Cinema.

After salad—shrimp salad with avocado—but before the entree, Abu-Nidal had the urge to visit the restroom. He was studied closely by a young man dressed in black slacks and black turtleneck who loitered at the showcases in the gift shop, just off the dining room. The young man's hands felt for the guitar string in his pocket while his eyes followed Abu-Nidal as he dined. It was noted that Abu-Nidal was wearing a white tee, navy cargo shorts, sandals, and white socks.

Thaddeus Murfee was acting alone this night. Christine had left the office building driving Thaddeus' car. A high-speed pursuit had erupted as soon as she bounced up onto Madison Street, Christine in the lead, two FBI vehicles close behind. The agents thought they were following Thaddeus, who had actually departed the parking garage in Christine's VW Bug and headed the opposite direction. He drove aimlessly for the first hour, making sure there was no tail. Then he headed for the Woodton Mall.

The deception had been simple and flawless. It would be an hour until Christine pulled into the Iron Skillet restaurant seventy-five miles south on I-55, giving the Fibbies their first real look at the occupant of the Tesla that had led them so far afield. She acted as if nothing out of the ordinary were happening as she parked and went inside, acting as if she drove off from work in Thaddeus' car every Friday night. When of course she did not.

Upon Abu-Nidal's departure for the restroom, Thaddeus called over the gift shop manager. How much for a five-minute thunderstorm? He slipped the guy $100 and thanked him. Two minutes later a gully-washer of an electronic thunderstorm, complete with rolling thunderclaps and lightning flashes, Surround Sound vibrating plates on tables and silverware settings, erupted throughout the restaurant. And the restrooms. Thaddeus fell in behind. The guy had a sixty-second head start. Thaddeus walked up to the restroom door and counted down another full minute before entering.

He slipped inside. An ancient gentleman in bulging slacks and golf shirt was carefully washing his hands. He finished up and switched on the hand dryer. Thaddeus walked up to him, took his elbow, and forcefully waltzed him right outside of the rest room. He hurried back in and checked the stalls. There he was inside the far stall: sandals and white socks.

Thaddeus removed the E string from his pocket, wound it tightly around his fists, and crept up to the stall. He removed a hairnet from the rear pocket of his black denim trousers and pulled it tight down over his hair and ears. Latex gloves completed the preparation. He raised his right foot and kicked with every ounce of muscle. The door flew back and slammed into the horrified Abu-Nidal, knocking his head back against the tile wall and reflexively snapping him forward, and at that exact moment Thaddeus formed a loop with the E string around the terrorist's neck and pulled with everything he had in his arms, back, and shoulders. In less than thirty seconds the guy went limp, the string cut into veins and arteries, and the bloodbath erupted. Thaddeus threw down the string and backed out of the stall. His footprints were everywhere, in blood, but that was okay. He would take care of it.

He crossed to the sink and one by one lifted his shoes into the sink and placed them under running water. Blood swirled off the rubber soles and ran down the drain. He stepped onto paper towels with the damp shoes and scooped the paper towels from the floor into his pockets. He strolled out and headed to the front of the restaurant, unhurried, almost nonchalant, standing aside so wait staff could pass by and so diners had access to the aisle.

Then he was out in the mall itself, hurrying for the main exit.

He made it to Christine's VW, climbed inside, and raced to the main road and freeway access.

Then he was gone.

He would make it home in time for a movie with Katy and Sarai. Probably *Little Mermaid*, again.

He sighed.

It just didn't get any better than that.

Tomorrow he would put the Bug's top down and take Sarai for a spin. He hoped Christine would enjoy the Tesla over the weekend.

It had been a fair trade.

27

The FBI CSI machine took command of the Jungle Zone crime scene that same night.

Known as Locard's Exchange Principle, the exchange-of-materials principle is what modern forensics relies on as the basis for all examinations. The principle holds that every contact a perpetrator makes with another person, place, or object results in an exchange of physical materials. If one is going to commit a crime and get away with it, Locard must be understood and respected.

Thaddeus knew all about the forensics of the restroom crime scene. He knew the footprint he left on the stall door would be lifted and analyzed. He knew it was likely the footprint would be compared to his own footwear when the FBI appeared at his house with a search warrant, which they surely would, as he was the individual with both motive and opportunity. He knew that the full and partial footprints etched in the victim's blood on the stall floor would be lifted as well. He prepared for that eventuality by stopping halfway home, pulling into a strip mall, and locating the

Dumpster behind the Mandarin restaurant. The Air Jordans on his feet were removed and replaced with loafers. The Airs were deposited into the Dumpster and covered with packaging materials he found there. They would never be found and, even if they were, they would never be connected to him. Too remote, no connection.

Then he removed the latex gloves from his front pocket, removed the hairnet from his rear pocket, removed the damp paper towels from his rear pocket, and wrapped everything inside the paper hairnet. He snapped a BIC and held the items away from his body, lighting them and watching them burn until he had to drop the package. He waited judiciously while it burned itself out and he then climbed back into the Bug and pulled away. The wind and alley traffic would quickly scatter the ashes and no trace would be left, even if someone came looking, which was mathematically all but impossible.

Thaddeus knew about the *Frye* and *Daubert* legal standards of proof by expert witnesses that might be used against him. He had cited and argued these rules to judges many times during his career as a trial lawyer. Under these standards, which he knew were historically distinguishable, the U.S. Attorney could call to testify against him various experts who would have collected evidence from the scene, tested the evidence and made comparisons, and who would try to connect him with the scene, especially through trace and transfer evidence. Trace evidence would be evidence he might have deposited at the scene under Locard's Principle, which could include strands of his own hair and fibers from his carpet and chair at the office as well as from home. To protect against contaminating the crime scene with trace evidence Thaddeus had stopped at a Target store and purchased the black turtleneck. It of course bore no hair and no fiber from either home or office. Likewise a pair of black denim pants. He changed in the Target changing room. On the way home, after the hit, he went back to the same Target for the stated purpose of trying on other items of clothing. In his briefcase he had brought along the suit, shirt, and coat he had worn that day to the office. He changed back into these and tossed the jeans into a trash barrel outside a Best Buy at the other end of the neighborhood mall. He pulled into a 7-Eleven two miles on down the road, went inside for a coffee, and on the way past plunked the turtleneck shirt into the trash barrel outside the doors. He felt comfortable driving home that night. He had protected himself against all such trace and transfer inquiries and techniques of crime scene investigation.

MANNY RODRIGUEZ WORKED LATE at the office.

He straightened his desk, flipping through the Chase Staples case, anything he might have missed that day. He pulled his MacBook out of his backpack. He scanned a stack of paper medical records from the baby's birth: hospital and doctor and nursing. He moved the scanned PDFs to the MacBook. He studied the screen, and then opened the finder. He browsed to Dropbox, where he created a new file titled "Chase Staples." He copied all scanned medical records on the Chase Staples case over to Dropbox. *Morgana says we're scrubbing Chase Staples? Not if I get there first, we're not. This kid is too screwed to let it happen to him.* He clicked the mouse and his laptop's desktop swam into view and the screen blinked.

"Here we go. Hudd Family wants us to screw this kid. Well, here's one nobody gets to scrub. I'm saving this entire mess to the cloud." He resumed scanning for another hour. Soon he had twenty-seven PDFs saved to Dropbox on his MacBook. Under his own name, on his own account.

Two floors below, XFBI recorded none of this. Manny's laptop did not happen to be connected to the Jones Marentz network. In fact, his personal laptop was running off its own broadband. No one knew the records were saved off-site. No one except Manny.

He returned the paper files to their accordion folder. He shut down the MacBook and unbuttoned his shirt. The MacBook fit flat against his abdomen. It was time to take it home.

He turned back to the Jones Marentz office computer and made an entry on the firm's intake screen. "Let me see. This is a new case about a baby born with severe brain injury. Dr. Phillip Payne, our client. Baby is named Chase. I like that, Chase. Well, Chase, your secrets are safe with me. Now good night."

It was after nine.

XFBI checked his backpack as he left the suite. The agent knew Manny, joked with him several times a day, and loved talking Bulls basketball with him.

"What about that Joakim Noah last night?" the guard said and whistled. "Bruiser, that guy."

"Sir Charles says he might be the best big guy in the NBA. I don't disagree."

"Good night, Mister Rodriguez."

"Catch you later."

Then he was gone, a complete set of original medical records safely onboard.

Now to decide what to do with them. He didn't know, at that point, what he would do. But he did know that the answer would reveal itself as they moved further into the case.

He shivered. Brain damage. How hopeless the parents must feel.

28

Prior to the visit with the pediatric neurologist, Thaddeus accompanied Latoya and Chase to the Chicago Office of Social Services. She had been struggling and Thaddeus was ready to do whatever he could to help. His role at the meeting would be to put pressure on Social Services to cough up financial help for the baby. At least provide in-home assistance with his care. Chase's needs were overwhelming and she needed help with the infant.

They were sitting across the desk from a rather obese woman who was intently snapping her Wrigley's and running her fingers across her monitor. Latoya held Chase in her lap. He was tightly bundled, as it was blustery and very damp outside that day. Thaddeus noticed the little boy's eyes were steadily focused on the overhead fluorescents.

The woman reported what she saw on the screen. "Uh-huh, you've been to see us twice now. Both times we've told you there's no in-home services for a severely disabled child.

Now we can help you find an institution that would be wonderful for him, but in-home is a no-no—way too expensive for Uncle, Miss Staples."

Latoya patted Chase's shoulder. "Please. Let me explain this again. Please write it down. This baby is my youngest of three. There are two others. One in pre-school and one in first grade. This one never will be. He was hurt so bad being born that he's never going to school anywhere. Which means I need help. I cannot do this by myself."

"What about your husband? Does he help out?"

"When he's not working days driving a bus and nights mopping floors downtown in some office building."

"It says here that your baby suffers spasticity and seizures. Is he getting his medical care for these things?"

"John has good health care from the Blueline Tours. So our baby is getting what he needs there, but it only covers outpatient doctors. There's nothing for doctors and nurses coming to us at home. I don't think you people understand. Bringing Chase down here with me today is an all-day job. First I spend two hours getting him dressed and fed and settled down. Then he takes all his medicine—he's on Dilantin. Then we get down here by bus because I can't drive, not alone with him in the car. That takes another full hour, meaning we change over on the green line and I have to wait at the bus stop with him. Now he's upset and throwing a fit because he's cold. He's always cold and I just can't get him warm enough."

"I understand all that."

Latoya started to cry. Thaddeus held out his arms to take Chase for a few minutes, but she refused.

The frustration at the situation overcame her. She became angry at the caseworker. "Do you? Does it say in your computer how my heart is broken? Does it tell you how

I cry myself to sleep every night? Does it tell you that I still cry even when all I'm doing is looking at him?"

Gently, the social worker said, "No, it doesn't say that. I understand, we all do. But in this economy we've had fifty percent cutbacks in all the services we can provide. No one gets their full needs met anymore. But I understand what you're going through. I really get it."

By then Chase was getting explosive. He was bucking like an angry young bull. The allure of the fluorescents had played out and his eyes roamed slowly around the room. A crying fit overcame him and he was crying while half-digested formula rolled from the corner of his mouth. Latoya reached in his bag and found a warm cloth to wipe his face. He jerked away from her touch and began sobbing. Her own tears followed.

"Do you really get it?" Latoya cried.

"I'm sorry. We do get it. But there's no money."

Latoya turned and looked at Thaddeus. "See, Thad? See what I mean?"

Thaddeus could only nod, but asked the caseworker, "Is there any kind of appeal process we can undertake? Or is your word final?"

The caseworker shrugged. "You can appeal, but all I'm telling you is that there isn't some fund of money we can tap if someone in appeals should order it. It's just not there and hasn't been for probably ten years. Let me tell you something."

She leaned forward conspiratorially.

"The wars in the Middle East shut off all funding. From Nine/Eleven and after it was like a faucet got turned. Funds dried up, we've been operating on a shoestring, and basically we've become a referral service."

"Can he get Social Security?"

"Maybe Medicaid. You'd have to see them about that."

"And there's no appeal process? Would filing a lawsuit help?"

"Be my guest. That still won't make money appear. No one has money, period. If we did I would love to help. If we did, Chase would definitely be at the top of our list."

Thaddeus looked helplessly at Latoya. She was struggling with Chase and trying not to burst into tears again.

He resolved he would look at all possible ways to sue the doctor and hospital that did this to the baby.

First he would need the medical records. They had been requested in writing.

Hudd Family Healthcare had promised the records by the end of the month.

Until then, his hands were tied and he could offer no other help to the little family with the gigantic problems.

They left, feeling frustrated and helpless.

Thaddeus hailed a cab and paid the fare for the duo's trip back home. When they were gone, he turned and began walking back to his office. He needed time to think. He needed time to collect himself after the failed system he had just witnessed.

More than anything, he needed to assess just how totally dependent on him Chase had now become. He accepted that responsibility a hundred percent. Now he had to begin laying plans. There would be a lawsuit and hopefully a full and fair settlement within the next ten or twelve months. He couldn't deliver it any faster than that and he was going to have to make sure Latoya understood the long wait she was facing before there would be money to help.

As for himself, he was more than willing to cut back legal fees if that would help.

If not, he would take Hudd and Dr. Payne to court and get a jury verdict.

29

Early that fall, Carson Palmer and A.W. Marentz went bird hunting. Killing domestic pheasants was an annual event. It made the men feel vigorous and virile: the loading of guns, the discussion of shot loads and muzzle velocities and shot patterns, the killing and cooking of game.

They hunted near the center of a picked cornfield, their shotguns raised and ready. A signal from the end of the picked row told them that a pheasant was about to be released from its pen. The bird fluttered up, trying to pick up speed, when both shotguns roared.

A.W. was upset. "That was my bird, Carse!"

Carson cracked open the breech of his gun and pulled the spent shell from the chamber. "Dead bird either way. I lost track."

"How many have we killed now?"

"Twenty-two."

A.W. held his hands to his ears. "My ears are definitely ringing. I've had enough for one day."

"At fifty bucks a bird we each owe five-fifty."

"Cheap at twice the price. Bill big, kill tame birds."

"Bill big, get boats and country clubs."

"Bill big and retire," A.W. laughed.

"Speaking of which, A.W.—"

"—Speaking of which I'm about ready. My protégé is winning her cases and my guy at Fidelity says I could live to four hundred ten and still have money left over."

"Your protégé Morgana Bridgman? I haven't spoken ten words to her since she walked out on us. I heard she was or is sick. How's she doing now? It's been what—six months since she came screaming back to us? What's she up to now?"

"She's settled eleven cases since the little hiccup. She's definitely seen the light and evidently enjoys her new partnership status. Not to mention the paycheck she drags off every other Friday."

"What's her trial calendar looking like? Surely not everything will settle."

"She has an upcoming trial. It won't settle. I'm thinking jury selection begins after Thanksgiving."

"I'd like you to keep a close watch on that one."

"Why's that?"

"First trial since she came back. Let's make sure she's up to it. There's a big difference between saying you'll engage in a criminal conspiracy and actually doing it."

They shot simultaneously at a final bird. Both missed and the bird escaped and became a dot in the sky.

Carson shook his head. "Is she keeping her files cleaned up? XFBI says there are no problems whatsoever."

"She must be, she's getting great settlements."

"Good girl."

30

The lawyers had the pediatrician's records. They thought Chase had a case—so far. Something had gone wrong during Chase's birth that had caused his damage. It wasn't something delivered to them as punishment from God (as her grandmother suggested) and it wasn't something genetic from the mother (as John's sister suggested). It was something done by the doctor who delivered Chase, or by the hospital, maybe both.

Which was why Thaddeus accompanied Latoya to the second meeting with Dr. Arroyo. The severity and kind of neurologic deficits suffered by the infant would add another piece of the puzzle. "The etiology of Chase's deficits," Thaddeus told her. "That's what we're going to need to pin down."

Dr. Arroyo entered exam room 4 and found Chase, Latoya, and Thaddeus waiting. Exam room 4 consisted of an exam table, chairs, nursery rhyme cutouts along the walls, worktable with computer and two screens.

Latoya sat with Chase on a frame chair, her knee bouncing up and down as she kept the baby moving--an exercise that helped to keep him happy.

"Hello, Mr. Murfee, and thanks for coming. Hello Mrs. Staples. How is young Mr. Chase doing today?"

"No change, Dr. Arroyo. He still cries and throws fits all night long.""

"Let's see. Chase is nine months old and he had his second CT scan last week."

"Nine months Friday. He's growing so fast."

"His crying and discomfiture can be explained. Let me just show you what a cross-section of Chase's brain looks like on the CT scan machine. Remember, a CT scan is just a series of X-rays. These are last week's study."

He positioned the computer screens so Latoya and Thaddeus could see the images. They watched as he flipped through several slides.

"Now the screen on the left depicts the brain of a normal nine-month-old child. The areas of the brain portrayed are synced to show the same areas as the screen on the right. The screen on the right will show the same views, but these films are Chase's brain. Please notice the differences."

"You took X-rays of my baby's brain. We've had this once before."

"That's right. The images we have obtained can be compared to a loaf of bread. I can look at each of these slices individually and see what's up with Chase's brain. Or I can combine them in a whole loaf and visualize the entire brain. Like this—"

—Clicking the mouse—

Latoya said quietly, "It's so small. His brain is so small."

"It's a normal size for his age group, and that's good."

For a fleeting moment Thaddeus could see she felt hope. She had told him that she always felt hope when a doctor or radiologist or nurse practitioner said something about Chase that contained the word "normal."

"Why is that size good?"

"Bottom line, it means we have possibilities to work with. If his brain was microencephelatic it would be much more dire. Not that Chase's situation isn't dire."

"How dire?"

"OK, look at this series of images here. Watch as I click through several of them."

The screen flashed several times, maybe a half dozen. The "normal" views changed likewise.

See?"

She choked back a cry. "It looks like there's a dark place inside his brain. Is there a dark place?"

"There is. And that's what we need to talk about. We believe that while Chase was being born he suffered a lack of oxygen, a condition we call asphyxia."

"That's what Thad says."

The doctor nodded at Thaddeus. But the physician wasn't smiling—this was dire and he wanted to impress her with just how dire Chase's situation was.

"I know. I've spoken with Mr. Murfee. It's my understanding he is prepared to file a lawsuit against Dr. Payne. Your lawyer believes the delivery was mishandled. He's probably right. Brain damage in newborns doesn't just 'happen.' It can always be traced back to some source. It's not magic. If everyone did their jobs properly we wouldn't see these cases. It's a crime."

"What did you tell my lawyer?" She looked at her attorney as she spoke.

"I told him that babies are capable of an amazing trick of nature. Babies are born with the ability to endure a short period of low oxygen levels. But when that brief window closes and Chase is still short of oxygen, life can go from wonderful to tragic in just a few breaths."

Latoya was crying now. Thaddeus placed a hand on her shoulder. He and the doctor could see she was facing the tough reality again. "And you believe that's what's wrong with Chase?"

"Look at this particular image. It's representative of this entire area of Chase's brain."

She followed the area he encircled with his pen. "Okay," she said.

"The risk of an oxygen shortage or asphyxia increases if your labor and delivery take too long."

She grew angry. "Which really pisses me off. Payne should have come earlier and none of this would have happened. We're furious with that man."

"You probably should be."

"My delivery took way too long. The nurses were scared to death, I could tell."

"After a period of time of low oxygen your baby becomes stressed. The lack of oxygen destroys the delicate tissue in the cerebral motor cortex of his brain. See this region back here?" Again, the images flipped across both screens until he found the one he wanted.

"Yes."

He placed his pen against the computer screen and indicated a large circular area. "This dark zone is the center of Chase's problem. He suffered this brain damage at birth. There's just no other possible explanation, given his health, your health, a normal pregnancy, the excellent prenatal care you gave him. He's suffering probably because he went too long without enough oxygen at birth. That's the best we can tell."

Thaddeus spoke up for the first time. It was time to pop the Golden Question that all plaintiff lawyers must eventually ask the treating physicians. "Doc, you'll say these things in court? To a jury?"

The doctor pushed his glasses onto his forehead. He sighed as he contemplated. "I suppose I'll have to. I'm his treating and my studies tell the story. Yes, I'll testify, I want to help. He needs advocacy."

"That's what Thad says you told him. He agrees and he's an expert." She smiled at Thaddeus and patted his arm. He squeezed her shoulder. This wasn't easy, not for anyone.

Whereupon Chase launched into a crying spell, bucking and tossing in his mother's arms. She patted, she whispered, she cooed, but nothing helped. His pain continued.

"You know, Latoya, I asked you to visit me with Mr. Murfee because he's a top trial attorney for this kind of injury to newborns. A colleague of mine from med school worked with him in Chicago."

"He has a quiet confidence. Chase and I love Thad."

Thaddeus smiled. "Thank you both. I'm sure I can help with this."

She patted Chase's back. "Chase likes him too."

"That's a nice thing to say, but I'm afraid there's not much truth to it."

"Oh yes, Chase can already tell the people he likes and the people he dislikes."

"Latoya, it's doubtful that Chase will ever be able to make those fine distinctions. That's why I asked you to visit me with Mr. Murfee."

Tears flooded her eyes now. "My poor baby won't be able to know very much, will he? Thad told me. He told me Chase is going to need special care all of his life."

"Probably more care than you and your husband alone are going to be able to give him. I'm thinking maybe Chase should be placed in a long-term care facility where he can get the additional care that he needs."

"No way! I'm not giving up my baby to some institution."

"You wouldn't be giving him up, you would just be turning him over to people who are experts in the type of care he needs."

"That will never happen. Chase is going to grow up with his mommy and his daddy. We're all he has."

"Yes, that's why I'm suggesting maybe he should have more. I'm just hoping we can at least open the door to discussion."

She was weeping and dabbing her eyes and nose with tissue. Never had Thaddeus felt more helpless than he did right then.

She said, "Chase is growing up with me and his daddy. The help he needs can come to see him in his house where he lives."

Dr. Arroyo said, "And that takes money. Millions and millions of dollars over a lifetime. Chase has a natural life expectancy of eighty-one years. That's a long time of daily—hourly—care."

"Thad is suing the hospital and the doctor. Chase will get the money he needs to live with his mommy and daddy at home," the mother confidently said.

"I hope you're right." He closed the chart and closed the CT scans and stood up. "OK, we've covered enough ground for today. I'd like to see you back in one month."

"We'll be here. This baby isn't going anywhere."

"Thanks, Dr. Arroyo," Thaddeus said, and shook his hand.

Latoya was busy with Chase's coat as the doctor grimaced at Thaddeus and shook his head.

This was going to be a tough one and they both knew that.

They would have to be at the top of their game, especially the young lawyer.

But he was confident. He had the treating physician ready to tell it all in the courtroom. Now he would add an expert witness from a local medical school, put the nurses and resident physicians on the stand, and Chase stood to win a whole roomful of money.

And that was a lot.

But first, he needed the Hudd records. They were due in two more days. He was certain he would find the smoking gun in those records. He knew they would show the doctor's late arrival, his neglect of his duties, and the clear liability for the injuries Chase had suffered. Records won or lost these cases.

And this time, he was sure he had a winner.

Chase, John, and Latoya would soon have the help they so desperately needed.

31

M organa's Porsche Cabriolet eased up the slope and nosed abruptly into its reserved parking space. The headstone said the slot was reserved for Morgana Bridgman, Esq. Morgana and Manny remained in the car to talk.

Morgana sighed. "So we've got another Phillip Payne case, Manny? Does this guy never stop hurting kids?"

"Evidently not. Even worse, I've been feeling like shit ever since you made me turn over the phony records."

"The meeting will be a walk. You've turned over the notes I said you could turn over. So what else? Give me a rundown."

"We got the Staples case a month ago. Dr. Payne is on the one o'clock. You met the guy a year or two ago. Similar case. He's going to need reassuring because he sure as hell was at fault. He could have killed this kid. Maybe it would have been better if he had. Kid's life is destroyed."

"What did you turn over?"

"What you said, the phony records."

"What all was missing from the records?"

"Only the nurses' notes. That made it easy. I destroyed the originals they sent us. We only scrubbed nurses' notes."

"Good man. Look, no one hates this place any more than me. It's a shit job and I get that."

"So why are you doing it?" Manny asked.

"Why are you? Same reason. It pays the bills."

"There's got to be a better way. What if we went out together?"

"And did what?"

"Open our own firm."

"Doing what, medical malpractice defense? No one would hire us."

"No, I'm thinking divorce, bankruptcy, some criminal, personal injury."

"I took a look at the numbers. I can't bankroll what it costs to start up plus pay my monthly nut."

"So we're screwed."

Morgana tapped her hand on the steering wheel. "What kind of injury is it again?"

"Anoxia. Brain damage, you've defended Payne on this very thing before."

"I vaguely remember."

"It settled, no trial."

"How much did we pay?"

"Policy limits. Five million."

"Not much of a policy."

"It's all Northwest Physician Reserve would insure him for. After they settled, they dropped him from the policy."

"So good old Hudd rushes in and picks him up."

"Who else would?" It was rhetorical. Both lawyers knew the answer.

"Jesus."

Morgana stared straight ahead. Her hands gripped and

loosened on the steering wheel. Her jaw worked as she contemplated.

Morgana turned and faced her associate. "So do we still have the original records?"

"I've got the original records. Just like we agreed when you came back to work here."

"Jesus."

"You want me to dump them?"

"No, no, you did fine," Morgana said, although she couldn't explain her hesitancy. Normally she would have insisted Manny destroy all originals. Not this time, though she couldn't say why.

"This is one messed up kid. I don't like this at all."

"But the firm would know if we turned the originals over to the mom's lawyer."

"How would they know?"

"For openers I'd probably get hit for fifty million by the jury. That would be a huge flag that something seriously went wrong."

"So what do I do with the real records? That is a pretty dense cloud of smoking gun."

"Let's just hold them in reserve and see how this thing goes. We'll prepare for trial like the original records don't exist."

"I don't like that, dude. If you change your mind on down the road and give them up, maybe you've committed a crime by then. Maybe you lose your license to practice law."

"Knowing Dr. Payne they've probably got him nailed even without the records. It's a miracle any insurance company will still insure him."

"That's the thing. He's left the practice just because of that. Nobody will sell him malpractice insurance. Even Hudd caved on him."

"Serves the bastard right."

"It does."

"So let's go hear about the baby he destroyed. Ready?"

"Ready."

A BLACK AND white marble tile floor demarcated the waiting area and at the far end a staircase to the second floor could be seen, back-dropped by six vertical windows, the upper three with lattice inserts. Beneath the staircase waited a wingback couch, flanked by end tables, fronted by a coffee table and surrounded by a flurry of wingback chairs.

Off the elevator stepped Dr. Phillip Payne, who cast an anxious look at the reception desk then averted his eyes as he approached. Busted.

The receptionist looked up and smiled at the doctor. "Good morning. Who are you here to see?"

"Phillip Payne, M.D. Here for Miss Bridgman."

"One moment, I'll buzz."

Moments later he was escorted into Morgana's office and the inquiry began.

"Just so I have this straight. Your wife threw your beeper into the hot tub?"

"That's right."

"And that's why we've got this brain-damaged baby on our hands?"

Manny rolled his eyes and said, "Somebody get the checkbook. This baby's going to get his needs met."

Morgana ignored her associate. "Let me ask this, Doc. The nurse's notes indicate you were scrubbing for C-section well within the thirty-minute window for decision to incision."

Manny added, "That's not what the real records say, of course."

The doctor looked puzzled. "What do the real records say?"

"That you're fifteen minutes late."

Morgana said, "We're going by the new records they gave us from the hospital, Doc. We're covering your ass on this one."

Manny shrugged. "Well, according to those records he made it with ten minutes to spare."

"Is that right, Doc?"

"I believe that's accurate."

"So your version has it that you made it to the hospital inside the thirty-minute window, correct?"

"Correct. Not my version, the truth."

"Then this baby shouldn't be suing us. Why is he suing us?"

"Pardon?"

"Doc, you tell me. Why do we have a bad baby on our hands?"

"There could be many reasons for an injured baby. Disease, maybe. Poor prenatal care, mother's drug or alcohol use, lack of proper nutrients—"

Manny scoffed. "Why don't you just pick one? What's the theme of our case? Wrong vitamins? We've got a bad baby because mom took prenatal E instead of A?"

"Let him finish. What else, Doc?"

"The thirty-minute decision to incision requirement is an arbitrary number."

A frown settled on Manny's face. "As in, someone pulled it out of thin air?"

"Studies have shown that babies in trouble during

delivery can withstand thirty minutes of compromised oxygen supply without lasting injury."

"So maybe Chase Staples is the exception? Maybe he couldn't take the full thirty minutes of oxygen deprivation?"

"That's what I'm suggesting."

Manny glowered at him. "Because that sounds better than the truth, which is just that you were too damn late to do the kid any good."

"Manny, shut the hell up. This is hard enough without your commentary. Now, let's hear this. Doc, the medical industry selected the thirty-minute window based on what?"

The doctor sniffed. He had been treated with rudeness. "Based on several studies."

Morgana asked, "So pretty much the whole obstetrics community believes that thirty minutes without full oxygen is survivable without brain injury?"

"The vast majority of obstetrical physicians believe so."

"So if the hospital's policy of thirty minutes decision to incision was based on those studies, the hospital met the standard of care?"

"The hospital met the standard of care in the industry. And so did I."

Manny looked skeptical. "Except we know you didn't because we know from the real records that you were thirty minutes plus fifteen. You were late, late, late and now some little kid is never going to know how to spell his name, which is S-C-R-E-W-E-D."

"Can we get someone else to help on my case?" said Dr. Payne, the frustration and fear driving him deeper in his chair.

Manny smiled broadly. "You're stuck with me."

"Manny will work his butt off for you when the time

comes. Cases get won because of Manny's meticulous, relentless study and research."

"But I don't trust you, Manny."

"That's probably the smartest thing you've said today. You shouldn't trust me."

Morgana was impeded in her effort to frame this correctly and it was showing in the deep lines cutting across her face. "Knock it the hell off, both of you. We've got our defense. The injury occurred because this particular baby was an exception to the general rule of thirty minutes."

The doctor looked at her closely. "Do I lose?"

"You do not. You win because the standard of care was thirty minutes and that was met. Nurse's notes say you were there at Decision plus twenty-one. Plenty of time to save the kid."

"Thank God."

Manny shook his head and waved his hand. "Did someone just cut one? It reeks like bullshit in here."

32

All gold shields and darting looks, they entered his waiting room at eight o'clock Monday morning. Special-Agent-in-Charge Pauline Pepper and partner George Washington.

Agent Pepper was all business, and that morning, wearing a silk Anne Klein six-button belted pants suit with Glock 19 stuffed in a shoulder holster, she looked all business. Washington was a black man from Yale, undergraduate in accounting, law degree from Georgetown. It only fit, he told everyone, George Washington at Georgetown. The humor was lost, of course, on the FBI, especially his senior partner Pauline Pepper. George Washington sported the mandatory FBI pinstripe. He was wearing Gucci eyeglasses with photo-lenses yet dark when Thaddeus received the page from the receptionist and found the agents impatient and refusing to sit.

He asked their business.

"Our business is you," said Pauline Pepper. She was unsmiling and grim. "We need to talk. Or we can just run you over to Metropolitan Correctional Center and book you. Your choice."

"What would you be booking me for?"

"How about a federal murder rap? Two down, four to go? Ring a bell?"

He shrugged. "I don't know what you're talking about. But come on in. Enlighten me."

They followed him into his office. It was a corner office, view of Lake Michigan, blue sky, and sailboats swooping across distant water, seagulls riding the thermals. And it was large, barely filled even by two couches, facing—Oval Office style— with silk-upholstered wingback chairs and marble coffee table the size of a Chevrolet Impala. His own desk was teak with a glass top. Arranged in a neat U were three computer screens, a Mac computer, two telephones, and a scanner. Law books were nowhere to be seen. The walls were covered with French Impressionists, most of which were originals. Thaddeus spent his days and many of his nights in that office, and cost was uncurbed when interior designs were drawn.

The agents took the couch facing the door and Thaddeus slumped on the facing.

"Get you anything?" he asked.

"We're good," said Washington.

Pepper nodded, yes, they were good.

"So what brings you here?"

"Two killings," said Washington.

"Look, let's cut right to the chase," said Pepper. "You obtained the names and backgrounds of two recent murder victims. We know you're the perp."

Thaddeus held out his wrists. "So, cuff me and take me away. I'm right here."

The agents traded a look.

Thaddeus nodded. "You can't because you don't have jackshit on me. You don't have opportunity, you aren't even sure you have motive, are you? Oh, that's right; motive is never required for federal crimes. But the FBI lives on motive. So all you need is some evidence."

"We're not here to arrest you. We're here to tell you that your little evade and avoid games have run their course. You're in our sights. You're interfering with a federal investigation and I'm about to go speak to the U.S. Attorney about charging you with something easy, something like obstruction of justice, just to get a bracelet on your ankle. Then you won't sneak off."

"Get the bracelet. Go for it. I've done nothing wrong here."

Pepper gave him a long, hard stare. "You're so close and you don't even get it."

"What don't I get?"

"We're going over the steam room and we're finding no DNA because there is none. We're going over the Jungle Zone restroom and we're finding no DNA and forensics netted a goose egg, but we can put you there that night, thanks to the security cameras. We've got you coming into the mall and leaving the mall. We've got you coming into the restaurant and leaving the restaurant. We've got somebody paying for an extra-long thunderstorm because he needs background noise for the door he's about to kick down."

"But what you don't have is evidence. Anything else you want to say? If not, I've got a deposition at nine on a bad baby case and I really need to get ready."

She scowled. Washington picked lint off his sleeve.

"Agents are executing a search warrant at your home as we speak."

"Be my guest."

"We have a search warrant for this office."

"Be my guest. The deposition is at the defendant's office. I'll be out of your way in ten minutes. Remember too that your search warrant does not allow you to browse client files. If I find that you have, I will sue you and get a judgment against you and collect your badges in my badge collection."

"My, my," she taunted, "aren't we getting snippy in our middle age?"

"I'm not thirty years old yet. So I don't know whom you're talking about. Just remember what I said, please."

"We have no intention of looking at client files. Client files didn't just kill Abu-Nidal."

"I don't know who that is, and I don't care who that is. I'll ask you to wait in the hallway now until I leave."

"No can do. We have to execute this warrant."

"Then I'll leave you to that."

They had nothing else.

He pulled on his suit coat, walked to the door, and left without another word.

But the game was on, he knew.

The game was definitely on.

33

The Jones Marentz pre-trial preparation room was huge, centered by a rosewood table the size of a backyard pool, surrounded by strategically placed whiteboards and giant paper tablets on tripods, surfaces that reflected the bright overheads back upon the tabletop, making it dazzle as if outdoors. Ten-foot ficus trees anchored the corners, and at one end was a series of six horizontal wide-screens where different size videos could be cued. Present were A.W., Morgana, Manny, Dr. Payne, Sandy, and Carson.

It was a sandpaper session. The witness/defendant would have his testimony rehearsed—aided, and abetted by his expert defenders—and the rough edges knocked off. Dr. Payne was sweating profusely and waved a white handkerchief in his hands in the copyrighted manner of Satchmo, as he gave proposed answers to practice direct- and cross-examination questions.

Morgana stood at a whiteboard on which she had printed "30 Minutes Decision to Incision."

"And at Decision plus twenty-one minutes, Dr. Payne arrives and is in the scrub room."

Manny nodded, following along on the trial script he had carefully prepared. "Right, and the nurse's notes indicate they have arrived in the OR and have been told Dr. Payne is scrubbing."

A.W. looked over at Carson. The two senior partners exchanged a smile. Morgana and Manny were performing like trained seals starved for fresh fish. It was all false, what they were laying out, but required.

Morgana continued. "Sandy, you're the head of Special Claims. Are these notes the originals we're looking at here?"

Sandy said, "They are. We've been over them downtown and they're the real thing."

Manny lowered his head. He literally was biting his tongue to stay out of what he wanted so badly to start.

Morgana continued. "What about Nurse Andrea? Has she seen the records since that night?"

Sandy looked at the ceiling for his answer. "Andrea's National Guard unit was called up. She's working a flying hospital between Ramstein, Germany, and Walter Reed. Not available."

Carson tented his fingers. "How convenient for us."

Manny's eyes narrowed and fixed on Sandy. "She's really unavailable?"

"She's really unavailable."

Manny's shoulder sagged in resignation. "Well, I just can't keep quiet about this. The nurse's notes you're going over right now are not the same as the original ones."

Sandy's face reddened with anger. "What's that supposed to mean?"

Manny sprawled back in his chair and crossed his legs in the manner of one no longer attending the meeting with the same sophistication as the other visitors. "It means someone at Hudd Family Healthcare screwed the pooch. They sent us the original nurse's notes and the doctored nurse's notes. Original records the kid wins. Doctored records the doctor wins. How ironic."

A.W. lifted a hand. "Which records have been turned over to the plaintiff?"

"Not to worry, sir. We're using the set that favors Dr. Payne. We're using the forged set. Now we can all go out to lunch and blow two hundred bucks on Hudd Family while this little kid gets ready for a lifetime of inadequate health care."

There, it was said. Manny had laid the egg in the middle of the table.

The room fell silent. Sandy finger-stirred his coffee and sucked his finger. Morgana continued writing on the whiteboard. Manny met anyone's gaze who looked his way. He was defiant, fed up.

After several stare-downs, Carson rose to the moment and took up the firm's banner.

"Morgana, I want you to replace Mr. Rodriguez on this case. Manny, please excuse yourself now. I'll come by your office and we'll talk about your concerns."

Dr. Payne was all self-righteous smiles. "About time. He's not helping the defense."

Morgana turned from the board. "A.W., I need Manny on this case with me. He'll work with me, I can promise you."

A.W. shook his head. He exhaled a long breath and said, "You heard the managing partner. It's his call who staffs what cases."

Carson gave Morgana what all understood was an order. "Pick one of your new associates. They can burn some midnight oil and get up to speed on the case in two or three nights."

With a thump of his chair shoved back against the wall, Manny stalked out.

Morgana nodded. "Whatever you say. Dr. Payne, let's close the loop with you. What time did you leave home for the hospital that night?"

"As soon as I got the page."

"Sandy, what time did the first page go out from the hospital?"

"The first and only page that shows up in the hospital's log is the one at six thirty-five that night."

"So you left home, you can say around six forty, right?"

"Right."

"And how long did it take you to drive to the hospital?"

"Well, rush hour was over by then. I would say maybe ten minutes. We just live out by the lake."

"Then the notes"—Morgana paged through the notes —"—the notes show the OR staff has been told at six fifty-three that you've arrived and that you're scrubbing. Sound about right?"

"I suppose so."

"No, you don't suppose so. You know so. "You know because—"

A.W. interjected, "Because I always time myself from home to the hospital."

Dr. Payne got it. "Because I always time myself from home to the hospital."

"Exactly. So you know you have arrived at Andrea's Decision mark at six fifty-three. And the baby is delivered at six fifty-seven."

Dr. Payne recited what they'd previously coached. "When the anesthesiologist is told I'm in the scrub room next door he makes the last prep to put mama under. When I walk through the door after that, mama goes to sleep."

"How long to cut and deliver?"

The doctor shrugged. "Minutes. Three tops."

Morgana looked at her watch. "So the baby—Chase—is delivered at—"

—Examining nurse's notes once again—

"—At exactly six fifty-seven. Is that what you remember?"

"It must be, but that's not what I wrote on the birth certificate."

Morgana encouraged him. "And you know that was inaccurate because you always—"

"—I always look up at the OR clock and call the time of delivery for the nurse to chart. But it isn't until later that I sign off on the birth certificate using the current time. That's why the birth certificate shows a later time."

Carson silently applauded, approving. "Beautiful answer. Gentlemen, we're on the way to a big win here."

A.W. took a swig of bottled water. "Dr. Payne, you're going to have to learn to be more sure of yourself and the answers you give. Get assertive, man."

"I can do that. Can I ask a dumb question?"

A.W. gave the standard trial lawyer answer. "There are no dumb questions."

Carson added, "Not when there's ten or fifteen million at stake."

"Or fifty," said Morgana.

"That's right, 'or fifty.'"

Dr. Payne understood. But he felt put-upon. Why were they even doing this? "Why don't we just settle? Why don't we pay the kid something and be done with it? Isn't that the right thing to do?"

Sandy said, "I've got that. Doc, this case wouldn't settle under fifteen million. Hudd Family Healthcare doesn't settle bad baby cases for fifteen mil."

Dr. Payne said, "You don't?"

"Hell no, we go to trial. We stack the deck and go to trial."

Dr. Payne tried it from a different angle. "What if we offered five million?"

"They'd spit in our eye. Thaddeus Murfee is known to hit big on these bad baby cases. He knows he's got a shot at fifteen to thirty million."

Morgana was ready to move it along. "OK, Doc, why don't you and I just run through it again while these gentlemen go have lunch. Can you do that?"

"I'm not doing much else these days."

"I understand that. This time, though, I want you to sit over here and pretend you're sitting on the witness stand. I'm going to ask you the same questions I'll be asking you in court. That way we can practice every answer, every look on your face, the whole nine yards. Cool?"

"I'm good with that. What should I wear to court?"

BACK IN MORGANA'S office two hours later, the inquisition was underway. They were seated opposite at the desk, and Morgana was pointing her finger in his face.

"You really hosed me out there. Just let me make one thing perfectly clear."

"I know, I've already heard. Jim Barnes is going to trial with you instead of me."

"That's part of it. Let me just ask you—do you still have those original nurse's records?"

"Staples case? They're on the cloud. I told you that."

"OK, take them down. Destroy them. I'm going to have to appear in court one of these days and tell Judge Moody the plaintiff has all her records. I don't want to go to jail for perjury later if someone manages to get their hands on them."

"Huge mistake. Just turn them over and get something else going in your life. There's other jobs, dude."

"Manny—"

"Got it. Consider them destroyed. Is that everything, oh Wise One?"

"It's never everything. Now get the hell out of here."

Manny was leaving but was met at the door by Carson, who entered the office, blocking Manny's exit.

"Not so fast, son. Sit your ass back down in that chair. Good."

Morgana said, "He knows he's not going to trial with me. I've explained it."

Carson said to Manny, "Are you purposely trying to run off our clients?"

Manny smiled. Morgana had to hand it to him. He showed no sign of being intimated by the managing partner. He said, "I'm purposely trying to help our clients see what this law firm is really about."

"I'll ask again, are you purposely trying to cost us clients?"

"All I want is for our clients to know their cases are being manipulated by the partners in this firm."

"And how long would it take you to box your things and leave our offices?"

"Why?"

"Because I'm going back to my office and I'm calling

security to escort you out. You're terminated. If security finds you here I'm going to have you arrested for trespassing."

Manny pulled out his iPhone and called for a taxi. Then he surreptitiously clicked RECORD on his phone.

"Mr. Palmer. You're saying I'm terminated and I'm no longer a member of the Hudd Family defense team?"

"You, sir, were never a member of the Hudd Family defense team. Now get your stuff and get out."

"Yes sir."

Manny exited and noisily returned to his own office, high-fiving people in the hall as he went, and slamming his door. He ended the iPhone recording. He slammed a box on his desk and began packing his personal items.

"Never a member of the defense team?" he said to no one. "That will come back to bite you in the ass, I'm almost certain of it."

34

The Niles neighborhood was a culturally diverse area that was popular among young professional couples. It was close enough to Chicago to hit the Art Institute and Theatre District, but far enough out to avoid some of the city's ills, especially poor schools. John and Latoya Staples decided to put down Niles roots and raise the kids in a safe part of town. They enrolled them in Catholic school to guarantee the best education for them. They had owned a condo in Niles for four years and were extremely happy in it. They were also twelve months ahead on mortgage payments. The future was bright.

But then the tragedy with Chase overwhelmed their happy home. They were beside themselves, at wits' end, and they were exhausted with trying to care for him. Help was needed and prayed for, but help was expensive and so far they hadn't figured out how to move things around on their budget to make it work, to get professional hands in place.

In the nice clean living room, John Staples and Attorneys Thaddeus Murfee and Morgana Bridgman were making small talk while Latoya poured coffee. John Staples was a casually dressed man in his mid-thirties, wiry and strong, who looked like he could hold his own in any alley. Latoya finished up playing hostess and joined the threesome in the living room.

Thaddeus led things off after the mandatory small talk was concluded. "OK, Mr. and Mrs. Staples. The court has given Morgana here permission to visit the house and to see Chase up close."

The father nodded solemnly, "We understand. Our older kids are at their grandmother's for the day."

Thaddeus added, "The reason that I'm making a Day in the Life film about Chase is that I plan to introduce it as evidence at trial."

"We understand that too."

A camerawoman had set up her tripod and camera in a corner, inconspicuous and staying out of the zone of influence. Thaddeus nodded at her and she switched the camera to ON.

"So why don't we begin by having you describe some of the peculiar things about Chase. Let's start with you, John, tell us some things about Chase that you have noticed from the older kids."

"Well, when our son was born he had a terrifying Apgar score. Plus his eyes diverged a little but they told us that was nothing to worry about."

Thaddeus asked, "So his eyes were open early?"

"He was practically born with his eyes open. I was right there just after. My mom came over to watch our kids. So I watched Chase. OK, so he cried a lot. He really cried a lot. He cried throughout most of the day and night. He hardly slept. I know, I was there in the hallway watching him like a hawk."

Morgana spread her hands. "Some children cry more than others, I suppose."

"No, Chase cried more than normal. He wouldn't stop crying for hours. Then he would exhaust himself and sleep for maybe fifteen minutes. Then he would wake up and start the whole thing again, crying and catnapping. I called it catnapping."

"Let me write that down," said Morgana. "Excuse me, I just need to figure out notes on my iPad. Okay, got it. Please continue."

"And the worst part was, when he did doze off he refused to sleep horizontal. He had to be held before he would sleep. Either me or Latoya or the nurses would be holding him while he catnapped. This was at the hospital. Then we got to bring him home. Tough little guy but he cried all the way home in the old Crown Vic we drive. Plus he threw up all over me not once but twice."

"Describe what home was like."

"OK, now we're home. Let me tell you what this is like in a typical day of Chase's life. Even now we have to take turns in the recliner all night, holding Chase while he catnaps. Then he'll be awake and for a little while he'll only be restless. But then it sets in again—crying."

Morgana nodded in agreement that it was extremely difficult. "You two must be very tired."

"At first we didn't know what the hell was going on. Now we do. This crying was a sign of possible brain damage."

"What else have you noticed about Chase?"

"OK, here's one. During his first two weeks he had a very low body temperature. Eighty-five degrees. We covered him with blankets and heating pads and did everything we could to keep him warm."

"Then what happened?"

"Eventually his body temperature climbed back up."

"Is it normal now?"

"It never has regulated well. Not like you and me. We're steady; you know what I mean? Not Chase, he still ups and downs. First he's hot then he's cold. Well, we learned this was another symptom of brain damage."

Latoya broke in. "These things start to add up. But you're only hearing one percent of what life is really like now. With me there's this constant dread of what's going to happen next. With the other ones I always knew that there would be stages, you know? Diapers, then training pants, then regular underwear. I don't count on that with Chase. They tell me he'll never potty train." Tears dampened her eyes as the reality again surfaced.

She added, "And that's just one tiny thing. Then I wonder about school, will he go to any kind of school? Right now we've got one in pre-school and one in first grade. The doctors tell me that Chase will never attend that kind of school. So I ask them what other kind of school there is and they just look at me. No one knows shit. Can I say that on camera?"

Thaddeus said, "The jury wants to see you like you are. That's fine to express yourself."

John said, "Latoya breastfed our other two kids. No problem. Chase struggled to be able to suck. He finally took some water from a bottle after two days. Latoya kept after him. After two more days she got him to finally suck. Two weeks of this kind of struggle and then he started breastfeeding regular. Another sign of brain damage."

Latoya hurried out and returned with a stack of tissues. She dabbed her eyes.

"Are you telling Miss Bridgman everything we've noticed?" she asked her husband.

He nodded. "I'm trying."

Latoya dried her eyes and straightened up. "Like I say, I've got two other kids. No problems, normal kids. Chase is different in so many ways. But he's going to come along just fine and be more himself as he grows."

Thaddeus softly asked her, "Latoya, is that being realistic?"

The tears started flowing. "No, it is not. This beautiful baby boy is not gonna have a life, Miss Bridgman. He's never gonna swim, never gonna go for a walk all alone, never gonna ride a bike, never write a check, never drive around town, never go shopping alone, he won't even know where to go for a simple haircut. Does this help you understand a Day in the Life? Does it?"

Morgana's cup rattled in its saucer as she held it. "I'm sorry. There's nothing else to say but I'm sorry."

His wife's tears unnerved John. Coupled with the frustration and stress of Chase, he bristled. "You damn well ought to be. You're defending the scum of the earth, a doctor who would let this happen to a precious baby. How could anyone even look at themselves in the mirror after something like this?"

"I don't know. I mean for me, it's my job. It's what I do. I have great sympathy, personally, for your situation."

"Do you have kids, Miss Bridgman?"

"Well, that's just it, we have one on the way, our first."

"Well, I'm gonna be praying for you that this doesn't happen to your baby. You've got to watch over them like a hawk when they're coming out."

"I will."

John asked, "And if there's any way you can think of, if we could just get some money now—kind of an advance—

we could get a nurse in here two nights a week and let us get some sleep. Right now we're zombies."

Morgana was taken by surprise. "I'm sorry, I—"

Thaddeus raised a hand. "What Morgana is trying to say is that we really have not discussed settling this case yet. We're still in the discovery phase."

Suddenly Latoya lifted Chase and placed him in Morgana's arms. Morgana was immediately flustered, trying to hold the iPad and restrain Chase's bucking and twisting in her arms. Chase arched his back and screamed.

Latoya folded her hands in her lap and watched. "There. Now you look Chase in the eye and tell him there's no money for him after what that fool doctor did to him. Go ahead, tell him!"

Morgana was totally off-guard. She tried patting the baby, she tried jiggling him up and down, but the frantic baby ignored her efforts. Finally, in desperation, she held the infant out to his mother. Morgana had tears in her eyes. She accepted the offer of a tissue.

Latoya said to her baby, "What, baby? Is the lady going to help my big boy? Did she say?"

35

T he three Middle Eastern men gathered at the Niles Denny's Restaurant, corner booth. They ordered—separate checks—and then launched into Arabic.

"I bought the video from the Jungle Zone," Ragman told the others. "Clearly it was Thaddeus Murfee."

"Poor Sayed," said Kilowatt. "Allah mourns."

"Allah rejoices. Sayed died fighting the infidels."

"Agree," said Maps, who raised his Diet Coke as a toast. His toast went unconfirmed.

"So. Here is his picture from our surveillance. A member of the South Chicago Cell took it last week. Notice no facial hair, six foot two, thick brown hair, round spectacles, plain Brooks Brothers suit."

"That's Gucci," said Kilowatt. "I have that suit."

"Okay, color me wrong," said Ragman. "A pinstripe suit. Like fifty thousand other lawyers in Chicago."

"Sorry," said Kilowatt.

"I'm just huge upset," said Ragman. "We're losing soldiers to this infidel."

"So what do we do?"

"I've turned him over to the Western Cell. They will hit him."

"When?"

"It better be before he comes after us again."

36

T haddeus reclined in the Emperor 1510 ergonomic chair, suit jacket and shirt removed. At his side perched a tattoo artist with tiny pots of ink and a well-broken-in Neuma tattoo machine. The artist focused on the portrait of a very small child being held in one very large hand, as it was injected onto Thaddeus' shoulder. Across the desk Latoya repeatedly poked a bottle of formula in the area of Chase's moving mouth.

Thaddeus looked up from the resolving tattoo. "So what are we saying here? You did read the nurse's notes I sent you or you didn't?"

Latoya held Chase away from her body like a sack of flour so she could respond. "I'm saying I did read them and they aren't what happened. It didn't happen like that at all. They're trying to make it sound like they paged Dr. Payne and twenty minutes later he comes screeching in to save me like Roadrunner. That's not it at all. It took at least forty-five minutes."

"And we know that because?"

"We know it because I was the one there. I was the one

waiting."

"Well, was there a clock in the room?"

"Not that I could see."

"Were you wearing a watch?"

"No, I was not. They took my watch and my wedding ring."

He frowned. "Well, did somebody tell you how long it took? No one's going to buy that. So you tell me."

"Simple. I knew how long it took because Andrea timed my contractions and she timed how long between contractions. Both took three minutes. Six minutes per cycle. And I went through this seven times until the doctor got there."

"You counted up to seven?"

"I did. I told myself I would go to ten and then I would get up and leave."

"I like your self-talk, girl. You're tougher than most of my clients."

"When I got to seven and almost said 'eight,' in strolls Dr. Payne. He was wearing his gown and I saw them put the gloves on him, then I went under."

"That will work. Six minutes times seven and you've got forty-two minutes from the time they paged until the time the doctor arrived. Add another three minutes at least to get the baby out and you're talking a forty-five-minute response time."

"Mm-hmm."

"But how do we know the contractions didn't get closer together?"

At last Chase took the bottle. He began sucking vigorously and his eyes played across the fluorescents embedded in the ceiling. "Because Andrea and Nancy timed them. Every time they said the same thing, three minutes. Then they timed in between and said the time. Every time that was three minutes. Seven times. Six minutes. Magic number, no more, no less."

"But the nurse's notes have him arriving eighteen minutes after the page."

"Horse puckey. I've told you what I know."

"So what are we saying here, the nurse's notes are wrong?"

"Contrived might be a better word. Those nurse's notes are wrong."

"Did you see other nurse's notes?"

"I did not. Who reads nurse's notes during delivery? Sweet Jesus, Thaddeus."

"Contrived? Are we saying these notes are fabricated?"

"Of course they are. Someone made up a bunch of bull-shit so they don't lose a million dollars on a nobody baby like Chase."

"We're after a lot more than a million here."

The tattoo artist spoke up. "Thaddeus, you're flinching. Try to relax."

"It hurts like hell."

The tattoo artist nodded at Latoya. "All great art hurts. Right, mama?"

She seemed to examine her baby with a critical eye. "This great art hurt. I can swear to that."

Thaddeus said, "What about the forty-two minutes. Can you swear to that?"

"I can."

"Under oath, before God?"

"Yes, I can swear before my Maker that it was forty-two minutes before he got there."

"Then we're done here."

"Not quite," said the artist. "Try to lean back and relax. We have a lot of decorating to add yet."

37

At the wheel of her Porsche, Morgana raced through Chicago Loop traffic while A.W. hung onto the passenger strap. Wide-eyed and jaw-dropped, the journey was clearly more than he had bargained for.

"For the love of God, Morgana, take it easy. None of these cabbies you're shooting through can read English and they all look alike. Hit one of them and they scatter like roaches. Then you have no insurance to go after."

She laughed and slapped the wheel. "This car will do one ninety-five, A.W. A little slashing and burning out here is small potatoes to her."

"Pull in here, Nouveau's."

They parked and Morgana followed A.W. into the restaurant. It was a man's menu on the wall: meat loaf, chili, corned beef and cabbage, pot roast. Few women were present but Morgana seemed not to notice and marched right in, leading the way.

They walked to the back, nodding to judges and lawyers as they went. The waiter followed them and waited.

Morgana asked, "What are you having?"

A.W knew what he wanted before he got there. "I'll have the roast hen and new potatoes. Water."

"Same. Iced tea. Now what do you want to talk about?"

"The Staples case. I'm going to trial with you."

"You're what? Jim Barnes is going to trial with me. I really like this guy; he's a Hoya too. Anyway, that's what Carson said."

"I know that's what Carson told you. Well, Barnes can sit this dance out. I'll be the one there beside you."

"Hey, climb aboard. It'll be just like the old times. We'll kick some ass, make a boxcar of money, and get drunk after. Just like the old times."

"I let the court know this morning. And by the way, Judge Moody wants counsel in his courtroom eight sharp tomorrow."

"Because?"

"You know Thaddeus Murfee. He's whining about the hospital records. I've already told the judge you've turned over all the records. I even told him that I had instructed you myself."

"So why the early court call?"

"He wants us to go on the record and swear under oath that all records are turned over."

Their food arrived, steaming and heaped on the plates.

"Which we'll do. Fine, here we are, let's dig in."

38

E arly Chicago morning, late fall, overcast, rainy and windy. Morgana and A.W arrived in A.W.'s chauffeured black Mercedes. They climbed out of the car in front of the court building. Thaddeus parked in lawyers' parking and walked around the building.

Elevator up to the twenty-third, passengers staring at the clicking lights over the door.

All attorneys took seats at counsel table.

Courtroom of Judge J. Albert Moody. American flag, sleepy bailiff, court reporter, court clerk, lawyers.

At eight sharp the bailiff came to life. "Oyez, oyez, oyez. The circuit court of the First Judicial Circuit will now come to order, Honorable James Albert Moody presiding."

Judge Moody floated in shrouded in his billowing black robe. "Be seated. Mr. Murfee it's your motion, please proceed."

Thaddeus climbed to his feet. He wanted to come across as someone who had been wronged by the withholding of records in the case. There had to be a whiff of frustration and anger. Latoya was seated beside him, with John Staples in the rear of the courtroom, holding Chase. He gathered himself for the assault.

Thaddeus began slow. "May it please the court. We've filed this motion to produce because we believe the defendant is hiding records."

There, he thought, it's on the floor and flopping around like a snake. A pile of trouble for the defendants.

Judge Moody looked down on the defendants' lawyers. "That's a serious accusation. Let's hear from the defense."

Morgana stood up. Her voice was strong and confident. "Judge that's just not true. Every record I was ever given has been turned over."

Thaddeus listened carefully. She wasn't saying she had turned over all records; she was saying she had turned over every record she had been given. Huge difference. He would circle back on this.

Before Thaddeus could launch into full attack mode, A.W. scraped back his chair and stood. "Judge, I can tell you that every record we received from the hospital and Dr. Payne's charts has been turned over. I personally saw to it that they were delivered to Morgana's office."

Judge Moody looked askance at the old lawyer. "You're certain?'

"I personally supervised it. There were three CDs turned over, thousands of pages of records and reports, doctors' entries and nurses' notes. It's all there, Judge."

Judge Moody's gaze shifted back to Thaddeus. "Mr. Murfee, what proof do you have there are undisclosed records?"

Thaddeus was ready for this. "There is no proof. Just a strong suspicion. My client sees things in the records that she will swear at trial are forgeries."

"Well, that's why we have trials, so your client can get to say those things."

Thaddeus decided to push it up another notch. "Let me ask counsel a question. Morgana, are the delivery room records complete and accurate?"

Morgana's face twisted at the insult. "Your honor, am I on trial here? I've already made my avowal to the court. The records I was given are all there."

Judge Moody saw it was going to go nowhere. The defense was presented with a situation where it was trying to prove a negative, which, as all first year law students know, is impossible. "Your point is well taken, you are not on trial. Unless there is something else we stand adjourned. Next case."

Thaddeus nodded. He felt better, having made his record. Now he would depose the hospital administrator on down to the lowliest clerk. Somewhere along the line somebody just might slip up and then he'd drag Morgana and A.W. right back in here on contempt of court charges. For now, he had done his job.

39

After court, Morgana and A.W waited on the sidewalk for the Mercedes to return. Morgana was fuming and standing apart from him. Finally she could hold it inside no longer.

"You made it sound like you have totally clean hands in all this. If this thing goes south, I'm the fall guy. Nicely done. You and Carson are genius at this bullshit."

A.W. looked away down the street, seeming to shrug it off. "I just wanted Judge Moody to know I've given you all the records I received from Hudd Family."

"But you left out the part about telling me to dump nurses' notes. And you left out the part about how some of those records are forged."

"How do I know they're forged? I gave you what they gave me."

Morgana turned her back to him. "I'm starting to see why our partners are such a close-knit group. If the truth about any of us leaks out we all wind up in prison."

"We're no different than any other firm. Welcome to the

practice of law in the twenty-first century. No one said it would be easy."

She swung back around. "Hard I can take. Illegal—that's a whole new world for me. You just want to be damn sure you have my back."

"And you mine. And that's how it works. Now where shall we have breakfast? Hudd Family is buying, we're still on their meter."

She was inconsolable. "Screw their meter and screw Hudd Family. I'm going back to the office and try to forget how I just lied to Judge Moody, a man I highly respect."

40

They followed Thaddeus into the deposition room reserved for his cases. It was tastefully decorated with expensive Western art on the walls, flocked wallpaper, and deep wool carpet. The mandatory wide screens and whiteboards surrounded the occupants, ready to serve. The court reporter set up his machine and ran a few inches of paper through the machine, finally nodding "Ready" at Thaddeus. He took the cue.

"We're on the record," said Thaddeus.

"Ready," said the court reporter."

"Morgana?"

"Keith Haley is appearing today pursuant to your subpoena. Your witness, Mr. Murfee."

Thaddeus launched in. "Before we took our break yesterday you had told us that you were the CEO of Hudd Hospital Chicago at or near the time of Chase Staples' birth, isn't that correct?"

Keith Haley hesitated, looking to his attorney Morgana for direction. He was a pink-skinned heavyweight, thick jowls, gray hair combed straight back from a widow's peak, bifocals perched on his fleshy nose, his face tilting up and down as he went from reading his notes to looking back at Thaddeus.

"Correct. He was born during my tenure as CEO."

Thaddeus nodded and reviewed his yellow pad. He had probably a page and half of questions for the CEO. He felt confident in his preparation and pushed ahead.

"And your position as CEO required that you enforce official hospital policy, correct?"

"Correct."

"Tell us what hospital policies were in effect the night of Chase Staples' birth, with particular regard to Caesarean sections."

"You mean policies that affect this case?"

"I mean all policies, sir."

"Hudd Family Hospital Chicago, like all Level I hospitals, had in effect a policy requiring a completed Caesarean section within thirty minutes of a staff member's page. This is called Decision to Incision."

Thaddeus smiled. He was going to close the noose around the guy's neck. "Exactly. Now tell me. Was that policy complied with or violated at Chase Staples' birth?"

"Complied with. In all respects."

"Let's take those respects one at a time. With regard to the nurse's notes, what do those tell us about the thirty-minute decision to incision policy?"

"Well, the page went out from the delivery room at six thirty-five o'clock in the evening, Dr. Payne was on the premises and the C-section was completed at six fifty-seven p.m. Well within the thirty-minute window."

"Mr. Haley, are those nurses' notes marked Plaintiffs' Exhibit Seven the only set of nurses' records from that birth?"

"What are you asking?"

"I am asking, sir, have you ever seen another set of nurses' notes from that same night, same delivery?"

"Never."

"Are those nurses' notes true and accurate?"

"Well, they're certified. That's this stamp right here in the corner."

Thaddeus felt his neck bristle. The guy was lying and Thaddeus knew it. That, or the guy had been terribly misled by his staff. "Do you know this for a fact? I'm asking, sir, did you personally review the hospital's records and determine for yourself that these notes are original and accurate?"

"I did not. No hospital administrator would ever do that."

"So you don't know if Exhibit Seven is a true and accurate copy of the actual nurses' notes in the hospital files at all, do you?"

"You're asking the same thing again. I did not personally check them, no."

"You realize you're under oath today?"

"I do."

"And you're standing by the authenticity of the notes?"

"I am."

The questions and answers continued another hour.

But Thaddeus had enough to impeach the CEO already.

THADDEUS AND ALBERT HIGHTOWER put their heads together. They made their trial plans. The first item on the agenda was whether they would take the depositions of Gerry Springer and Nurse Nancy, who had been on duty during Chase's struggles to be born.

Records were examined and re-examined. As near as the attorneys could tell, neither doctor nor nurse had made entries in the delivery room records. Nancy was a student nurse at the time and it would have been unusual for a student to make entries into the nursing notes during a troubled delivery. Same for Gerry Springer, as he was a brand new physician who wasn't writing orders during the delivery. In the end it was decided that neither would be deposed and neither would be called at trial to testify.

41

Chase Staples clutched spasmodically at empty air as he flopped upon the examining table at Hudd Hospital ER. On either side of the exam table, Latoya and John Staples tried to touch and comfort their child as the ER staff and doctor worked feverishly to get drugs into the baby's system to control the seizure.

His name was Nathan Tonopah and he was a first-year intern. He said, "OK, Mr. Chase, you've got Dilantin onboard. Come on now, baby."

Latoya clutched her heart and rolled her eyes skyward. "Sweet Jesus, help this baby!"

John asked, as if from a distance, "How long will it take?"

"He should stop seizing in thirty to sixty seconds. Here we go; he's relaxing now as we speak. There we go."

Chase relaxed and fell back against the table as if the levitating force had dissipated. The mother gently laid her head on the baby's chest and whispered to him. "We're right here, baby. Sssh-sssh, Mommy and Daddy are right here with you."

The doctor asked, "Is Chase getting in-home medical care of any nature?"

John responded, "No, we're waiting for Medicaid to help with that."

"What's the holdup, anything I can help with?"

Latoya sadly shook her head. "Case manager tells us they're underfunded anymore. It's the economy, she says, there's just no money to help this baby."

The doctor shook his head. "Jesus."

"Yes."

"Is there any insurance for him?"

John spoke up. "They busted our collective bargaining agreement down at the bus line where I work. We lost our insurance coverage two weeks ago."

"Have you tried the federal program?"

"We're in the process. But none of them we found so far have in-home full-time care for Chase. Not like we need."

"Well, who else have you tried?"

"There's no one else."

Doctor Tonopah rubbed Chase's belly. All was calm. "You did the right thing bringing him here tonight. I'm going to write a script for Dilantin that should help control future problems. But this baby is still going to need regular in-home nursing and medical care. He's gaining weight every day and these lab values will be changing. Dosage will need constant adjustment."

"We know that. We just don't know how."

"Do you have a lawyer working on his case?"

"We do. Thaddeus Murfee."

"He's very good. You might want to give him a call and see if there's any kind of insurance help he can get at this stage of the case."

"I've asked him all that until he's sick of hearing from me. But I'll call him tonight."

"Yes, at least tell him what's going on now with the seizure development."

"I will certainly call him."

42

I t was late afternoon and the ski crowd was thinning on Aspen Mountain. Clouds were low in the valleys and fresh snow was floating down. As the shadows disappeared to dim light, A.W. and Morgana gave a quick look, nodded, and set off on a downhill race. Morgana fell behind and obviously was allowing A.W. to win. By the time she reached the bottom of the run, A.W. had wandered off to find after-ski drinks. As she was stepping out of her skis the cell phone in her pocket buzzed. It was Thaddeus Murfee.

"Hello?" she said.

"Morgana, Thad. We've got problems on the Staples baby case."

"Go on."

"Chase Staples seized tonight. Grand Mal seizures. Bottom line, the ER doc wants him to have in-home care as follow-up. Problem is Mom and Dad don't have insurance for that. They don't have any insurance. I need to get their case settled and get some money for this child. Is your client ready to talk sense?"

"I—I don't know what to say. Hudd Family isn't in any

kind of position to settle. Where's the liability that I can recommend settlement? What did our doctor and hospital do wrong?"

"Look, it's a jury question whether Dr. Payne arrived in time for emergency C-section. You've got a fifty-fifty chance of losing that. Surely to God that means something to Olde Heartless Insurance Company?"

She poked her pole around the snow, thinking. "That's your assessment. We've got records to prove the treatment was well within the standard of care."

"Look, lady, I'm not going to argue the case with you. Can you at least ask your client if they have any motivation to settle? You do have a duty to ask your client now that I've opened the issue for discussion."

"You're right. I'll ask my client. I'll recommend against, but at least I'll ask."

"We'll take ten million, not a dime less."

"Right, and it's snowing in Phoenix."

"Ask, please."

"Goodbye, Thaddeus."

SHE SAT FIDGETING at the table next to the stone fireplace at Aspen Mountain Lodge. It was time for a little *après-ski*, as A.W had suggested, and Morgana was toying with her Diet Coke and Caroline was sipping brandy as A.W and his wife worked on their second martinis.

Morgana felt nervous and knew her skin was glistening but didn't know if the damp was from the proximity to the fireplace or a result of the very negative feelings she was having over her complicity in the Chase Staples cover-up. Alternatively she felt nauseous and loss of appetite followed by a craving for something sweet. Caroline had assured her that none of it was a return of the cancer, which had been in remission for seven months. Her health had been good, she knew, and so the sadness and sense of loss she felt was definitely about her role in the case. Maybe she could bring it to a head and get the damn thing settled, she told herself. And there was no time like the present to make a stab at it.

She caught the eye of A.W. "I had a call from Thaddeus Murfee. The Staples baby is in a bad way."

He was suddenly in business mode. "Ladies," he said to his wife and Caroline, "could you give us ten minutes here? Go off to the gift shop and look around?"

Caroline said, "Sure, we can do that. C'mon, Marilyn, we'll look for ski-wear for pregnant ladies."

The two lawyers leaned in across the table.

"What did young Mr. Murfee have to say? Twenty million or thirty?"

She ignored him. "This baby is having seizures. We should try to help."

He tasted the martini and nodded with approval. "Realistically, though, are the seizures our problem?"

"What do you mean?"

He shrugged, indicating that he felt like he had clean hands in the matter. "Is the baby's lawyer using his client's health problem to win a settlement in a loser case?"

"We've got some exposure here. Settlement wouldn't be all that unreasonable."

"No. I've studied the deposition summaries, I've seen the medical records, there's no need to settle. Besides, it would be premature to settle now. We don't even know that the baby will be alive at the time of trial."

"Christ, how can you say that?" She hated herself more by the second. *Was this really her life now? Gambling on the hope*

that Chase Staples might die before his trial? I mean what the hell!
Her mind screamed. *What have you gotten yourself into?*

"I can say that because I am a businessman. We're in the business of saving our client money."

"This is my case and I say we recommend eight million to settle. We've got phony records and a very appealing child against us."

He'd had just enough to drink to allow a smirk. "You've got phony records. I don't."

"What the hell does that mean?"

The smirk remained on his face, terrible and completely turning her off to the man who she had once thought was a great mentor. She'd been allowed a peek inside her law firm and all she saw was evil. "It means you told Judge Moody the records were true and accurate. It wasn't me."

She flopped her chin against her chest. "That's it. I can't do this anymore. I want to be taken off this case. I've lost the stomach for it."

"Morgana, do you know how we got out to this beautiful resort in these Colorado mountains? Do you know how many people can't afford to come here? In case you've forgotten, we're here because clients like Hudd Family Healthcare pay us huge sums of money to defend them."

"I don't need to hear this. This place is as empty as my soul right now."

"They paid for our airfare, paid for this incredible hotel and our suites with Jacuzzis, paid for our lift tickets, paid for our poles, our boots, our drinks we're drinking right now, the crap our wives are plunking down plastic to buy in the gift shop this very minute. All of it—thanks to our client."

"Balance that against a baby that's fighting for its life. What side do we fall on, A.W., are we only about money?"

"Short answer? Yes."

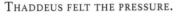

Thaddeus felt the pressure.

It wasn't an altogether uncomfortable feeling, more like the feeling of needing to punch your opponent in the boxing ring but the first bell hasn't yet rung. That dancing around, throwing-air-punches-moment in the mind of the trial lawyer that comes after the jury has been selected and it's time for opening statements.

Judge Moody had presided over jury selection at the Daley Center courts building. Thaddeus was somewhat satisfied with the jury, eight women and four men, chosen because they reported they knew nothing about the case, had no family members with brain damage, had no lawyers or doctors in the family, and hadn't made similar claims against hospitals or doctors on account of some medical procedure gone wrong.

In other words, the jury was of one mind.

More or less.

Thaddeus had to smile, however. It was the stuff that was hidden away—that was the good stuff. And it never came out during jury selection; it always came out after the trial, when it was too late to do anything about it. Stuff like kids who were mentally challenged or stuff like a seething hatred for people who filed cases and came to courts looking for money, or a general dislike of lawyers who helped injured people—that was the hidden stuff. You just never knew for sure whom you had allowed to slip through during the jury selection process, and he knew that. He was no novice at picking juries, having been at the helm of seventeen major medical malpractice trials by the time Chase's case came on for trial.

Joining Thaddeus at counsel table were Christine Susmann and Latoya Staples. Christine had actually done all the heavy lifting while working up the case. She was every bit as anxious as Thaddeus to get the fight underway. She was always the ex-soldier, always preparing, preparing, preparing for the moment when the battle would rage and she would be called on. And, as always, she was ready. It was the Army training that always took over for her and impelled her toward engaging the enemy and winning. Thaddeus believed Christine had caught all the issues and addressed them, those for and those against. She was the brightest trial assistant anyone could ever hope to have at counsel table. For that, he was eternally grateful to her that she stuck by him. She had even uprooted her family when it came time to move the law firm from Orbit to Chicago. She was loyal, above all else. She was also highly paid, now earning in the mid-six-figures.

Seated at defense table were Morgana, A.W., and Phillip Payne, M.D. The Hudd CEO would be joining them as the hospital representative in the afternoon session. For now, his presence had been waived by the defense.

Behind the bar sat Sandy Green and a higher-up in risk management, a silver-haired woman named Rosemary Washington. Their role was to keep a lid on things by way of settling the case PDQ if it looked like a runaway-jury situation. Such situations developed in trials where a judge's rulings on evidentiary issues were taking a decidedly plaintiff-oriented bent. Long story short, if the plaintiff was winning on objections, it was a clear telegraph from judge to jury exactly whom the judge favored. Sandy and Rosemary knew only too well that juries in such cases would most often take their lead from the judge and unconsciously begin siding with the plaintiff too, just because. Such cases called for quick, dirty settlements, usually for way too much money, early in the case. Which was every defense lawyer's nightmare. No one, especially the two lawyers from Jones Marentz, wanted such a nasty result on their balance sheet. Better to have settled up front before trial than settle during the plaintiff's case when the price tag would be much, much higher.

Having issued his instructions to the jurors and made sure everyone was comfortable and equipped with a steno notebook, Judge Moody turned his attention to Thaddeus and his case. It was time to move into the witnesses.

"Please call your first witness, Mister Murfee."

Out of habit, Thaddeus stood. "Thank you, Your Honor. Plaintiff calls Doctor Phillip Payne as an adverse witness."

Whispers broke out across the gallery. The jurors sat up, alert and ready to take notes. It was unusual for the plaintiff to open by calling the defendant doctor as its first witness. But that was exactly what was happening.

Dr. Payne didn't have far to walk, from the next table to the witness stand. Phillip Payne was a tall man, all of 6-3, who walked with a baboon slouch. His posture said he had been beaten by the world and bent over for good measure. Which, to an extent, was true. His blue eyes were chronically watery and sad, his heavy jowls road-mapped with spider veins, his dark hair receding dramatically back from the widow's peak where a small tuft of hair still claimed the day, hanging on until it would finally be forced to surrender to the encroaching bald front too. He stoically proceeded to the front of the courtroom and took the witness chair, maintaining eye contact with no one. He didn't even give the jury a nod or a smile.

The defendant slowly raised his eyes to Thaddeus; the look on his face said he knew this wasn't going to be an enjoyable ride.

"State your name."

"Phillip Mounce Payne."

"What is your age and occupation?"

"Fifty-seven. I work as an advisor on medical malpractice cases."

Thaddeus studied his notes. "You're a medical doctor?"

"I am. Retired now."

"And why are you retired now?"

"Business decision."

"Describe that business decision, please."

"Objection!" said Morgana, rising from her chair. "Approach the bench to make a record?"

"Come," said the judge.

Both attorneys crossed to the judge's throne and leaned toward him to whisper. The court reporter moved her steno machine close in so she could make a record of what was being said.

"Miss Bridgman, state the basis of your objection," whispered Judge Moody.

Morgana said, "Your Honor, the question seeks to reveal to the jury that Dr. Payne is no longer able to procure medical malpractice insurance. Which is objectionable because, first, evidence of insurance coverage is never admissible in a tort case and, second, because his inability to procure physician's errors and omissions coverage would be highly prejudicial where he's on trial because of an alleged error or omission."

The judge nodded. "Mr. Murfee? How is the question relevant? Better yet, how is its relevance not outweighed by the significant prejudice it could cause this defendant?"

Thaddeus smiled. "Your Honor, the question seeks only relevant information. It does not seek insurance coverage information and can be answered without revealing the presence or absence of insurance. I was simply asking him to describe the business decision that he made which resulted in his no longer practicing medicine. He can be cautioned by his counsel not to go into medical malpractice insurance. Not only that, all questions prejudice one party or the other. They're supposed to do that."

"Very well," said the judge, "I'm going to allow the question and overrule the objection. However, Miss Bridgman, we'll send the jury out for an early morning break so you can confer with your client out of their view and caution him not to mention insurance when giving his answer to the pending question."

"Thank you," said both attorneys in unison, whereupon they re-took their seats.

The judge sent the jury out and exited the courtroom, unzipping his robe as he returned to his chambers. Thaddeus explained it all to Latoya, and while they were whispering, he could see that Morgana was explaining the ground rules to Dr. Payne as well. Then Thaddeus got back to reviewing his direct exam questions for Dr. Payne and Latoya went back to relieve John in holding Chase.

Ten minutes later the jury returned, court was reconvened, and they went back on the record.

Thaddeus set in again. "Doctor Payne, please explain to us the business decision that went into your ceasing the practice of medicine."

"I retired."

"You retired because you had been sued by two mothers for the birth injuries you cause their newborns, isn't that so?"

"Objection!" said Morgana. "Counsel has been advised where this could potentially lead."

"Your Honor," said Thaddeus, "I only am asking about past or present lawsuits. Nothing else."

"I'll allow it," said the judge. "Please continue."

"Please answer the question," said Morgana.

"My decision to retire had nothing to do with the lawsuits against me," said Dr. Payne. But then he could be seen visibly losing the battle to shut up and leave it at that. He just couldn't keep himself from adding, "And those lawsuits alleged negligence against me that simply was untrue."

Thaddeus' head jerked up. "Let's look at those lawsuits, since you opened the door. First, we have the mother who alleged in her case that her baby suffered cerebral palsy because you failed to properly monitor the infant during birth. Do you recall that lawsuit?"

"Yes."

"And are you saying today that the baby doesn't have cerebral palsy?"

"I'm not saying that."

"So the baby was born with cerebral palsy?"

"That's my understanding."

"Doctor, where does cerebral palsy come from? What is its etiology?"

The physician poured a glass of water from the pitcher and took a long swallow. Clearly he was reviewing what he was about to say. "The disorder is characterized by a lack of oxygen during the time of a child's birth. This lack of oxygen can lead to serious health problems very quickly, a baby could suffer cerebral palsy and permanent brain damage from mere seconds without air."

"So CP is caused by a baby not getting enough air while being born, long story short, correct?"

"That's the current thinking, yes."

"Doctor, that's not just the current thinking, that's medical fact, correct?"

"Correct."

"Now let's please review some ways in which newborns can have their oxygen compromised. Will you help me do that?"

"Yes." He took another drink.

"Potential causes of oxygen starvation during birth can include cord prolapse, correct?"

"Correct."

"And cord prolapse is when the umbilical cord leaves the uterus before the baby, correct?"

"Correct."

"Cord occlusion is another injury mode, is it not?"

"Yes."

"Placental infarction? Tell us about placental infarction."

"That would be where there was a growth of extra tissue or lesions on the placenta."

"What about a nuchal cord. What's that?"

"That's when the umbilical cord wraps around the newborn's neck."

"By the way, that's what happened with our baby, Chase, is it not?"

"That was his presentation at caesarean section, yes."

Thaddeus looked over at the jury. Many were busy scribbling notes. "What you're telling us is that when you cut Latoya open, you found the baby Chase's umbilical cord wrapped around his neck, correct?"

"Pretty much."

"Yes or no."

"Yes. In part."

"Really? Which part? Fifty percent? Ninety percent?"

"Closer to ninety percent."

"Well. Tell us about some other ways a newborn can suffer oxygen starvation."

"Well, it may also result from excessive maternal sedation by anesthesia, placental abruption, breech delivery (also known as breech birth—when the child comes out of the uterus foot or bottom-first, rather than head-first), uterine rupture or prolonged labor."

"Was Chase's a prolonged labor?"

"Not especially."

"So we're left with a situation where the baby was being strangled by the cord, correct?"

"Yes."

"Is that what caused Chase's brain injury?"

"I wouldn't know. I'm not a neurologist."

"Well, let's do it this way, then. Look over there and tell the jury what you believed caused this baby's catastrophic injury."

He poured another glass of water. A small trickle appeared at the corner of his mouth as he tried to mouth breathe and drink at the same time. Clearly rattled, thought Thaddeus. Good.

"I can't think of any reason."

"You do know about the umbilical cord wrapped around the child's neck, correct?"

"Correct."

"And you've already told the jury that that alone can cause brain damage, correct?"

"Correct."

"And you saw no other mechanisms at work that you've listed that could cause oxygen starvation, correct?"

"Correct."

"So wouldn't you be able to say within a reasonable degree of medical probability that Chase's injuries were caused by the umbilical cord around his neck?"

"I would say that."

"But you weren't willing to say that before I asked the question, were you?"

"I guess I didn't understand."

"You didn't understand the question?"

"I didn't understand where you were going with it."

"Doctor Payne, has anyone told you that you have to understand where I'm going with something in order to answer my questions?"

"My lawyer told me to be sure I understood your questions before I answered."

"And why did she tell you that?"

"She was afraid you might try to trick me."

"Have I tried to trick you?"

"No."

"Have you heard her object to any of my questions as tricky?"

"No."

"So she was wrong about me."

"Evidently."

"When you told the jury that Chase suffered his brain injury because the cord was wrapped around his neck, were you tricked into saying that?"

"No."

"Because?"

"Because it's the truth, I suppose."

"Now, a compromised umbilical cord doesn't always result in brain damage, does it?"

"Definitely not."

"In fact, it usually does not result in brain injury, correct?"

"Correct."

"How is brain injury prevented?"

"By careful monitoring and making sure the delivery happens within a certain number of minutes of certain warning signs."

"Whoa, let's break that up, shall we?"

Whereupon an elderly juror in the second row raised her hand. She sent a note to the judge. She had bladder problems and needed to use the restroom. Trying to hide his agitation at the interruption, the judge called a second morning recess. The jury was anxious for the case to move along so their service could end and they could return to their real lives, but they were helpless in the face of the older woman's bladder.

43

Thaddeus used the break to hit the restroom.

Christine sat at counsel table and explained to Latoya what was happening. She didn't need explaining and even suggested follow-up questions for Dr. Payne. Meanwhile, Morgana and Dr. Payne disappeared behind a door marked ATTORNEYS leading off the courtroom. Sandy Green and Rosemary Washington followed close behind.

Ten minutes passed. Thaddeus returned to counsel table and anxiously tapped his fingers, waiting, waiting. Judge Moody finally returned, the jury was settled in, and all was ready.

Then they resumed trial.

"Your honor," said Thaddeus, "Plaintiff would call Dr. Helmut Andersen, out of order, reserving the right to recall Dr. Payne after Dr. Andersen."

"No objection," said Morgana, who clearly was happy for her client to get a break from testifying.

"Proceed," said the judge.

The bailiff retrieved Dr. Andersen from the hallway,

where he had been waiting with his files and books. He briskly followed the bailiff up the aisle and took a seat at the witness stand. He was a bearded forty-something with long flowing white hair, white beard, and wire spectacles, with the prehensile face of a surgeon who might perform the most elaborate of surgeries. He nodded at the judge and smiled at the jury. Clearly a pro.

"Good afternoon, and tell us your name and occupation for the record."

"Helmut Andersen, professor of obstetrics, University of Chicago Medical School."

"How long in that position?"

"Eleven years."

"Doctor, I want to cut to the chase here. We've just left off with Dr. Payne and we were about to ask about fetal monitoring. Do you hold in expertise in this area?"

"I teach it every day of the school year at UC Med."

"Fair enough."

"And I write about it. In journals, professional magazines, those things."

"Doctor, explain fetal monitoring during delivery."

"Fetal monitoring is defined as watching the baby's heart rate for indicators of stress, usually during labor and birth."

"Explain the modalities used to monitor a fetus. What's available?"

The doctor nodded and launched into the field of fetal monitoring. He discussed the fetoscope, which he said was a special type of stethoscope for listening to a baby. However, he added, regular stethoscopes work just as well. Then he described Doppler monitors. These were handheld devices that transmitted the sounds of the baby's heart into earpieces. The Doppler's could generally pick up heart tones after twelve weeks gestation. He continued on, describing electronic fetal monitoring that involved an ultrasound device used during labor and birth to record the baby's heart rate. Then he finished off with a look at internal fetal monitoring, where an electrode is inserted inside the mother and attached to the baby's head to record heart tones.

"Which types were used with Chase Staples? Describe the monitoring."

"Objection. Multiple."

"Sustained. Please restate."

"Doctor, describe the fetal monitoring in Chase Staples' labor and delivery."

"Stethoscope. Electronic was added."

"And the risks and benefits of the stethoscope?"

The doctor nodded. "This method is non-invasive, simple to use, and has a live person on the other end. This can prevent some of the errors that are mechanical. This gives mother the mobility to deal with her labor, shower, and so on. It does require that the person using it be trained, although it is a standard procedure taught in every medical and nursing type institution. In the case of high risk, induced, or with certain medications, it cannot provide the round the clock monitoring that may be necessary."

"So Chase was under-monitored, given his situation."

"That would be my opinion, yes."

"So that's why electronic was added to his care."

"Certainly. I'm sure that was the thinking."

"And whose thinking would that have been?"

"From the records I was given to review, that would have been the nurses' decision, to use electronic fetal monitoring."

"Who usually makes that decision?"

"The OB doctor."

"Why wasn't that done here?"

"Probably because he wasn't present and had no idea about the case."

"Why would they have used electronic fetal monitoring?"

"EFM provides a beat-to-beat view of the baby's heart tones, in relationship to mother's contractions. This may be used either continuously or intermittently. This is a benefit for the high-risk mother."

"Was she high risk?"

"Well, not going in. There's nothing to indicate she was high risk."

"But she became high risk?"

"The labor became high risk."

"Should an OB doctor have been prepared for that possibility?"

"Always."

"Was Dr. Payne prepared?"

"Evidently not. The doctor had left the building."

"How should fetal monitoring be done in a case such as Chase's?"

"ACOG is the national organization for OB/GYNs in the U.S. It has an official policy statement that intermittent fetal monitoring is just as safe and effective as continuous. Their recommendations are a twenty-minute baseline strip, then once every half hour (for sixty to one hundred twenty seconds) in first stage, and every fifteen minutes in second stage, as long as everything looks normal."

"And in a birth where the baby is in trouble?"

"Continuously."

"What else should be done with a child in trouble?"

"Obviously, one needs to discover the problem and correct it."

"Including timely caesarean sections?"

"Including timely caesarean sections."

"Have you reviewed the notes in this case?"

"I have reviewed doctors' notes, nurses' notes, and hospital records."

"And what is your opinion of how this birth injury happened?"

"Umbilical cord compromise. Wrapped around Chase's neck."

"Why did that happen?"

"Obviously the caesarean wasn't timely."

"It was late?"

"It was late.'

"How do we know that?"

The doctor's smile was a smile of irony. "Because we have a catastrophically injured newborn. That never should have happened and was one hundred percent preventable."

"How could it have been prevented?"

"By getting that baby the hell out of that mother in time. Excuse my language, but what I see here makes me very angry."

"Because?"

"Because a human being's life is ruined. By a careless doctor. An entire life, and family, destroyed."

Thaddeus seemed to be reviewing his notes. While the courtroom was quiet, waiting, the expert's words sank in. And the jurors were solemn, quiet and still.

Finally, when the effect had been maximized, he continued.

"Now let's talk about caesarean, fetal distress, and time limits."

"Generally, audit of the speed with which such caesarean sections are performed is important for clinical governance and risk management. Thirty minutes has been adopted as an audit standard."

"What are common risks?"

"Delays occur both in getting the patient to theatre and in achieving effective anesthesia, though delivery within thirty minutes is more likely if the patient gets to theatre within ten minutes."

"Tell us about the thirty-minute audit standard."

"The audit standard of thirty minutes has become the criterion by which good and bad practice is being defined both professionally and medico-legally. The implication is that caesarean section for fetal distress that takes longer than thirty minutes represents suboptimal or even negligent care."

"Thirty minutes decision to incision."

"Yes."

"Do you agree with that criterion?"

"Thirty minutes decision to incision? I certainly do in this case."

"Because."

"Because that criterion was ignored and a birth catastrophe was the result."

"And you said medico-legal criterion defines good and bad practice."

"Yes."

"Beyond thirty minutes is bad medical practice?"

"Yes."

"It's medical malpractice?"

"Objection!"

"Restate."

"Doctor, do you have an opinion based on a reasonable degree of medical probability whether the delay beyond thirty minutes fell below the standard of care?"

"I do."

"State your opinion."

"The doctor and hospital were both negligent."

"Because?"

"The doctor plain wasn't present. His negligence is plain and simple. The hospital's negligence is predicated on the fact it wasn't staffed with an experienced OB to manage this case where the treating didn't show."

"Thank you, that is all."

Morgana spent ten minutes trying to cross-examine the doctor, but he refused to budge from his opinions and was too experienced to be tripped up. She finally, quietly, sat down and said she had no more questions.

FOLLOWING THE LUNCH RECESS, the trial continued with Thaddeus recalling Dr. Phillip Payne to the stand.

"Doctor, I had previously established with you that a compromised umbilical cord doesn't always result in brain damage. Do you recall that?"

"Definitely."

"In fact, it usually does not result in brain injury, correct?"

"Correct."

"I then asked you, how is brain injury prevented. Recall that?"

"And I told you by monitoring the birth telemetry and making sure the delivery happens within a certain number of minutes of certain warning signs."

"Exactly. Did that happen here? I'm asking, was there careful monitoring?"

"By Dr. Gerry Springer and nurse Andrea Mounce, yes."

"But not by you."

"Not minute-by-minute, no."

"Though minute-by-minute was definitely called for?"

"Not by me. That's what residents and nurses are for. To assist the physician."

"Which gave you the freedom to go to a Little League game?"

"Yes."

"Which made you late for the caesarean?"

"It was done within your own expert's rule of thirty minutes."

"Can we agree to disagree about that?" Thaddeus asked. There was no use arguing what was going to be a question for the jury. The amount of time that went by from the decision to incision was hotly disputed. Thaddeus knew the guy wasn't going to admit any more than he already had. So he stopped and the doctor was excused, with the defendants' right to recall during the defense case.

"Congratulations," Thaddeus said to Latoya and John as they made their way out of the courtroom.

"For what?" asked Latoya.

Thaddeus smiled. "We just made your case."

"What about the thirty-minute disagreement?"

"That will be up to you. Will the jury tend to believe you over Phillip Payne? I think they will."

"We're praying," said John.

"Good idea," said Christine, "and let's kick ass along with that prayer business."

"We're counting on Thaddeus for that," said Latoya.

"You've come to the right guy," said Thaddeus. "Christine and I happen to specialize in whoop-ass."

44

After reviewing the day's testimony with Dr. Payne, Morgana was burnt out. Her head ached, her joints ached, she was still angry with Caroline for a snide remark that morning, and she didn't feel like going straight home. She called Manny and asked could he meet her for a beer? Turns out, he could.

Their favorite haunt in Chicago was a hidden Irish tavern called Carlos O'Brien's. It was just off the Loop and easy in and out after rush hour abated.

They sat across from each other in a small booth. A pitcher of dark beer and two pint mugs completed the table setting. Manny scrounged a basket of stale nuts and began disarticulating shell from nut and scattering remnants on the floor, as the management desired.

"Ambiance," he said, and tossed a shell skittering across the floor.

"I'll drink to that," said Morgana, and she raised a brimming mug.

They clinked mugs and drank deeply.

"So I told Payne after today's testimony that I thought he was in deep shit. Did you hear any of the trial?"

Manny nodded. "I was there for most of it. Thaddeus Murfee rocks. That guy is cold and deadly."

"He gets right to it, I have to admit. I asked Payne whether he found moving his bowels any easier now that he had been reamed out."

"Shit, you didn't!" Manny laughed.

"I did. Can't stand that guy. He all but killed that baby. Asshole."

"I know. Poor little kid, hosed by a hack doctor."

"I'll drink to that," she said, and again they clinked mugs. Old friends enjoying a few together. They let their eyes roam around the tavern, which was filling with the rush-hour-avoidance-types like themselves, making it harder to be heard above the din.

Morgana shouted to be heard. "So you open your damn mouth and now I'm in trial without you and you're shit-canned. Screwball!"

"You could have used me, no doubt. Payne looked really bad."

"Dr. Payne sucked. That part about taking off to catch his kid's Little League baseball game was inexcusable. He blew it, we have a bad baby, and no one will admit it. No one on our side. I told him to put his house in trust where no one can find it."

"You didn't."

"No, I didn't, but I should have. These bastards should just pay policy limits and settle. But no one on my bench seems to know that."

"Except you."

"Me. And that's it. Since you left I've had to become the firm's conscience on these cases."

"Screw them, lady. Your ethical sensibilities in your little finger puts them to shame as a group."

She ignored that. "The firm's conscience is about money. The sooner I realize that and accept it the happier I'll be as a lawyer. Nothing is like what they taught us in law school. It's a dirt job and I need to get hold of that."

"Can you really accept that?"

She scoffed, meaning to deflect his question. "Let me tell you something. As of yesterday you're on the street with your hat upside down trying to learn to play the guitar. My partners don't mess around with their staff. They'd just as soon dump us as dump records."

"You're afraid of these guys? Since when?"

"These 'guys' as you call them are the most well-connected guys in the country. They can ruin me and they will if I pull your brand of junior Batman shit with them."

"You're got a baby here, a real human being, who got screwed over by an incompetent hack of a doctor. Do you care about him?"

"Of course. Nobody wants that."

"Then who takes care of this kid if he loses this trial?"

She didn't hesitate, an attestation to how she had rationalized the problems away. Even as she said it, however, she knew it was a rationalization and hated herself for it. "His parents take care of him. My mom took care of me after my dad split. She worked three jobs. We all worked to put food on the table and warm coats on our backs. His folks will work too."

"He needs more than that, so—"

"—Screw that, Manny. I can't save the whole damn world. Maybe you can, but I can't. Maybe Carson's right, maybe you didn't belong at Jones Marentz."

"He said that?"

"After you left. He ranted and raved for ten minutes. He sure as hell didn't appreciate you bringing up about the missing records over and over. You're not a team player, as he put it."

"Not that team. I'm on my own team from here on. So screw him."

Manny slid out of the booth and snapped his overcoat from a hook. He began sliding into it.

"And why don't you say the rest of that. Screw him and screw—"

"—OK, screw you too, Morgana. You've sold out, big time. Of all the tough people I never thought would cave, you've definitely caved, lady. Do yourself a huge. Turn the real records over to Thaddeus.

"Sit back down. Let's talk this through."

"What, rationalize? No thanks; I'm already gone. Eagles, 1977."

45

Second day of trial.

Judge Moody called court to order and Latoya was the first witness. She testified quickly about the delivery, the C-section, and the problems with Chase since he came home. She completed her direct exam and then Morgana launched into her cross-examination.

"Good afternoon, Mrs. Staples."

Latoya tossed off a look at Thaddeus, who only nodded. Proceed.

"Afternoon," Latoya answered.

"You've told us you know at least forty-five minutes went by from the time Andrea sent out the C-section page until Dr. Payne removed Chase from your abdomen, correct?"

"Correct."

"And you know this because you were counting contractions, correct?"

"Correct."

"And so you want the jury to believe your version of the events based on the number of times you had a contraction, correct?"

"Correct."

"Do you recall Andrea and Nancy timing each and every contraction?"

"I—I—mostly I do, yes."

"Mostly you do. Is it possible that some of the contractions weren't timed?"

"I suppose it's possible."

"Yes, and it's possible that those contractions that weren't timed might have been less than three minutes long and less than three minutes in between, correct?"

Thaddeus stood. "Objection, there's no evidence any of the contractions went untimed, there's only counsel's suggestion."

Judge Moody gazed at the ceiling, and then said, "Overruled. You may continue."

"Thank you, Your Honor," said Morgana. "Miss Staples. I asked you whether the times could even have been less than you can remember."

"I suppose anything's possible."

"And you would agree, then, that Dr. Payne might actually have been there in under thirty minutes—wouldn't you agree?"

"I don't think—"

"—Keeping in mind that you were in tremendous pain and that you cannot specifically recall each and every minute that passed."

"Okay, he might have been there under thirty minutes. But that's not what happened."

"At least not according to your best recall."

"That's right."

"Which we can all agree might be impaired."

"It might not be perfect, but it's very close."

Morgana didn't respond, instead lowering her head and busying herself with an exhibit. After several minutes of flipping through pages, she looked up. "Latoya, I'm going to hand you what's been marked Defense Exhibit 67. Would you look it over and tell the jury what it says at the very top of page one?"

"Sure." She received the documents and gave them a once-over. "They are nurses' notes."

"Does it say what hospital?"

"Hudd Family Healthcare, Chicago."

"And look at page two, about halfway down. Can you see an entry there at six thirty-five p.m.?"

"I see that."

"Read it for the jury, please."

"'Nurse Andrea Mounce calls stat for C-section.'"

"The time that call was made?"

"It says six thirty-five."

"P.M.?"

"Yes. Nighttime."

"All right. Now moving on over to page seven, two-thirds of the way down. Can you see an entry there at six fifty-five?"

"Yes."

"What does that say?"

"Dr. Payne arrives OR. Initials are 'AM.'"

"Andrea Mounce? Nurse Andrea Mounce?"

"I wouldn't know. I guess so."

"Well, your lawyer wouldn't want you to guess. I'll connect that up with another witness. But here's my question to you. If the stat call for a C-section was made at six thirty-five and the doctor arrived gowned in the OR at six fifty-five, how much time has gone by?"

"Twenty minutes."

"Clearly within the thirty-minute Decision to Incision window?"

"Yes. But that's not what actually happened."

"Move to strike, Your Honor. Non-responsive."

"The comment 'But that's not what actually happened' is stricken from the record. The jury is instructed to disregard."

"But that's—"

"No further questions," said Morgana, and sat down.

Thaddeus was immediately on his feet. "That's not what, Latoya? That's not what happened?"

"No, that's not what happened. He wasn't there within no twenty minutes."

"Did you see by any timepiece what time he actually arrived?"

She tapped her head. "Only by the one in here. I was counting contractions times three minutes."

"And you have previously testified on direct examination that he arrived no earlier than seven fifteen that night, correct?"

"That's right."

"And you know this because?"

"Because I was counting contractions at three minutes each."

"From the time you heard the stat call over the hospital public address until the time Doctor Payne actually came into the OR, how many contraction did you have?"

"Objection, asked and answered on direct exam."

"I'll allow it," said Judge Moody. "It's harmless."

Latoya said, "Can I say?"

"Please do. How many contractions from stat to arrival?"

"Thirteen or fourteen."

"Times three minutes per cycle, so between thirty-nine and forty-two minutes went by?"

"Yes."

"Which would have Dr. Payne actually arriving at seven fourteen to seven eighteen or so?"

"Yes."

"So you disagree with the nurses' notes."

"Yes."

"That is all. Nothing further," said Thaddeus.

A look of panic crossed Latoya's face. "That's not all," she blurted out. "I left something out!"

The attorneys and judge froze. Before any response could be made, Latoya locked eyes with Morgana.

"I left out that I'm praying for you, Miss Bridgman. I'm praying that you do the right thing and admit this doctor hurt my baby."

Morgana couldn't have been more gracious. "Thank you for that."

46

Following Latoya's testimony, Morgana hurried into the women's restroom. She was just washing up when Manny Rodriguez entered.

"I know it's the ladies' restroom. Call me a peeping Tom."

"A peeping Manny."

She rolled out several sheets of paper towel and began drying her hands.

Manny scowled. "Did that feel good to nail the mother in court just now?"

Morgana. "That damn well hurt. I'm hoping I lose this mess but I keep winning even when I don't mean to."

"Sandy looks ecstatic. I know they think you destroyed the kid's case. I do too."

"You heard it all?"

"I've been here since opening arguments. Haven't missed a word. Your opponent is excellent with expert witnesses, by the way."

"Thaddeus?"

"Yes. That doctor for UC Medicine was terrific. Jury was

hanging on every word. Unfortunately, Thaddeus can't get around the doctored nurses' records. He's going to lose because of those."

"I guess you're right. Crap. I feel horrible for that baby."

"That makes two of us. I have half a mind to go to the judge and ask him to call me as a witness."

"You'd wind up putting me in prison."

"You've got leukemia. They'd have mercy."

"I'd lose my law license."

"True that."

"So please. Keep still. Something will happen."

Manny leaned with his hands against the sink and studied his eyes. "You're very good in there, Morgana. "You don't need the help of these criminals to win your trials."

She balled up the paper towel and tossed it at the wastebasket. "This case should have been settled. This is inexcusable."

"You can still make something happen. Settle the damn case, do the right thing."

"I can't. I recommended ten million to Sandy and he laughed at me a few minutes ago. He knows we're chewing them up and spitting them out on the nurses' notes part."

"Because he's got the phony records."

"And Nurse Andrea is in Europe some place on active duty with the National Guard. Thaddeus probably can't locate her to ask about the notes."

"Figures. Settle the damn case, girl. It's the only act of redemption you have left."

She violently shook her head. "Stop! Is settlement the best I can do? If it is, we're all hosed, not just Chase, all of us. No, you and I need to figure this out. We're smarter than these idiots."

"Now you're talking! Let's sabotage the bastards."

"Lay a trap."

"What are you thinking?"

"Maybe I'm thinking you should testify, like you mentioned. Maybe that's a pretty hot idea."

"Just let me know when and I'll take the witness stand."

"You know, this just might be a great idea. What if we actually got you on the stand? Could you help?"

Manny pushed away from the sink and straightened his shoulders. "Try me. I'll nail these assholes to the door."

"Let's think about this. Did you ever talk to Nurse Andrea?"

"I did," he said. "When I was first reviewing the doctored notes. I wanted to know about the real notes. So I tracked her down."

"Where is she?"

"Ramstein Air Base, Germany. She works out of the hospital there."

"I wonder how Thaddeus would like to know that?"

"Want me to tell him?"

"Give me a day. Let me think it through."

"I won't wait until it's too late."

"I won't either. Trust me, Manny."

"You know I do."

"Gotta get back. It's been fun."

"Later."

47

A t 4:35 p.m. on the second day of trial, the judge recessed for the day with the last witness called and cross-examined.

Immediately Sandy, Morgana, and A.W. met in the court conference room. A.W. loosened his tie and Sandy pulled up a window and sat on the sill and lit up. He blew cigarette smoke out the window.

"That's healthy," said Morgana.

"I'm hooked. Dying for a weed," said Sandy.

Morgana shook her head. "Well, I'm not staying unless you put it out right now. Secondhand smoke is all I need."

Sandy doused the cigarette in his coffee. "Your wish, oh smart one."

"Thank you."

"I've got to meet the missus," said A.W. as he checked his watch. "Let's wrap up."

"So how'd we do," Morgana asked, though she already knew the answer.

Sandy smiled his best smile. "Well, on behalf of Hudd

Family Healthcare let me just say that went exceedingly well."

A.W. agreed. "Yes, Morgana, excellent cross of Mrs. Staples."

Morgana tossed her head and scowled. "Gentlemen, this baby is catastrophically injured. Sometimes I think about him and it brings tears to my eyes. I know that if I feel that way and I'm adverse to him, then the jury is going to be crying its eyes out and award him a bundle if this thing goes south. I am going to counsel you that I believe it's time we seriously consider settlement. Run ten mil by Thaddeus and see if he bites."

Sandy shook his head. "I have seriously considered settlement and I've rejected the notion. We have the smoking gun in our nurses' notes and the time differentials between Mrs. Staples and the nurses' notes. No reason to settle, not that I can see."

She slowly shut her eyes and counted. Her face reddened. "But we all know those notes are fabricated. They're a lie and a hoax. When are we going to get real about this baby's severe injuries that our doctor caused?"

Her senior partner disagreed. "That cross-examination was real. You just proved to the jury that you're relying on the nurses' notes too in order to trip up Mrs. Staples' testimony."

She slammed a fist into the table. "What the hell! Is anyone hearing a single damn word I'm saying? There is a real baby somewhere out there with real, catastrophic injuries that our client caused. Hudd Family Healthcare owes him. I recommend an offer of ten million dollars."

Sandy laughed. "Hudd owes him nothing. It's up to his lawyer to prove we owe him something. So far his lawyer has fallen far short of proving us negligent."

"Don't be an asshole, Sandy. His lawyer hasn't had the benefit of seeing the real records in this case. If he did we would be dead in the water. You'd have hundred-dollar bills shooting out of your ass like lightning."

"There's an image," said A.W. "Nice."

Sandy wouldn't budge. He said to Morgana, "You've done your job well, you've protected the truth."

"I've lied."

"You've acted as a lawyer."

"That's what I just said. We're miserably pathetic."

"Just close your eyes and plow ahead. You'll be richly rewarded for your work here."

A.W. added, "It's a war, Morgana, and you're the—"

"—I know, I'm the warrior. You just don't get it, do you? I've got to pee."

48

Thaddeus was playing a video for the jury. It depicted a day in the life of Chase Staples. It recounted the moment he awoke until midnight when he would finally drift off to sleep for fifteen minutes or so, but never more than a half hour at one time.

The video showed the baby in various degrees of distress and upset, of crying fits, seizures, and general chaos.

Chase's life was disturbing and deeply moved the jury and the trial participants, including Morgana.

When the lights went back on in the courtroom there were no dry eyes. Even the judge was dabbing his eyes with a tissue. The ordinarily unflappable bailiff turned away, hiding his red eyes and he refused to turn back around for several minutes. Then he was staring at his desktop. The court reporter had swiveled in her chair to view the video and she now turned back around and retrieved a handkerchief from her purse. She noisily blew her nose and dabbed her eyes. Several jury members passed along a box of tissues and all of them were grim-faced, unsmiling, and very restrained.

Thaddeus nodded to himself. The video had had the desired effect. If you couldn't overwhelm the twelve jurors with the facts, then hit them with emotion. Which was exactly what the video had done.

He had sent Latoya and John out of the courtroom while the video played, as there was no reason for them to again review the tragedy that was their son. Chase was with his grandmother, besides, so it gave the couple an abnormally long time together in the witness room outside the courtroom where they could talk and even, at one point, agree to lay down the gloves and quit fighting between themselves, if for no reason other than the children.

But Thaddeus was perplexed and struggling. The video was as good as his case was going to get. Without some way of attacking the nurses' notes he could invent no other plan of attack.

"That nailed their ass," whispered Christine when the lights went up. "Well done, Thad."

He whispered back at her. "Yes, but we're out of bullets. I got nothing else."

"How about we put a blanket on the floor in front of the jury and have Latoya feed him, change his diaper, try to show him love, and just let them see how hard it is from her standpoint. We haven't shown her side of it, yet."

"Excellent idea. We'll recess for the day and have her bring Chase in first thing in the morning. Then we'll recall Latoya to the witness stand. Find her and tell her to bring a blanket and Chase in the morning. Have them bring Grandma, too, for quality control."

"To manage the baby."

"Exactly."

"Done."

Christine left the courtroom in search of mother and father.

∼

THEY RECESSED for the day and Morgana gave A.W. a lift back to the law firm. They swung into Morgana's parking place. She shut off the engine.

A.W. spoke first. "Don't let that Day in the Life crap run away with your feelings."

She shrugged. "Naw, you know I'm tougher than that."

"I know you are."

"I'm going to go upstairs and work on a motion to dismiss to present to the judge in the morning. We'll ask the court to dismiss the case after the plaintiff rests."

"They have no case. You've eaten them alive."

"I have, haven't I?"

"Sandy is ecstatic. He told me he was ordering the champagne tonight for the victory celebration that's coming down the road. What will this be for you, thirty-one straight?"

"Thirty-one straight. A record most lawyers would die for."

"You've earned it."

"Yes, I have."

She kept it as light and noncommittal as possible, she was sure. No promises to the old man, no arguments about settlement. Just appear to be going along with the scam.

Appearances were acceptable.

If he only knew.

49

Morgana stayed late and prepared her motion to dismiss the plaintiff's case. This was a standard motion, called for in all medical malpractice cases, that asked the judge to dismiss the case at the close of the plaintiffs' evidence on the basis that all the evidence admitted so far, taken in the light most favorable to the plaintiffs, wouldn't sustain a finding of negligence against the defendants. In short, the motion said, as Morgana put it when she taught trial tactics to bar association groups, "You just hit me with your best shot and you still lose."

Once the motion was drafted, she emailed it to Manny for his review. She was still paying him, under the table, of course, and he was giving her feedback on trial strategy and pleadings, as the trial hurried along.

Morgana received his reply twenty minutes later. One word: "Cool." Now she could file it; he had found nothing objectionable. She had to smile at the thought: nothing objectionable except the entire fraudulent defense. They had cheated their way all the way through the plaintiffs' case with the phony records, which led to the phony cross-examinations of Chase's witnesses, which led to phony arguments to the judge, which led to that night's phony motion to dismiss.

It was all a sham.

She shivered; she was in it up to her neck.

She could and probably would go to prison for what she had done. She refused to kid herself about that. Manny was determined to spill the beans to Thaddeus and his clients. Knowing Manny, he would do just that, even if it cost Morgana her law license and her freedom. He was just that committed to doing the right thing. *Too bad, she thought, she wasn't likewise so steady in the boat. I'm a lightweight,* she thought, as she clicked FILE on the court's computer screen. The web page confirmed that she had filed her motion and automatically distributed a copy to Thaddeus. *I'm a lightweight and I hate myself very much.*

With an exhausted sigh she pushed away from her desk and headed down to the parking garage.

Out on Armory Street she made a right and went down to Middleton Street, which she followed north. Just as she turned north, her cell phone chimed. Dr. Rabinowitz. Her heart sank.

"It isn't good," he immediately said to her. "The tests are back and the cancer has metastasized. You have a tumor on your pancreas. Inoperable, we fear. But the tumor committee is meeting tomorrow to officially confirm all this. In the meantime, hope and pray that they recommend a heroic measures treatment of some sort."

She was so frightened she feared she would drive up onto the sidewalk. "Heroic measures?" she whispered into the phone. "What's that mean?"

"Well, where a case is hopeless an untested, unapproved treatment modality is tried. Maybe a new drug, maybe a surgical technique, maybe a kind of radiation we haven't used. That kind of thing."

She found herself saying, "I wouldn't be interested in that. I want to leave a pretty corpse, not something hacked up."

Dead silence at the other end. Then, "Very well, Morgana. We'll talk again tomorrow. And—I'm so sorry, but I wanted to call you myself."

She was shaking from head to toe. It was a death sentence. Now all she needed to do was tell the judge about the deceit she had been engaged in and there would be a second death sentence, this time to her career.

She took a deep breath. At least she didn't have to worry about prison or doing any time. She wouldn't live that long. She would be dead and a memory before they could prosecute her and put her away. Of course they could and would arrest her, if it all came out. And she would spend her final weeks or months away from Caroline. She couldn't allow that to happen. Not now.

She took her foot off the gas and almost coasted to a stop. Tears flooded her eyes. She steered with her knees and tore a handkerchief out of her purse. Tears flowed and she sobbed as she steered the car through a wet haze.

She waved a tailgater around and he gave her a dirty look, as in, "How the hell could anyone drive in the fast lane at the speed limit?"

She shot him a nice smile and spread her hands. *It's just where I'm at*, she thought. *Just where I'm at tonight*. Suddenly there was no hurry, no hurry about anything. All tasks seemed irrelevant. The trial seemed irrelevant, the trial court record was laughable—none of it could turn her head from that moment on. There were no deeds to do, no promises to keep.

She switched on Sirius. Dizzy Gillespie lit up the interior of the car with his horn. She drummed her fingers on the steering wheel.

It was time to help that little brain-injured boy. Tears again came to her eyes, but this time they weren't her tears, they all belonged to him.

Chase Staples, she thought, I'm coming for you now.

50

From her home office, Morgana phoned Manny.

He answered on the second ring, "Hey, dude, what's the haps?"

She cut right to it. No explanations. "I need the web address."

"The cloud?"

"The cloud. And I need the password."

"OK, I'm emailing you a link right now. Tell me when you get it."

"Got it. Are the original nurses' notes still there?"

"Just like I told you in the bathroom."

"Thanks for not following my orders to destroy them."

"I knew you'd want them sooner or later."

"Thanks again. I'll write you from prison."

"I'll come see you. You'll be out in twenty-four months. Just like Martha Stewart."

"Now that's damn reassuring. Now about your testimony, I think I've got that dialed in."

They continue speaking only minutes longer, then said their good-byes.

Morgana called Thaddeus.

"Thad, Morgana. Can you access your office email from home?"

"I can. Why?"

"Because you're about to win this case. I want you to read some nurses' notes you've never seen before."

"I'll look for the email. Morgana, you're doing the right thing—"

"—Yeah, yeah. Screw you, Thaddeus."

"Okay, my friend."

Morgana hung up and prepared an email to Thaddeus. She inserted the web address and the password. Next she typed the body of the email to Thaddeus: "Thaddeus, there's no way to say how sorry I am. The best I can do at this time is see to it that Chase gets the care and comfort Hudd Family owes him. Andrea Mounce, Chase's delivery room nurse, is on active duty overseas. You need her testimony with the records I'm sending you. Tomorrow I will join you in a request to the court for a full day continuance of the trial in order for her to attend. Call me after you've seen the records. Morgana."

She waited ninety minutes before the phone rang.

"Thaddeus. Jesus, Morgana, what a slimy bunch you work for."

"Don't forget to include me in that bunch. I'm one of them too."

"We need Andrea's testimony. Any luck locating her?"

"Ramstein Air Base, Germany. You still got that jet?"

"Sure."

"You're ready to bring her back to the States?"

"Sure."

"Let me make some calls."

51

A nother trip to the oncologist and a wordless drive home.

There were no words, yet.

The news wasn't good. The cancer had become systemic. Scans and tests had revealed that Morgana had developed cancer of the pancreas—a death sentence in all but a minority of cases.

Cancer doctor Rabinowitz was blunt. "There's very little I have to offer to you by way of treatment," he told Morgana and Caroline. "Your cancer is extremely aggressive."

Morgana wiped tears from her eyes. She was no longer in great fear; growing to live with cancer had taught her there was no longer any degree of certainty in her life. Her life expectancy was now limited, Dr. Rabinowitz explained.

"How much time does she have?" Caroline asked. They were sitting together in the doctor's office, not an exam room. In a way the office meeting place was a statement: no need for exam rooms, there's nothing further medicine can do for you. No need for exams.

He shook his head. "Life expectancy is really hard to judge in these cases."

"But we need a number," Morgana said. "We have things to attend to."

"Ninety days, give or take."

"Ninety."

"I'm afraid so."

"How bad will it be?"

"We can offer palliative care. We can all but keep you free of pain."

"At the end."

"Yes, at the end," he said.

The women saw how passive the doctor had become. When Morgana had been in treatment mode he was always animated and spoke aggressively about steps they would take. Now he was letting them know through his slow-moving body language and suppressed speech that the time for medical action had passed. They had moved on. This was new territory to the women, old to him.

They drove home in silence. Morgana insisted on getting behind the wheel. "I need to feel normal, like driving is something I'll be doing for the next sixty years."

At home they made coffee and took a seat at the kitchen table. In their condo the kitchen was open to the family room, which itself was brightened by clerestory windows that were admitting high noon sunshine. It was a cheery setting, though no one felt cheerful. Not then.

"I don't want to hurt," Morgana said. "I'm a sissy when it comes to pain."

"We won't let you hurt. He already said so."

"And I don't want to drag it out. No life-extending measures. No heroic measures."

"All right. I disagree, but you're the patient."

"You would be selfish."

"Yes, I would."

"But I'm the patient."

"I know. Your wishes count, not mine. I'm just the girlfriend."

Morgana violently shook her head. "You're my spouse."

"Not legally."

"True, so let's fix that?"

"Get married?"

"Why not?"

"I would like that. I'm a go on that."

They reached and held hands across the table. Tears flowed and coffee went untouched.

After ten minutes of silence they went upstairs to their bedroom, where they stretched out on the bed, fully clothed, and held each other.

Then they cried. Hard, wracking cries without letup.

It would be a long afternoon, and it had only just begun.

THE WOMEN MADE love that afternoon. Caroline held Morgana and gently kissed her face and mouth. They removed their clothes and turned down the covers. They lay side by side and touched for an hour or more, before giving into their desires and strong feelings for one another. Hands touched between legs, mouths tasted open bodies. Sated, they finally spooned and drifted off for another thirty minutes. Then they awoke and started all over again. Following the second round, they held on and cried.

By sundown they were cried out and starting to make jokes about small, insignificant matters in their lives.

Morgana bounced out of bed at six o'clock and

announced she was going downstairs to her office to look into Iowa's same-sex marriage laws. Caroline said she wanted to make Morgana's favorite, beef stroganoff. They dressed in lounging clothes and parted ways, feeling closer and more bound together than they had in months.

They were both free to love fully and completely.

Adoring looks were exchanged and hands touched as they parted.

MORGANA and A.W were seated at defense table while Thaddeus was whispering to Christine at the plaintiffs' table.

Judge Moody took the bench and looked down at the litigants. The jury was in the jury room and all but a few mostly disinterested spectators had taken up seats in the courtroom.

The judge spoke, nodding first to the reporter to indicate they were on the record. "Counsel, you asked to present a motion prior to the jury being brought in. So who goes first?"

Thaddeus stood. "I do, Your Honor. Judge, we've been able to get in touch with a missing witness. Now we've learned that we can get her here but not until tomorrow."

A.W's head jerked up. From the look on his face he clearly had no idea this was coming.

"So you're asking for a continuance for one day?"

Thaddeus nodded. "We are, Your Honor. She's a mission-critical witness for us. A *sine qua non*."

The judge looked over at Morgana. "And what about you, counsel, what is the defense's position on this motion to continue trial for one day?"

Morgana quickly began, "Judge, we really have no objection—"

Whereupon A.W leapt to his feet. "Hold on! We do too object, Your Honor. Sit down, Morgana."

Morgana sat. A small smile danced at the corners of her mouth but she stared straight ahead.

"And what's the basis of your objection?"

A.W said, "We have our own witnesses scheduled for today. We have experts we've flown in to testify today, experts from Los Angeles and Atlanta. Everyone's meter is running and we want to put them on to testify without delay."

"Thaddeus?"

"Your Honor, I will be happy to personally guarantee payment of their witness's' invoices for a full day of testimony today. We want to be fair about this."

"You'll pay out of your own pocket, win, lose, or hung jury?"

"Yes I will, Judge."

The judge nodded and cast a look around the courtroom as he pondered. The baby's father sat alone in the very rear of the courtroom, a pleading look on his face.

"Very well. Based on counsel's affirmation to the court that a day's continuance will be paid by plaintiff's counsel I see no reason why we can't all take a day off today. Personally I could use the respite and I'm sure the jury has errands they would like to run and family they would like to catch up with. Motion to continue granted. I'll see all of you back here tomorrow morning at nine sharp."

A.W said under his breath to Morgana, "I'll see you back at the office. We need to have this out."

She climbed to her feet and pulled herself fully upright.

"Let's meet at The Judges' Chambers across the street. Give me a chance to toss down some eggs and bacon."

"See you there."

~

THE JUDGES' Chambers, a local eatery and watering hole directly across the street from the courthouse, was bustling and blew the smell of bacon frying and eggs sizzling right out the door onto the busy sidewalk.

A.W. and Morgana had just ordered and the waitress was walking away. Morgana stirred her coffee. A.W. was red-faced. His hands clenched at nothing and unclenched several times over.

"No objection to a continuance? What, are you kidding me?"

She was light and breezy. Dying, she thought, makes you that way.

She tasted the coffee and wiped her mouth. "I think it's time we make a serious offer and settle this case. We could use this day to do just that. So I didn't object, I thought we could make good use of the time."

"Have you been paying attention, girl? Sandy won't authorize one dime to settle!"

"He should think about that. There's a new witness on her way."

"Do you even know what witness they're bringing in on Friday?"

"Well, by the process of selection I can compare the witness list to who they've already called and see who's left to call."

"You know what I'm saying. Who are they bringing in?"

"Nurse Andrea. They found Nurse Andrea."

"The delivery room nurse? I thought we had her buried overseas!"

"We did. They dug her up."

"And you know this how?"

"Thaddeus told me just before the judge came in. He asked me if we wanted to settle and gave me a huge smile."

"Jesus."

"That's what I'm saying. I think it's time we tuned up Sandy and put some money on the table. If they've really found her then we're going down hard."

"Girl, are we having some kind of problem here?"

"No more than usual, why? Boy."

It hung in the air. Equals were faced off. No more girl, girl, girl. She had nothing to lose. Absolutely nothing. And everything to gain."

"How did they find her?"

"You know Thad. He's one hell of a lawyer, A.W."

"Let's call Sandy, see if he knows anything about this. Or her."

A.W. jabbed at his cell and punched it on SPEAKER. It rang twice.

Sandy came on. "What gives, old man?"

"New development, Sandy. I'm hearing they've located Andrea Mounce, the delivery room nurse."

"That's impossible! She's in Germany. They'll never find her."

"Morgana tells me they found her. And this morning they got a continuance until Friday to put her on."

"Not to worry. My people have already taken her statement. She'll say the records are her handwriting."

"You're absolutely sure of that?"

"I'd bet on it."

Morgana interrupted. "Sandy, Morgana. Are you willing

to bet twenty million on it? Cause that's the minimum we'll get hit for if she takes the stand and denies the records are hers."

"I'll take that bet. We've statementized her and she's golden."

"Even if she is, this is the time to put some money on the table. I want this on the record and I'm delivering a letter to you this afternoon that I'm recommending settlement."

Sandy laughed derisively, as if dealing with an upstart teenager. "You're already on that record. You've been on that record for months, Morgana. You need to relax and let us handle this part of the case. I'm telling you she's golden. I was headed to court, but I'm turning around. See you both Friday."

They hung up.

A.W scowled at Morgana. "What, are you trying to lose Hudd Family as a client with your cold feet?"

"I'm only trying to save my client. You should be too. This continuance is Thad's shot across our bow. He's known for knocking down big targets and we're in his sights right this minute. Only you guys don't hear me."

"We've got her statement. Relax and eat your breakfast."

"You eat it. I'm out of here."

She stomped to the door and threw it open. The cold air rushed over her face. It felt good. Getting away from the old man and his cronies suddenly felt exhilarating.

She walked down the sidewalk and never once looked back.

52

On the final day of trial the jury was brought in and seated. They were smiling and whispering to one another, restless and ready for things to begin. Thaddeus could tell they could smell the end of the trial coming when they would be freed of their duty as jurors. Once seated and settled down, Judge Moody looked over at them and smiled. He was wearing his black robes and his glasses perched on his forehead.

"Good morning," he said to the jury. Heads nodded, smiles exchanged; they were friends, judge and jury, and Thaddeus liked the symbiosis he was witnessing. "I hope you all enjoyed the day off," he said, and many of the jurors nodded emphatically. "Good."

The judge looked down at Thaddeus. "Counsel, you may call your next witness."

"Plaintiff calls Andrea Mounce."

Her starched military fatigues swishing as she strode up the aisle, Andrea Mounce had a stern look on her face. She looked to Thaddeus like she was studied and serious. Studied in that she had reviewed the trial transcripts he had provided her when they were flying on his Gulfstream back from Germany. "Can't believe what I'm seeing here," she muttered at one moment over the Atlantic.

She took her seat and nodded at the jury. Smiles were returned; Americans love their service members.

"State your name for the record."

She pursed her lips thoughtfully, and then launched into what she had come to say. "Andrea Mounce."

"Andrea, you're deployed by the National Guard to an air base in Germany, is that correct?"

"That is correct."

"And your rank in the military?"

"I am a major."

"What is your job with the military?"

"We fly American soldiers from the U.S. Hospital there in Germany to Walter Reed Hospital."

"So you help take care of American soldiers in transit?"

"I do. In a hospital aircraft."

"Now directing your attention to July fifth, last year, what was your occupation at that time?"

"I was a nursing supervisor, responsible for several different practice areas in Hudd Family Hospital Chicago."

"And as part of those duties did you participate on the delivery team for Mrs. Latoya Staples?"

"I did."

"While you were serving as a nurse, were you in the delivery room with Latoya?"

"Delivery room and I scrubbed in for the OR part of the delivery. I'm a certified OR nurse."

"I see. Now, as part of your role that evening, were you entering nursing notes into Latoya's chart?"

"I was."

"I'm going to hand you what's been marked at trial as Defendants' Exhibit 4. Can you tell me what that is?"

"It appears to be nursing notes and appears to be connected to Latoya's delivery."

"Have you ever seen those notes before?"

She pulled a small pair of readers from a chest pocket and examined the exhibit. "Well, they have what appears to be my initials but none of this is my handwriting."

A.W leapt to his feet. "Objection, surprise!"

Judge Moody gave the old attorney a long stare. "Surprise, counsel? I've never heard of an objection to testimony by surprise."

A.W continued. "We had no idea until just now that they would be calling this witness."

The judge turned his attention to Thaddeus. "Counsel, is Major Mounce listed on your witness list submitted to the court?"

"She is, your honor. And I told Miss Bridgman yesterday morning that I would be calling Major Mounce today."

The judge focused on Morgana. "Miss Bridgman?"

"That's correct, Your Honor. We were warned she was coming to testify."

A.W whispered angrily to Morgana, "Warned? What the hell does that mean?"

"Objection overruled," said the judge. "You may continue, Major Mounce."

Thaddeus picked up where he'd left off. "We were discussing the notes that the hospital and doctor provided me before during the discovery phase of this case. These notes they gave me are not in your own handwriting? Even where your initials are placed alongside each entry?"

She again reviewed the exhibit. After a minute or more

she looked up and shrugged. "This is not my handwriting. I don't know what else to say."

"Even where it says the page for C-section was made at six thirty-five p.m.?"

"Not my handwriting."

"And even where it says Dr. Payne arrived at six fifty-three p.m.?"

"Not my handwriting."

"Do you have the original nurses' notes?"

"I do."

"Objection!" cried A.W. "The originals are already in evidence!"

"No," said Andrea, "those are not the originals."

"Let me rule, Major," said the judge. "The witness can testify to what she knows. Please proceed, Mister Murfee."

"Please give me the original nurses' notes," Thaddeus said to the Major. She arose and walked back to where she had left her overnight bag. Everyone watched as she unzipped the top of the red nylon bag and removed a sheaf of papers. She retook the witness stand. She handed the papers to Thaddeus. He reviewed them for a moment and then addressed the court.

"Let me ask the court reporter to mark an exhibit."

The court reporter marked the sheaf of papers from Thaddeus.

"Now let me show you what's been marked Plaintiffs' Exhibit 21. Can you look these over?"

"OK, I've paged through them."

"Can you tell us what these are?"

"These are nurses' notes. In my handwriting. Some of the entries are in another nurse's handwriting, as well. But I know her and know that's all her own, too."

"Where did you get these?"

"Some man in the hallway handed them to me as I got off the elevator."

"Did he say who he was?"

She nodded. "He said he was from the hospital."

"And what is what's been marked as Exhibit 21?"

"These are my nurse's notes from the Latoya Staples delivery of her baby by C-section."

"And according to these notes, what time did you page for a C-section?"

She reviewed the exhibit, drawing a line with her finger as she read. "Let's see. I made the page for a C-section qualified OB at six thirty-five p.m., eighteen thirty-five hours."

"Did anyone answer that call?"

"Well, Gerry Springer, M.D., came to help."

"Who is Dr. Springer?"

"He was a first-year OB resident. He had only been in the rotation for three months and had never performed a C-section. He wasn't qualified."

"What did he do?"

"He told me to page Dr. Payne."

"And you did that at what time?"

"I paged Dr. Payne at six thirty-five p.m."

"What time did Dr. Payne arrive?"

"Let's see." Again reviewing the notes. "Forty-five minutes later we had the baby out. He got there at seven fourteen. Thirty-nine minutes after the page. The baby is delivered at seven nineteen. My notes, my handwriting."

"Which means Chase would have gone about fifteen minutes longer than any baby can without suffering damage from lack of oxygen?"

"That's correct."

A.W again pushed himself upright and complained to the judge. "Objection, Your Honor. She has not been qualified as an expert and does not have the knowledge or training to testify about anoxia in fetuses."

"Counsel, you're telling me that even though she's a certified OB nurse she can't testify about this baby's lack of oxygen for thirty-nine minutes?"

"Correct. That's what I'm saying."

"Overruled. Counsel, we're going to take a fifteen-minute break. My chambers, please."

The attorneys followed the judge through the doorway back behind and to the left of his lofty plateau.

Moments later they were all clumped around his desk. Judge Moody had unzipped his robe and loosened his necktie. He waved the attorneys into the ring of chairs scattered around his desk.

He took a swig out of a cold Starbucks on his desk, and said, "Someone owes me an explanation."

The attorneys looked at each other. Then they stared at the floor, all except Thaddeus, who maintained eye contact with Judge Moody.

The judge was impatient. "Well? Who wants to go first?"

A.W went first. "Your Honor, I think we're putting the cart before the horse here. We were just preparing to make a settlement offer to the plaintiff and her attorney."

Thaddeus shot back, "Rejected. We don't wish to settle, Judge."

A.W looked him in the eye and shook his head. "But you haven't even heard how much. You can't reject without knowing."

"How much?"

"Fifteen million. Take it or leave it."

"I've already spoken to my client. She's told me to reject anything less than fifty million."

A.W all but shrieked, "That's preposterous! She can't just reject fifteen million!"

The judge lifted a hand. "Apparently she can, and she did, Mr. Marentz. Now let's get down to the real deal. Months ago you came into court and told me all records had been turned over to Mister Murfee. Do you recall that?"

A.W looked at Morgana, indicating she should speak. "I do."

"I'll ask you again, were all records turned over?"

A.W chimed in. "I can answer that. We've discovered a second set of nurses' notes. We're trying to sort out which ones are real."

Thaddeus smiled a wide smile. "Give me five more minutes with my witness after the break. She's prepared to sort that out for you. She's going to save you a lot of stumbling around in the dark, Mr. Marentz. Stumbling around in the dark like you've had me doing this past six months. Yes, we're going to tell the jury about real records and phony records. Judge, can we return to the courtroom now and let me finish with my witness?"

"We can. Counsel—" He looked directly at A.W. Marentz. "We're not finished here. We will get to the bottom of record turnover before we're finished here today."

They returned to the courtroom, whereupon Thaddeus remained standing and addressed Judge Moody.

"Judge, I would like to call another witness at this moment, a witness about the nurses' notes. Then I would like to recall Major Mounce after that."

"No objection," said Morgana. She and A.W gave each other a quick look of relief to see the trial going sideways, even for a minute.

"Very well," said the Judge, "call your next witness."

Thaddeus spoke loud and clear. "Plaintiff calls A.W.

Marentz to the stand."

General pandemonium broke out against a backdrop of both defense lawyers bolting to their feet, whispers among the gallery, and the jurors nudging one another.

"Silence!" said the judge. "You may proceed."

"Objection!" cried A.W. "I can't be called as a witness. I don't know anything!"

Thaddeus responded to the judge. "Your Honor, Mister Marentz just told you in chambers that he was working to sort out the new records that he had discovered. I just want to ask him what he knows, since he's been in the chain-of-custody of those records."

The judge looked at A.W. "Do you wish to respond? My inclination is to allow Mr. Murfee to go forward."

"Sure, Judge," said A.W., doing a complete about-face. "I'll be happy to tell what I know."

He took the witness stand, gave his name, professional address, and answered several questions about his role in the case as defense counsel.

Then Thaddeus asked, "How come the jury now has two totally different exhibits of nurses' notes from your client, the hospital?"

"Sir, I don't know," the old man said. "But we're looking into that."

"Well, let's do it this way. The nurses' notes that you first turned over. Where did those come from?"

"From my client, Hudd Family Healthcare."

"And where did they get those notes from?"

"From their records in-house, I would imagine."

Thaddeus nodded. "Did you ever talk to the records custodian about the origin of those records?"

"I did not."

"So you just assumed your client was telling you the

truth when they told you they were giving you their records?"

"I assumed so, yes. Why wouldn't I?"

"Now we've found Major Mounce has been given a second set of nurses' notes. From a man who said he was from the hospital, correct?"

"That's what she said."

"Who would that man be?"

A.W. shrugged. "I can tell you, I don't have the slightest idea. He wasn't anyone I know about."

"Do you deny that he turned over to her the real nurses' notes?"

"I wouldn't know."

"Well, you were in the courtroom when she testified and you heard her?"

"Yes."

"I mean, there's nothing wrong with your hearing?"

"Nothing wrong there."

"So you have no reason to disagree with what she said, that the records you gave the jury were a complete fraud?"

"I can't disagree. They weren't meant as a fraud, however."

"You don't disagree they are a fraud?"

"Depends on what you mean by a fraud."

Thaddeus moved a step closer. "Well, let's think about that. If the jury had sent this brain-damaged baby home without a cent because of your phony records, would that be a fraud?"

"I can't answer that."

"Can't, or won't?"

"Both. I think I need to talk to my own lawyer."

"Are you taking the Fifth Amendment now?"

A.W.'s face had drained of color. His normally pink

cheeks were white like chalk. "I certainly don't intend to sit here and incriminate myself."

"Do you think you might be guilty of a crime?"

"No—I don't know. That's why I'd like to talk to my lawyer first."

"So there might be a crime, it's that serious, to your way of thinking?"

A.W let out a long sigh. "Perhaps. I don't know. I just don't want to take a chance."

Thaddeus stepped back. "That is all. You're excused. Unless attorney Bridgman wants to question you."

Morgana stood. "No questions."

"You may be excused," said the judge. "And we'll break now for our afternoon recess."

Thaddeus allowed the courtroom to clear out ahead of him. He remained behind for ten minutes. Then he heard the courtroom door open behind him in the otherwise empty courtroom.

"Hello, Mr. Hudd," Thaddeus said.

"Counselor," said Manny. "How goes it today?"

Thaddeus smiled and chuckled. "I hear you now work for the hospital."

"Only long enough to pass a stack of records to a certain Major this morning."

"Well done."

"Indeed."

"Are you ready to testify?"

"Indeed."

Thaddeus smiled and shook his hand. "Welcome aboard. I've been looking for a smart young lawyer to help with my cases."

"You've been busy, then?"

"Indeed."

53

On the fifth and sixth days of trial the defense pulled out all the stops. But it was clear from the start that the defense case had been gutted by the truth about its records. "A bell once rung cannot be unrung" had never been truer. The jury had heard about the fraudulent records and had all but turned on TVs and succumbed to knitting as they ignored everything the defense witnesses had to say. At long last—blessed relief—the defense case was all in.

A.W made it official. "Defense rests, Your Honor."

Thaddeus took to his feet. "Your Honor, the plaintiff has one rebuttal witness to call."

Judge Moody looked up. "And who would that be?" he inquired.

"Manny Rodriguez."

A.W was instantly on his feet, objecting and sputtering about the sanctity of the attorney-client relationship and how Manny couldn't be called to testify about his client.

Thaddeus said, "We have the right to call him, it's rebuttal."

Judge Moody moved his hands forward and pointed an index finger at Thaddeus and A.W. "Gentlemen, approach the bench."

The jurors as one rolled their eyes as the lawyers took up their spots before the judge's throne and began speaking in angry whispers.

A.W went first. "Your Honor, this is unethical and must be barred. Further, counsel for the plaintiff should be censured by the court for this."

"I'm only trying to call a witness, Judge."

The judge looked sharply at Thaddeus. "Mr. Murfee, don't try the feigned innocence with me. You know damn good and well you cannot call a former member of the defense team to testify."

Thaddeus leaned in and raised his voice a notch. "That's just it. He was never a member of the defense team."

A.W. exploded and his whisper carried throughout the room. "Ridiculous, of course he was!"

Judge Moody extended a palm. "Keep your voice down, Mr. Marentz. Mr. Murfee, ask Manny Rodriguez to step up here."

The waters parted and Manny joined the bench conference.

The judge began, "Mr. Rodriguez, were you a member of the defense team in this case?"

"I was not."

A.W reared back and roared, "That's a blatant lie! Of course you were!"

Judge Moody indicated *come here* to A.W. "Raise your voice once more in my courtroom and you'll spend the weekend in jail. Do you understand me?"

A.W. meekly replied, "I do. Sorry."

Manny continued. "According to the Jones Marentz

staffing partner, who is also the managing partner, I was never a member of the defense team."

Judge Moody frowned, frustrated. "A.W. says you were, you say you weren't. Mr. Murfee, I'm afraid the defense wins on this one. He cannot testify."

Manny held up his iPhone. "Judge, can I play a recording off my cell phone?"

"What would I be listening to?"

"The staffing partner, Carson Palmer. Then me. It's just a single exchange, but it will make the point."

"Very well. But keep it low."

Manny clicked PLAY. "Mr. Palmer. You're saying I'm terminated and I'm no longer a member of the Hudd Family defense team?"

Carson Palmer, on the recording, answered, "You, sir, were never a member of the Hudd Family defense team. Now get your stuff and get out."

Thaddeus smiled and Manny returned the phone to his pocket. Judge Moody glared at A.W.

The judge made his ruling loud enough for those even out in the hallway to hear. "Mr. Murfee, you may call your final witness, Manny Rodriguez. The court specifically finds that Mr. Rodriguez was never a member of the defense team."

All attorneys resumed their seats at counsel table. Manny took his place in the witness chair.

Thaddeus began, "State your name."

"Manuel Rodriguez."

"Mr. Rodriguez are you prepared to tell the jury what you know about Hudd Hospital Chicago and Dr. Phillip Payne and how medical records were altered by these two defendants?"

A.W. leapt to his feet. "Objection!"

"Overruled," the judge said almost nonchalantly. "Please continue."

Manny continued his testimony. He explained how records were altered, records were shredded, records were switched out and phony records switched in, and how records were saved to the cloud computing location.

When he was finished, Thaddeus proffered the witness to A.W.

"No questions," said the founding partner.

The jury stared at the floor.

Defense table eye contact was avoided and no one was smiling.

54

The afternoon light lay low across the courtyard, a horizontal plane seeking entry into the dim court-room. Overheads had been clicked to BRIGHT settings and everyone was tired. The jury was out, the judge had retired to chambers, and the lawyers were sitting with their feet propped up, making calls on their cell phones and surfing on their laptops.

At long last, the bailiff stuck his head in and announced a verdict. Immediately the lawyers hopped to, arranging themselves and straightening ties, leaping to their feet as Judge Moody appeared as if an apparition that walked through the wall, floated to his lofty place and spread his wings as he settled. The jury filed in and took their customary seats in the jury box.

Judge Moody said, "Madam Foreperson, has the jury returned its verdict?"

"We have, Your Honor."

"Please read the verdict out loud."

"We the jury do find in favor of the plaintiff Chase

Staples and award him damages in the amount of fifty million dollars."

Judge Moody nodded solemnly. "That's it, then?"

"And we award punitive damages for destroying records and conspiring to destroy this baby's life of one hundred fifty million dollars. Now that's it."

Bedlam erupted. Chase cried; John Staples swung him in his arms; Latoya sobbed; Christine shook Thaddeus' hand; and Manny cheered from the back row. Until the judge gave him a long, severe look. Then the lawyer left the courtroom.

THIRTY MINUTES later a scene took place on the courthouse sidewalk. Morgana and A.W were standing toe to toe. A.W was gesturing furiously.

"Those records could only have come from you!" the senior litigator cried.

"You're right."

"But why?"

She shrugged and wrapped her arms around herself. "Let's just say I decided to settle the case without you or Sandy."

"I have already called the office. Your check has been seized. No more pay for you. Your benefits have been cut off. Your 401(k) is frozen pending the result of our lawsuit against you. Which will be filed at eight o'clock in the morning."

"I'll get another job. Or maybe not."

"Your American Express is canceled."

"I have other cards."

"Your partnership is rescinded. You've been terminated."

"I never liked my partners. You're all crazy as bat shit."

"And Judge Moody has turned this case over to the U.S. Attorney for prosecution. You're headed for federal penitentiary time for perjury."

"You've got me there."

"You'll lose your law license. That's a given."

"I'll coach junior high girls' basketball."

"We'll see that you never coach at any school."

"No, that I doubt you can do. This is a pretty big country and there are lots of little kids who need a great coach."

The old man's Mercedes pulled to the curb and flashed its lights.

A.W. stormed away and climbed into the back seat of the black limousine. It roared away from the curb and disappeared into traffic.

Morgana watched the limo disappear, and then looked up and down the street. No cabs were in sight. Just then, a weathered old Crown Victoria pulled over to the curb. It was Latoya and she leaned across the seat and rolled down the window.

Latoya smiled and motioned her over. "Going somewhere?"

"I have six blocks to walk to my car."

"Need a ride?"

"I do. I do need a ride."

"Hop in. Climb in back with John and Chase."

Morgana crossed around to the traffic side and climbed in the back seat. Chase sat next to her in his car seat. For once the baby was reasonably happy. Morgana sat back, put her arm up around Chase, and a smile came to her face.

Morgana tweaked his foot and laughed, "Chase, could you spare me a hundred until payday?"

The old Crown Vic rolled away from the curb in a haze of smoke and disappeared into rush hour traffic.

55

They chose Iowa City because of the college influence and the validating effect that liberal institution would have on same sex couples.

Caroline and Morgana piled their luggage into the yellow cab's trunk and climbed in the back seat. The flight from Chicago had been uneventful though bumpy due to low-hanging cumulus over central Iowa. They rode the cab into downtown Iowa City and the driver pulled in at the Sheraton Hotel drive-through. After check-in they found their room and ordered room service.

"Now to find City Hall," said Morgana. "And get a license."

"Is there a waiting period? Blood tests? Any of that crap?" asked Caroline.

"Unknown. Let me call City Hall."

They found that they could obtain the license from Johnson County and there would be a three-day waiting period. They had arrived on Thursday so the license would be valid on Monday.

They took a cab, went to the Johnson County desk, paid the thirty-five dollars, signed papers, and had their license.

They ran back outside, squealing and laughing, Morgana waving the license and showing pedestrians, who would smile and nod and step around her.

They caught a cab back to the hotel, ordered room service again, and began scanning for in-room videos. It was going to take Friday plus the weekend, but they had plenty of sightseeing planned and exulted at being together with no interruptions.

"We're putting the honeymoon before the marriage," said Morgana. "Any objections from the crowd?"

"Not here," Caroline laughed.

"Hearing none, let the movies, lovemaking, and sight-seeing begin. Not to mention the seafood. I want lobster tonight."

"Done."

"By the way, do I have a job yet?"

"None!"

"Then let the party begin!"

56

They were married eight weeks when the pain became too difficult to bear without a constant drip. She found herself tethered to a pole. Which meant she was spending long periods in bed. Morgana's pancreatic cancer was a death warrant. She was Stage IV and the five-year survival rate was one percent. Morphine was the treatment modality for the severe back pain she was experiencing.

The pain grew worse, much worse. The added morphine was leaving her increasingly drowsy and nauseous.

Ten weeks out, the morphine's effectiveness abruptly fell off. Additional opiates were prescribed, which would help for a few days, then those would fall away as well.

Caroline was with her constantly, leaving her bedside only to bring water and obtain medical marijuana. Illinois had at long last implemented a pilot program and twenty-two grow labs around the state were selling out faster than the pot could be produced. Dr. Rabinowitz prescribed the marijuana for Morgana's nausea and the pot did actually help her in occasionally eating, though by then most sustenance arrived in a tube that snaked into the back of her hand.

Twelve weeks out she was in constant pain so severe that when she was conscious she was crying and begging Caroline to do something.

"I've called Doctor Rabinowitz. He wants you to go to hospice."

"I won't leave our home!" Morgana cried. "This is where I choose to die, at home, in my own bed!"

"I'll call him again."

But she was dying and there was no more help. Dr. Rabinowitz paid a house call and held Morgana's hand while he spoke to her in very soothing tones. "There's nothing else I can offer, Morgana. We've done all we can for you. We can step up the morphine but you'll be rendered unconscious. Is that what you choose for me to do?"

Morgana thought it over. "Yes," she said. "That's my choice."

"We'll give you very specific instructions so you do not overdose. We don't want that."

"We don't?" whispered Morgana, fighting off a wave of unrelenting pain that now covered her entire torso and paralyzed her legs. Caroline would carry her to the bathroom when there was time, or would change diapers day and night, usually both.

"We don't want an overdose for you. For one thing, there's no physician-assisted suicide in this state, if that's what you're thinking."

"It is what I'm thinking."

"All oncologists in Illinois know the law by heart. You're a lawyer. You can read it on your laptop at Sec. 12-34.5. Inducement to commit suicide. The law is very clear that I would be committing a class two felony were I to help you commit suicide."

Caroline raised her hand. "Hold on a sec. What if I help her do it?"

"Same law would apply."

"Even though I'm not a doctor?"

"Right. The law applies to everyone, not just doctors."

Caroline seemed to know where she was going with this. "All right. You do your part by increasing the amount of morphine she needs to stay pain free."

"And?" the doctor said.

"Don't ask," said Caroline gravely. "Just please, don't ask."

"Very well. I'll make the orders and instruct the nurse."

"Thank you, Dr. Rabinowitz," Morgana moaned. "For everything."

"Of course. Now I need to get back to the office."

"Sure."

"But I'll see you again."

"Of course."

He squeezed Morgana's foot and shook Caroline's hand. "God bless," he said, and headed downstairs.

AT MIDNIGHT her body was wracked head to toe with pain and she couldn't stop crying. The new morphine load would take her under, but fifteen minutes later the pain would again overwhelm and wake her up. The inline morphine pump had been replaced by a handheld and she was able to self-medicate and eventually close her eyes again. But then it would return and she would be crying out and screaming for Caroline to hold her.

Caroline was at wits' end. She called the doctor and he again recommended transfer to hospice. Morgana again refused. She was determined to die at home.

"I want to ask you something," Morgana said to her friend and lover. Morgana's once beautiful face was now gaunt—hollow cheeks, sunken eyes, mostly bald head from the now-discontinued chemo.

"What can I do for you, my love? Just ask."

"I want to press the plunger as many times as I can and then pass out."

"Well—I don't know."

"Then when I'm out I want you to press it until it's all gone."

"You want me to help you commit suicide, in other words."

"I'm begging you."

"I can't do that."

"If you love me, you can and will. I'm begging, Linus."

Linus. The most endearing name for her lover. Caroline's heart was already fragile and the term of endearment just pushed her over the edge. She would have to help.

"Do we have to do it tonight?"

"Right now. I can't do this any longer."

"Understand."

Morgana patted the bed beside her. 'Come up here and lie down beside me. You need to hold me while I do it."

Tears were streaming down Caroline's cheeks but she was restraining herself and crying inaudibly. She kicked off her house shoes and climbed up on the bed. Hands and knees, she positioned herself alongside Morgana.

"Perfect," said Morgana. "Now you tell our baby hello from me."

Without another word she pressed the pump ten times,

counting each one out. The normal dose was one pump every five minutes. Almost immediately Morgana's eyes closed and her lips parted as her breathing grew shallow. Caroline spooned her and grasped the pump in her hand. She began clicking the plunger without counting. She held her friend and kissed the back of her neck. She wept until there were no more tears.

Fifteen minutes later the breathing had stopped.

Caroline lay very still and held her breath. She listened for breath sounds. She released the plunger and pulled away. She propped up on an elbow and listened, placing her face on Morgana's face. Already the skin felt cool on her cheek. She heard nothing.

She climbed off the bed and sat again in her bedside chair. The clock downstairs chimed three times. Without moving, she sat watching the next hour, looking for any sign of life.

But there was none.

She called the crematory service.

It was done.

In the morning the home health nurse came to collect the medical supplies. She looked quizzically at the morphine bag but said nothing to Caroline. Clearly the bag was empty, a vacuum where the self-administering plunger had withdrawn all air. Curious, she placed the items inside her nylon bag and left.

She would definitely have to report this to the director of nursing.

Someone would need to write it up and she didn't want to be the one. It would be like ratting out a friend. The home health nurse had grown to really like these two women.

She would report it, but she wouldn't write it up.

57

I t was a straightforward motion on a case involving a woman to whom nitrous oxide had been administered while having a tooth shaped for a new crown.

Call it an overdose, call it her surprise allergy to the drug, she had lapsed into a coma from which she still hadn't awakened twenty-five months later.

The dentist's lawyer had filed a motion for directed verdict seeking to have the case dismissed. The motion was based on an expert witness report defense counsel had bought and paid for, and it totally exonerated the dentist.

Thaddeus had countered with an expert report of his own when responding to the motion. It was a battle of the experts, both of whom were purchased, both of whom said what the lawyers wanted them to say, and both of whom had sleazy ethics but that was okay, it was how the game of medical malpractice experts was played. Or as the lawyers put it, my guy can kick your guy's ass.

The court had "carefully considered both motions," as the judge recounted, had listened to arguments of counsel, and was now ready to rule.

Thaddeus knew going in that he would win on the motion. The defense won about once out of a hundred times. Defense counsel to pad their bills to the insurance companies mostly used directed verdict motions. Fourteen hours of research @ $600/hour + eight hours of motion drafting at $600/hour + three hours of in-office conference time to discuss the motion, + two hours of travel back and forth to court + three hours to prepare to argue the motion + two hours of oral argument + one hour post-motion to discuss the motion with plaintiff's counsel, and so forth. That was the idea. It was the sort of practice that made people hate lawyers, and with good reason.

Thaddeus had no such golden goose at his disposal. His fee would be paid out of the jury verdict he was planning toward. It was a crap game and in some ways he hated it. He thought he had left gambling behind in Vegas when he got out of the casino game, but here he was, still betting the odds.

The upside was that injured people got access to a lawyer and his or her firm without up-front money. So that day, he was patiently going through the motions of going through the motions, knowing that at some point the defendants' motion practice would burn out and then the case would probably settle. That would be when the golden goose had been totally de-feathered by hourly billings. At the end of the court session, he was bored, tired, and ready to head back to the office.

The judge droned on about this legal citation and that, for the sake of the record, giving his reasons for denying the defense motion, and the lawyers were half-listening, wishing only to pack their bags and head out.

At last the judged uttered, "It is so ordered. We stand in

recess," and everyone stood up and stretched as His Honor fled his throne.

Thaddeus was throwing things in his briefcase when he felt the eyes on his back. He turned around.

For the most part the courtroom was empty. There was nothing to attract attention to a rather mundane argument of technicalities on a rather mundane medical malpractice case on a rather mundane late Tuesday afternoon. Except for one man, wearing sunglasses, seated at the rear of the gallery, who was paying close attention and appeared to be texting on his phone. But nobody noticed the man, nor should they have. He was obviously Middle Eastern and oddly interested in a nothing-to-recommend-it legal proceeding. The man had gone through courthouse security, was found to be carrying no weapons and nothing that might pose a threat to other courthouse habitués, so he of course was waved right on through and allowed to proceed upstairs. Now he seemed to be fixated on Thaddeus.

Defense counsel cleared out, the bailiff took flight, the court reporter sprinted to the elevator for her next hearing, and the clerk of the court trundled out beneath his epic stack of files from the afternoon's doings. Now it was just Thaddeus and the dark man.

Thaddeus pushed open the gate at the bar and began walking up the aisle toward the double doors. When he drew abreast of the man, the stranger stood and removed his sunglasses.

"Could I have a word with you?" he asked Thaddeus.

Thaddeus stopped. He checked his watch. "Sure. What can I do for you?"

The stranger came closer. "I have your daughter."

Thaddeus felt his heart thump against his rib cage. "Say again?"

"I have Sarai."

"Not funny, pal. Now excuse me."

The man stepped into the aisle, blocking his way. "No, excuse me. If you want to see her again, you'll come with me."

"How do I know you have my daughter?"

The man gave a vague smile. "I notice the mole on her left shoulder has grown since I last had custody of her. You really should have that looked at."

He felt the sweat roll down his back. The guy really knew and the description of the mole was a hundred percent accurate. It had grown and her dermatologist was monitoring it. "What do I have to do? All I want is my daughter back."

"You will have her back. But you'll have to accompany me to fetch her."

"I'll do whatever you say."

"Just follow me to my car."

"I'll do that. Please, lead the way."

They left down the back stairs, avoiding the elevator and the FBI agents waiting in the lobby. They made their way to Lot D on the north side of the courthouse. It was hot out, and windy, but Thaddeus noticed none of it. He was sweating profusely, a million thoughts racing through his mind, none of them taking hold as acceptable strategies. The problem was, dark man had given him just enough detail to convince him he knew minutiae about Sarai's physical appearance, minutiae that wouldn't be casually noticed.

Her shirt had been removed for such an observation to be made.

His heart was pounding by the time he climbed inside the Ford Bronco.

Before turning the key, the man turned to him. "She's

still here in Chicago. Whether she remains here is entirely dependent on the next three minutes. Do I have your attention?"

"Yes."

"Do you understand that if you try to overpower me while I'm driving I will not make my next check-in call and she will be moved?"

"I understand. What do you want with me?"

"Bright boy. We want information."

"What kind of information do I have that you could possibly want?"

"You have killed some friends of mine. Is that enough for now?"

He knew better than to deny it. Realizing they had caught up with him, he felt himself slump back against the seat and heard the air leave his diaphragm as he totally succumbed.

They had Sarai; they had him. All that mattered now was the protection of his daughter. His own existence had no value beyond taking care of his baby. Whatever they wanted from him was as good as theirs already. But he wouldn't tell them that. While they thought he might still resist them, he had at least an ounce of bargaining power. It wasn't much, but he knew he had nothing else in his favor.

"Can I call her mother and tell her Sarai is okay?"

The man violently shook his head. "Pass me your cell phone, please."

Thaddeus retrieved the phone from the suit's breast pocket and handed it across the seat.

"Is this the only one?"

"Yes."

He passed it back. "Open the back of the phone."

Thaddeus inserted a thumbnail under the release on the back of the phone. "Got it. Now what?"

"Remove the SIM card."

Thaddeus removed the tiny circuit board. "Okay," he said.

"Lower your window and throw it out."

Thaddeus complied.

"Now pass me the phone again."

Once the man held the phone again, he drove several miles further on. Then he lowered his own window and threw the phone out.

"Now you may call Katy. Oh, you don't have a phone? Then I guess you can't call. Now sit back and say nothing more until we exit the truck."

Thaddeus closed his eyes and forced his mind to stop wheeling through space at 11,000 miles an hour. He envisioned Sarai's face, her smile, and let himself hear her voice. He almost panicked when he lost the image, but forced himself to stop trying.

He began to consider what information they would want from him and what they would do with it. He knew he was only one step ahead of his own death. These were not people who would suffer his trespasses against them. Not at all. They would want their revenge and they would have it in spades. First, of course, they would take care of the business of their cell. He could only guess what their role was in the grand scheme of jihad. But he knew he had interrupted them in their strivings and for that there would be pain.

They took the Palatine exit from I-90 and headed north. The city fell away and houses stood further and further apart until, as if scenery were gliding by in a dream, Thaddeus realized they were in the country. It was getting dark, early evening, the highway was heavily tree-lined, and, once it became two lanes, the shadows from the western side began covering the highway. He didn't know the road, though he knew the general area. There was a massive Cineplex in Palatine that he and Katy at one time enjoyed, and there was a medieval-themed restaurant where knights jousted while the guests dined on roasted chicken and cheered the pageant. Sarai had been left that night with her nanny. When they had returned home at eleven, she was sound asleep in her own bed, warm and safe. Right then he would have given every dollar he had or ever would have if only he could be in the same position of arriving home to find his family safe.

But it wasn't that way. His drive to exterminate these people had left him blindsided. How could he not have foreseen that they would come for him? What had they done, obtained surveillance video from the mall or the Jungle Zone? How could he not have foreseen that they would identify him and immediately track him down?

They kept rolling north and soon left the familiar behind.

Then it was nightfall and headlights were burning a path through the gloom.

58

When he regained consciousness the first thing he knew was that he was completely immobilized. He had been strapped to a spinal board made of hard plastic with four hand-size openings along the length of each side. Each opening anchored adjustable nylon belts that were passed insufferably tight across knees, waist, chest, and head. His arms were pinned at his sides where the first waist belt went up over his waist and the second waist belt was passed beneath his lower back, pinning his arms to the board. He immediately panicked; breathing was labored, thanks to the chest belt. His lungs and chest cavity could expand to grab a breath only one inch. He closed his eyes and told his mind to slow way down. He told himself that he had been breathing even while they had drugged him so there was enough oxygen passing in and out to sustain him. Calm settled over him.

He moved his eyes right and left. He could see only ceiling and partial wall to the left; he could see only ceiling and partial wall to his right. His shoulder burned, and he remembered being injected. Whatever chemical they had

used had formed a bolus just under the skin that was emit-
ting a burning sensation throughout the shoulder. Relax, he
told himself, the burning won't kill you. In fact, there's no
indication at all they want to kill you.

Coming from somewhere above him was the sound of a
baby crying. Through the fog shifting and curling inside his
brain he formulated the notion that from the sound of it the
baby would be about a year or less. It erupted into an even
heavier caterwaul, and for a moment he thought that he
might have been mistaken, that maybe it was the sound of a
cat being tortured. He drifted off and then returned when
the crying broke into a series of choking sobs. Definitely a
baby. He knew from having Sarai—

Then he remembered: Sarai. It was coming back, bits
and pieces. They had pulled off the highway onto a long
gravel road. It was dark and the headlights bounced off trees
and heavy brush as they picked their way along the gravel.
Then the house had loomed up out of the blustery gloom
and they had driven around back and parked. He had
voluntarily followed the dark man inside, expecting to find
Sarai held there, as they had told him.

But there hadn't been Sarai awaiting him. There was
only the room with the backboard set up across three
sawhorses. They had forced him to fully undress and recline
on the board. Then came the straps.

"Where is my daughter?" he had asked.

But there was no answer. Instead, as an apparition just
beyond his peripheral vision once he was strapped in, a
hypodermic floated by and the next thing he knew he was
falling, falling down a deep bottomless well. Then he was
gone.

He sensed a presence in the room.

"Where am I?" he groggily asked. His mouth and throat were parched. "Can you give me water?"

"We're going to give you water. More than you will ever believe."

"Can you show me Sarai? I need to know she is safe."

The voice laughed. "Sarai. There is no Sarai here."

"So it was a lie?"

"I don't know what you're talking about. You've been away."

"How long?"

"One day. They're looking for you by now."

"What is going to happen to me?"

"What do you know about us? Let's start with what you know."

"Nothing. I know nothing about you."

Wordlessly he felt sharp jabs of pain on the bottoms of his feet, excruciating, piercing pain on his genitals, biting pain on his nipples, stabbing pain on his ears as they fastened alligator clips. They left him like that for a long period of time, several hours, he guessed. While it was quiet and still around him, the pain receded and soon he was numb where he had been wired up.

The sound of the crying baby brought him back around. The child was in obvious distress and it sounded as if it had been abandoned and was hungry, hurting, or both. His pain had receded but part of his consciousness had fled along with it. He vaguely knew where he was and then he drifted away.

The potentiometer was switched from OFF to ON. And then quickly switched OFF again.

He literally arched up from the spinal board as the electric current shot through the contact points and sizzled along the length of his body. A long agonizing scream issued from his chest and throat, entering his mouth and blasting at the ceiling. He urinated on himself and muttered helplessly, ashamed and shredded and totally terrified of the current returning.

"My, aren't we the touchy one," said the voice at his head. "You are capable of sound other than your lies."

"What—what do you want?"

"The truth. Let's start with that."

"I swear I'll give the truth. What?"

"How did you find out about us?"

He turned it over in his mind. The "us" the voice was referring to could only be the cell. Ragman and his group. He would answer as if.

"I obtained a file. From the FBI."

"Where is this file now?"

"At my office. On my computer."

"What does it say about us?"

"I—I don't know what you mean."

OFF ON OFF. The charge shot through him and this time his scream was silent and long. Then he passed out.

How long he was out he had no idea, as the light above his head slowly refocused. It could have been minutes; it could have been days. He had no idea.

"You were away," said the voice. "Welcome back."

"Please. I'll tell you everything."

"Let's take up where we left off. What did the file say about us?"

"The FBI is watching you. They have agents in your mosques."

"Agents?"

"FBI agents. They are very close to you."

"Do they know specifically about our task?"

"Don't shock me again! But I don't know, honest to God! The file doesn't say anything specific about your task."

"Well—that's good news for you."

"Thank you."

"Do they have our names?"

"Yes."

"And they are following us, of course?"

"Yes. Everywhere you go."

"And you have been following us too."

"Yes. Sometimes."

"And you have murdered three of my brothers."

"You took my daughter. I couldn't let that happen again."

He clenched his teeth and squinted, expecting a freight train of electricity at any second.

Which didn't come.

"But you got your daughter back."

"She won't talk."

"That is unfortunate. We meant her no harm. It was only about the money you took from Mr. Mascari."

"Is that her crying upstairs?"

"There is no one crying upstairs."

"But I heard crying! A baby—Sarai?"

"You need to forget about Sarai. This is about you now. Only you. Are we clear on that?"

He tried to nod his understanding. But his head wouldn't move. His hands and arms were asleep and sharp needles were creeping up along his arms as the blood flow remained impeded. Then the shaking set in. He began involuntarily to shudder from head to toe. His teeth chattered and his eyes burned. "Water, please," he muttered.

"There is no water here. There is only electricity. As you know beyond all doubt."

"Water."

"Tell me this. How many agents are working against us? Which of us are they following? Do they know about our location in the Sears Tower? What else is there?"

"I don't know about the Sears Tower—it didn't—"

OFF ON OFF.

Again the fiery comets of electricity shocking him up from the table, stretching every muscle along his body, shuddering his eyes in their sockets as he fought to make it stop. He heard the howling of an animal and abruptly realized the wrenching sound was his own. Then his brain swam to the other shore and he was gone again.

A different voice spoke. "He has told us everything."

"Agree."

"Get rid of him."

"Agree. What should I do?"

"Burn this place to the ground."

"And the child?"

"Mother saw your face. Leave them too."

A look passed between them. Jihad was happening and lives were easily expendable, infidel and believer alike.

"We will catch up to you."

"Excellent."

59

When he didn't come home from work and the sun had set, Katy called paralegal Christine Susmann. Did he say anything about stopping off anyplace after court? No, Christine said, and she immediately went on alert. She knew it wasn't like Thaddeus to just disappear and not tell anyone. The way it had been since Sarai's kidnapping was a matter of constant communication so Christine, Katy, and Thaddeus knew each other's whereabouts night and day. Their lives ran on calendars and expectations of comings and goings that were preplanned and communicated three ways. Always three ways. For him to just disappear after work could only mean one thing. They had him.

She couldn't tell Katy about her fear. She would push it back an hour while she made inquiries on her own. Then they would talk. She communicated this to Katy, who reluctantly agreed to wait to hear from Christine.

Paralegal Christine Susmann had received her professional training in the U.S. Army. Following basic training, she had begun her career working as an M.P. and had served two years at a Black Ops detention center in Baghdad. She was under lifetime orders to never discuss what she had seen or done on that post, which was fine; she never wanted to discuss it anyway. Following two successful years working hand-in-glove with CIA field officers, she had her choice of army schools and selected paralegal school. She had seen all she ever wanted to see of detention centers, prisons, jails, or any other institution where people were held against their will. Paralegal training had dragged on for almost a year, but when she finished, she was assigned to a JAG unit of busy lawyers in Germany.

Christine was five-five and average weight, but that's where "average" ended for her. For one thing, she was beautiful and had won Miss Hickam County in the summer of her senior year, right before enlisting. For another thing she was built like an NFL safety: broad, heavily muscled shoulders and upper arms; muscular thighs and calves; and she could still press 275 while weighing only 135. She worked out religiously at the Central Chicago Athletic Club with her boss, Thaddeus, on lunch hours where he wasn't already spoken for.

Christine returned to the office after the frantic call from Katy. She had locked up two hours earlier at five o'clock. She had assumed—wrongly, she now knew—that he had gone from court straight home. That had been the plan. She kicked herself for not checking to make sure he had arrived. She always checked to make sure where everyone was. But tonight she had expected his bodyguards to drive him safely home. What she didn't know was that the guards had been lax. Amos Stamplett, who had accompanied Thaddeus to court, had walked to the end of the hallway outside the courtroom to take a call on his cell. He had moved beside the nearest window, hoping to improve the microwave signal. When he had reentered the courtroom, he had found it empty. His package had disappeared.

Why hadn't he immediately called Christine? BAG headquarters had tried, but she hadn't answered. She had taken the EL train home and amid the clatter and clack of the train and its noisy occupants she had missed the call. It was coming together as she called around and pieced it together.

One thing was certain. He was missing.

The hair along the back of her neck prickled. She was certain they had him.

There was only one place she knew to go and that was the white duplex on Milwaukee Avenue where Ragman lived. She would begin there.

She headed downstairs, pressing 6 on her cell phone as she went.

Bat answered. "Hello, Christine? What can I do you for now?"

"We've got trouble. The package is missing."

"What!"

Bat—Billy A. Tattinger—was the firm's head investigator. He had relocated from Las Vegas to Chicago when Thaddeus returned to Murfee and Hightower Law Firm, Chicago. Bat had been rescued off the streets by Thaddeus, trained by Thaddeus, and schooled at Thaddeus' expense. Bat loved the man, figured he owed him everything, including his licensed investigator status with the state, his return to the human race from the sidewalks and alleyways of Las Vegas, and even his own wife and son, newly acquired since Thaddeus had worked his magic of rehabilitation on Bat.

"Come by for me," said Bat. "I'll be waiting out front."

"Bring a gun."

"Christine."

"Okay."

"You come packing, too."

"Always," she said, and punched off. She was ready to roll.

She picked Bat up in front of his house in Glen Ellyn. The man was earning in excess of $150,000 per year, plus his wife's salary as a radiographer, so in theory they could have lived in any suburb of Chicago they chose. They chose Glen Ellyn for its easy proximity to Chicago by train.

"Milwaukee Avenue?" he asked after climbing in beside her.

"Uh-huh."

"How long has it been?"

"He left court around three, according to the order signed by the judge."

"And it's what, seven now?"

"Just about."

"Which means he could be anyplace."

She swerved around a fast-lane sightseer, pulling across the double line momentarily.

"Shit!" he cried.

"It's me, remember?"

He put a hand on the dashboard. "I do remember. You still drive like a bat out of hell."

"We're talking Thaddeus here."

"I'll shut up. So what do we do when we get to Mr. Towel-Head's house?"

"Here's what I'm thinking. Tell me what you think."

She explained it all to him, how she saw them moving along in their investigation. He nodded several times and agreed with how she wanted it to go down. "You're on," he said at last. "I like your thinking, girl."

"That's woman, to you, pal."

TWENTY MINUTES later they drove slowly past the duplex. The garage door was shut.

All lights appeared to be off. But Christine knew these guys. Lights meant nothing. Everything was a cue and nothing was a cue. Misdirection was their roadmap to anyone who happened to be watching them, every moment carefully choreographed and calculated to mislead and cloud what was really going on with them.

She pulled into the Mobil lot, zipped around the dozen pumps to the far side of the station, and shut it off. They climbed out and headed west, parallel to the duplex's property line, but a full lot north.

Special Agent Stanley Ciuffa clicked on the comm. "They're headed west. Evidently coming around behind." He was parked across from the Mobil in a windowless yellow van. What he was able to see was made possible by three TV lenses mounted along the van's roofline, a new feature that used the same nighttime visual capabilities as found on the Apache helicopters in Iraq and Afghanistan. In fact, Ciuffa had served in both theaters and had been wounded, but not disabled, and had thereafter joined the Fibbies. He was second in command to Pauline Pepper and worked terrorist organizations while she had come up through gangs.

That night, she was down at the other end of the block and around the corner, riding a Harley panhead and accompanied by two other agents on street Harley Softails.

It was a new look for the FBI, the bikes, being tried on for size in Oakland, Chicago, and Miami. Places where biker gangs were notoriously active and violent. The riders wore leathers and were heavily armed with semiautomatic

firearms and small shotguns. To say they were itching for a
fight with the occupants of the duplex would have been an
understatement that rankled all of them.

Pauline Pepper spoke into the comm fastened to her
jacket. "Let them go. I want Christine first in on this guy. If I
know my girl, she'll get Thaddeus' location before we ever
could."

"Roger that," said Ciuffa, as he watched the infrared
couple round the corner and head back south, out of sight.

"Rolling," said Agent Pepper, and she kicked it into first
and edged ahead to the intersection with Milwaukee
Avenue. She inched around the corner, lights off. Running
without lights on the new Harleys was of course impossible,
but Mechanical and Armaments had intervened and the
normal lights-on wiring had been interrupted with a switch
on all bikes. She left the motor running and was quiet
enough with the heavily baffled pipes that all agents swore
by. If there was any giveaway in all this, it was the fact the
bikes avoided straight pipes in favor of silent running. No
Harley rider in his right mind would have settled for quiet.
But this was a very different ilk of rider than the norm.

Christine and Bat crossed the imaginary property line
separating the first house from the duplex on the west side.
They would have to enter the adjoining house's backyard,
pray there were no watchdogs, and then go up the outside
fire stairs to the upper entrance. Her gut instinct told her
Ragman was inside. She would have bet the farm on it; in
fact, she was making that bet. If she lost the wager and the
guy wasn't actually there, then she would have zero idea
where to begin looking for her boss. She said a silent prayer
and lifted the gate latch to the abutting backyard and
stepped inside. Bat followed, his hand against her back so
he didn't overstep on her. Silently they crept across the

backyard and came to the fence that set off the rear lot line. It was a standard six-foot fence, wood, and she felt along its surface. She could see well enough by now to make out the absence of a gate. So now what?

"You step on my hands," Bat whispered. "Then go on over."

"What about you?" she whispered back.

"Hey, for an old street guy a six-foot fence is nothing. Now let's worry about you."

He joined his two hands together, interlocking fingers, and Christine stepped onboard and he lifted. Her free leg swung up and over and in one easy move she was on the other side, waiting for Bat. He easily pulled himself atop the fence and jumped down the other side.

"Ready?" she whispered.

He nodded.

They set out across the backyard.

Then they were at the stairs. She went first. Bat followed close behind.

She stepped on the outer edges of the stairs as she went up, in order to avoid squeaks from boards that would otherwise give underfoot. Bat followed her lead and climbed likewise.

They made the first landing. She pulled her .40 caliber Glock from its shoulder holster and waited while he extracted his nine-millimeter as well. Then they proceeded up the second flight. They quickly made the upper landing and waited, breathing as shallow as possible as they listened. Both were crouching and Christine's ear was pressed against the wood door. She heard nothing.

She turned and pressed her non-shooting ear to the door. She had better hearing in the ear that was furthest from weapons as she fired them. It was true of all who had fired thousands of rounds through military-issue guns. However, even through the better ear she still could make out no sounds.

She reached above her head and touched the doorknob. She tentatively twisted it counterclockwise. It gave in a full 180-degree turn. She nodded at Bat, indicating it was unlocked. This was a trick she had taught Thaddeus several years ago. Let them come inside without a sound, she had taught him. Then you can easily track them across the room and let them come to you before their eyes fully adjust to the blackness inside.

The door opened and she stuck her head inside. She could make out a washer and dryer piggyback. Her eyes quickly adjusted and she looked through the next doorway into what appeared to be the kitchen. There was no one there, so she moved from a crouch to a half-stance and moved inside. Bat followed close behind. They had previously agreed that when they went into the living room she would own the right half and he would own the left. An old Special Ops trick that was going to perhaps come in very handy tonight.

Without a sound she crossed the kitchen floor and stopped. The living room was next and she didn't want to reveal herself. So she didn't peer within.

Incredibly, she hadn't long to wait.

Ragman himself came marching into the kitchen like he owned the place. Which he did. But what he didn't own was the space and its occupants. They had made it inside without a sound and he didn't have a clue. He snapped on the kitchen light and found himself staring at point blank range straight into the very nasty-looking muzzle of a very large caliber handgun. Holding the handgun was a woman he'd never seen before, but his instincts told him to freeze at just the same moment she said the same word.

"Freeze!" she cried, and jammed the gun against his forehead.

He quickly raised both arms.

"Who else is here?" she said. "Fast before I fire."

"Just me," he blurted. "Everyone is gone."

"Where's Thaddeus?"

"Who?"

"Okay, we'll do it that way," she said, fully understanding that this guy wasn't going to give them anything. Which was fine; she had her own Plan B for such an eventuality, courtesy of the CIA spooks she had been assigned to in Baghdad.

"Bat, pull the kitchen table away from the wall."

"Got it."

"Little more. Give me two feet back there. You're going to need to fit on that side."

"Done."

"All right," she said to Ragman. "Up you go."

"What?"

"Up on the table, asshole. On the table on your back. Now!"

She slipped her finger inside the Glock's trigger guard.

The man complied, sitting backwards on the table and then scooting over and reclining onto his back.

"Spread your arms wide open."

He complied and she removed the nylon belt she was wearing. "Bat, do what I'm doing with your belt."

"I don't have a belt."

"Find something, then."

Bat went over to the blinds above the sink and ripped away the heavy cord.

He returned to the table and tied the man's left hand to

the table leg on his side. Meanwhile, Christine had secured the right hand on her side. Now the guy was spread-eagled.

"Open for business," she said. "Go to the bathroom and get a towel."

Bat returned with a towel.

"Now, where we came in through the laundry room, there's a bucket. Retrieve, please."

Bat returned with the bucket and took it to the sink. "Fill?"

"All the way," she said.

He handed the bucket to her.

"Now hold him down, stretch out across his legs."

She placed the towel across Ragman's face. Then she began a steady stream of water down into his mouth. Within seconds he was struggling his head side to side.

"Reach up here with your hands and hold his head still."

Bat did as he was told and the pouring resumed. Now the choking began and didn't stop. The man's head was jerking violently against the water but Bat held him steady. This went on for much longer than a bystander might have predicted.

Finally she relented and the flow of water stopped. The bucket stood half full.

"Now I'm going to ask you again, asshole. Where's Thaddeus?"

"Umf-dun-kniw," choked the voice beneath the towel.

"You don't know? Maybe this will help your memory."

She again poured water down into the towel, mouth level, until this time the bucket was empty and the struggling had ceased. She ripped the towel from the man's face. His eyes were open and water gurgled out the side of his mouth. She turned his head to the side and slapped his face. Again, harder. He jerked back to life and began whimpering.

No, no, no, no," he begged.

Without a word she again covered his face and repeated with another half bucket. Again the struggling ceased and again she uncovered him and slapped him back to consciousness.

"Son of a bitch is out cold," Bat said with no small amount of glee. "I never seen that before."

"I'll keep it up until he drowns, if that's what it takes," she said to the open, frightened eyes. "More?"

"He's out by Palatine. North."

"Give me the address."

"2500 North Randolph Drive. It's on the east side. Of the road. Back along gravel road."

"Is he alive?"

"Don't know."

"Well, I'll tell you what, asshole. If he's not alive you're about to meet your seventy-two virgins. With my help."

"He was left alive."

"And?"

"That's all I know."

"That's not all you know. Give me the rest of it or I'll float it out of you."

"No, no. They were going to burn the place."

"Wait here, asshole. We're going to go find our friend. If he's dead, I'll be back. If he's not dead, I'll be back anyway. And when I come back I'm going to make sure you don't scare off those virgins with your manhood. Get my drift?"

"No, please."

"Save it. I'll be back, so don't leave."

Bat said, "I'll get something tied around his legs. Give me five."

"You've got it."

Christine two-fingered a Marlboro out of a hard pack

and lit up. She smoked it a third of the way down and tapped the ashes over the man's face.

"So you remember me," she said.

Then she lifted his shirt and angrily ground it out on his belly. Howls erupted and the motorcyclists out front saw Special Agent Pepper smile in the dark night. "Got him," she said.

"Remember me," said Christine. "I'm coming back for you, mother. I want your balls."

"Please."

"Save it for someone who gives a shit. Kidnap a little girl? You and I have only just begun."

The agents stopped them downstairs.

Christine gave Pepper the sit rep.

"We'll lead the way. Gentlemen, lights up."

The agents turned on their flashing red lights and put Christine and Bat into the van.

Then the procession roared off Code Three for Palatine.

Two agents were left behind to take Ragman into custody. He was taken to the jail, fingerprinted and booked. He would make bail and walk free within twelve hours and the agents knew that. But for now, he was in custody and they were going to make inquiries of him. Lots of inquiries. It was going to be a long night for Luis M. Sanchez aka Ragman.

60

She was twenty-three, the victim of a home invasion while her husband was in the city, and had a fifteen-month-old to care for. They came into her farmhouse and locked her, with her baby, in the upstairs master bedroom closet. The makeshift lock consisted of a chair pushed backwards up under the doorknob.

The baby's diaper was overflowing and she was starving. Two hours past her bottle and she wouldn't stop crying. So Teresa Merrill did what all good mothers would have done. She placed her back against the closet wall, raised both legs with feet against the locked door, and kicked with every bit of strength she had. Surprisingly the door easily swung open and crashed against the exterior wall.

She climbed to her feet and inhaled a huge lungful of smoke.

The house was on fire.

Without another thought she scooped up her baby and tore downstairs. Which was when she saw the man, nude, laid out on the backboard. He was strapped from head to toe and it was unknown whether he was breathing. So she placed her baby on the floor and released all straps. His eyes were still closed. She patted his face. Nothing. So she slapped him—once, twice. His eyes fluttered open and she shook him

"C'mon, mister, they've put us on fire."

He shook the cobwebs from his brain. The smoke curled into his nose and he abruptly regained consciousness. He sat up.

"What?"

"The house is on fire. Let's get you outside."

He swung his legs over and stood. Wobbly at first, he reached for her shoulder.

She didn't mind. She had seen nude men before. Besides, this one was no threat; he could hardly stand. She picked up the baby, snagged Thaddeus' suit pants, and led him outside onto the porch. Smoke was everywhere, as the place had been doused with kerosene from the barn and then set ablaze.

He wanted to go back inside for his shirt. She refused to allow that.

"Sit tight," she said. "The neighbors will notice and call someone."

At which point he fainted dead away.

She heard sirens approaching.

"That didn't take long," she remarked to her baby.

They pulled in, a van with flashing lights and three bikers with flashing lights.

"Call the fire department!" she cried, which was unnecessary. Special Agent Pepper had already made the call from several hundred yards back down the road.

The house wouldn't be saved. The accelerant gave the fire too much of a head start.

But the occupants were saved. They were transported by

the EMTs to the hospital. Thaddeus was treated for smoke inhalation and kept overnight. Minor wounds were cleaned and dressed. The FBI agents posted local police officers at his door. The FBI gave Bat a ride back to Christine's car. Christine remained behind at Thaddeus' bedside. She would spend the night there, upright and alert, her Glock in plain view.

The mother was examined in the ER and released. The baby was given a bottle of formula from the hospital nursery. The crying subsided and the mother breathed a prayer of thanks.

Christine confirmed what she had guessed all along: Sarai was home safe and sound with Katy. She had never been taken away at all. Thaddeus, Christine knew, couldn't accept the odds of betting on that however. The mere threat of a kidnapping had easily overcome him.

As for Christine, she would have done the same thing had it been one of her own kids.

Some odds escaped the roll of the dice.

61

S aturday morning Thaddeus worked until nine-thirty.

The cleaning crew arrived and Juan Marenzenga appeared with his cart on the twenty-ninth floor of the American United Building.

Thaddeus knew the FBI agents were downstairs, waiting for him to leave on foot or by car. They would be stationed in their black cars along the curb. Another car would be waiting across from the building's parking garage exit ramp. He knew there would be no shaking them by normal means.

He waited until Juan was inside his office, switching on lights so he could clean the wastebaskets and vacuum. Thaddeus met him in the client waiting area.

He stuck out his hand. "I'm Thad. What's your name?"

"Juan." The small Mexican man looked suspicious. For one thing, he was expecting to find the office empty. For another, he was surprised and startled that a gringo was taking the time to speak to him. Strange, indeed. He took a step toward the door. "Should I come back later?"

Thaddeus smiled at the man. "No need. But I'm

wondering whether you would like to earn an extra five hundred dollars this morning?" He reached inside his wallet and extracted five hundreds. He held them out to Juan.

Juan refrained from accepting the money. But he wasn't disinterested. "What do I have to do?"

"You know the loading dock where you take the trash?"

"Yes."

"I want you to take me there."

Juan's look was totally quizzical. "Why don't you just take the elevator there? You don't have to pay me no five hundred dollars for that."

"No, you didn't understand me. I want you to take me there."

"How could I do that?"

Thaddeus pointed at the trash cart. It was five feet long, four feet high, on four six-inch wheels. A broom and two mops thrust upward from a canister on one end, a push bar extended across the other. It was black and said "49" in stencil characters.

Juan eyed the cart. "You mean take you in that?"

"Yes. I need to get out of the building without being seen."

"Is this your office?"

"It is."

"Are you running from the police?"

"I'm not. Would that make any difference?"

Juan grew perplexed. "No. Not really."

"Look. You want the money; I need a ride. Deal?"

Juan extended his hand as he nodded. "Deal."

"Let's go."

"Wait. What will you do at the loading dock? Do you have a gun?"

Thaddeus spread open his suit coat and did a 360. "No

gun. No knife. Just a harmless lawyer."

The weapon strapped to his ankle would have said otherwise.

"*Abogado.*"

"*Sí, soy abogado.*"

"*Sí.*"

"Are you ready?"

"Please, let me help you in."

"No need."

Thaddeus swung his legs up and over and settled back in the trash. The cart was half full of discarded paper towels from the restroom, discarded copy paper, and dozens of *Chicago Tribune*s and *Daily Sun*s. He immediately began covering himself. Juan joined in and Thaddeus crossed his hands on his abdomen and settled in for the ride.

THE CAB RIDE from the American United Building back over to Schaumburg ate up twenty-five minutes, as Saturday morning outbound traffic heading was peaking. Stop and go, stop and go. Thaddeus sprawled across the back seat, staying low.

He smiled. Ragman's new American girlfriend sent him to the Barrington Farmers Market every Saturday morning without fail.

THE MARKET WAS OUTDOORS, canvas stalls lined the street, and the pungent smell of barbecue spread. The crowd numbered in the hundreds, all drawn there by the promise of fresh fruit and vegetables.

Lost in a throng of shoppers, Thaddeus squeezed in beside his man. Getting next to him was easy, as Ragman was checking out the young women in their halter-tops and shorts. Thaddeus knew what was going on behind those driving glasses, knew they were seeing young flesh and ignoring the rest. Nobody would miss this guy. He was Mr. Hip, Slick, and Cool.

Perfect, thought Thaddeus, as he watched Ragman ostensibly shopping for bananas but secretly shopping the girls. Even very young ones; the elevens, the twelves.

When a young mother with a thirteen-year-old daughter gave Ragman a frosty glare, his eyes darted down to the banana display. She didn't move, which unnerved him.

Suddenly, he lifted a bunch of seven fruit to the sun, turning, turning. It appeared he was looking closely for spiders, for the fruit was known to ship from Latin America to Chicago with tarantulas stowed onboard. He held the bunch at the proximal portion of the vine and carefully examined it. Waiting, waiting, while the angry mother moved on.

Ragman bent to replace the bananas in the display. Thaddeus, at his side, took one step back and jammed the 9 mm behind the man's ear. He pulled the trigger three times.

The yellow-lensed sunglasses flew into the display. He splayed forward across the yellow fruit.

Thaddeus almost laughed as he pulled back into the crowd and disappeared. Bananas, he thought with a rush. The guy had actually let his guard down over a bunch of bananas. Thaddeus turned and put his back to the clamor as the looky-loos formed a circle around Ragur Amman Hussein, aka Ragman. "Is that blood?" the woman in the yellow shorts coveralls squealed.

Christine had left the Tesla parked along Monagle

Street. Thaddeus strolled nonchalantly through the crowd. He snapped the latex gloves from his hands as efficiently as the heart surgeon following transplantation. The gloves were stuffed inside a front jeans pocket. Fingerprints could be lifted from the inside of the gloves. No clues, not for the retinue of CSIs that would overrun the scene.

He opened the car and congratulated himself. Three down. The targets had multiplied. It was like when Thaddeus was a young boy stripping the bark from rotting cottonwoods. The scorpions, exposed to the glaring Arizona sunlight, would scatter by the thousands. Same thing here. While not as many, they were every bit as deadly.

And the original six—now three—who formed the group. Special Agent Pepper had referred to them as a cell. What of them? He slid across the seat, an angry scowl pulling at his face.

They were a matter of national security, that much was now known.

The why and the where and the when remained to be found out, though he already had a pretty good idea of the why.

For him, he was finished with it. Let the FBI clean up the rest.

He had his man facedown across a fruit stand. The new and improved Ragur Amman Hussein arrived in paradise at ten thirty-one a.m. Thaddeus wondered what the welcome was like.

Once the body was removed the merchant would spray and sell the yellow fruit anyway.

The guy wouldn't be out a nickel.

THE END

ALSO BY JOHN ELLSWORTH

FREE BOOK FOR EMAIL SIGNUP

Signup for my email list and receive a free Thaddeus Murfee book today! Your email will not be spammed and will only be used to notify you of new book releases, book sales, and free drawings, so please signup now.

—John Ellsworth

ABOUT THE AUTHOR

I'm an independent author. I'm independent because I enjoy marketing, selecting covers, reader communications, and all the rest. But I do need you to tell others about my books if you like them. Also, if you liked *The Defendants*, would you please leave an Amazon or Goodreads review? It would mean a lot to me.

Presently, I'm working on my 29th novel. I published my first book, *The Defendants*, in January 2014. It's been a wild ride and I was self-supporting four months after my first book came out.

Reception to my books has been phenomenal; more than 2,000,000 have been downloaded in 60 months. All are

Amazon best-sellers. I am an Amazon All-Star every month and a *USA Today* bestseller.

I live in San Diego, California, where I can be found near the beaches on my yellow Vespa scooter. Deb and I help rescue dogs and cats in association with a Baja animal shelter. We also work with the homeless.

Thank you for reading my books. Thank you for any review you're able to leave on Amazon.

Website and email:

ellsworthbooks.com
johnellsworthbooks@gmail.com

CPSIA information can be obtained
at www.ICGtesting.com
Printed in the USA
LVHW081418010221
678013LV00033B/769